"You're both going to be worn out when we land,"

Anson said softly.

Julia nodded and closed her eyes again.

"I could suggest a hotel...maybe get you settled...I mean...if you don't already have definite plans..."

She opened her eyes and stared at him with a searching intensity that made him nearly weak with guilt. Then her gaze softened, and she sighed as though surrendering in some way.

"Yes, I would appreciate that." Her voice was low but unmistakably practical.

"I need a decent place"—she glanced down at the child—"but one that's not too expensive...perhaps offering weekly rates." She looked suddenly unsure. "Is it possible, do you think?"

And with that last question he knew he had her. She trusted him. That was what he wanted, wasn't it? That was what he needed in order to carry out his plans.

So why the hell did it make him feel so awful?

Dear Reader,

Spellbinders! That's what we're striving for. The editors at Silhouette are determined to capture your imagination and win your heart with every single book we publish. Each month, six Special Editions are chosen with *you* in mind.

Our authors are our inspiration. Writers such as Nora Roberts, Tracy Sinclair, Kathleen Eagle, Carole Halston and Linda Howard—to name but a few—are masters at creating endearing characters and heartrending love stories. Their characters are everyday people—just like you and me—whose lives have been touched by love, whose dreams and desires suddenly come true!

So find a cozy, quiet place to read, and create your own special moment with a Silhouette Special Edition.

Sincerely,

The Editors
SILHOUETTE BOOKS

CAITLIN CROSS
Shadow of Doubt

Silhouette Special Edition

Published by Silhouette Books New York

America's Publisher of Contemporary Romance

SILHOUETTE BOOKS
300 East 42nd St., New York, N.Y. 10017

Copyright © 1987 by Caitlin Cross

All rights reserved, including the right to reproduce
this book or portions thereof in any form whatsoever.
For information address Silhouette Books,
300 East 42nd St., New York, N.Y. 10017

ISBN: 0-373-09380-2

First Silhouette Books printing May 1987

All the characters in this book are fictitious. Any
resemblance to actual persons, living or dead, is
purely coincidental.

SILHOUETTE, SILHOUETTE SPECIAL EDITION and colophon
are registered trademarks of the publisher.

America's Publisher of Contemporary Romance

Printed in the U.S.A.

Books by Caitlin Cross

Silhouette Special Edition

High Risk #272
Catch the Wind #341
Shadow of Doubt #380

CAITLIN CROSS

has lived in California, Oklahoma and New York and has traveled extensively throughout the U.S. and Canada. She has owned and raced her own quarter horse and has been closely connected with professional rodeo, during which time she co-authored the *Basic Bullriding Manual*. Caitlin has been in love with books and writing since she was a child but did not publish until after attending the University of Oklahoma's Professional Writing Program under Jack Bickham. She is currently writing full-time with the support and encouragement of her three small children.

CANADA

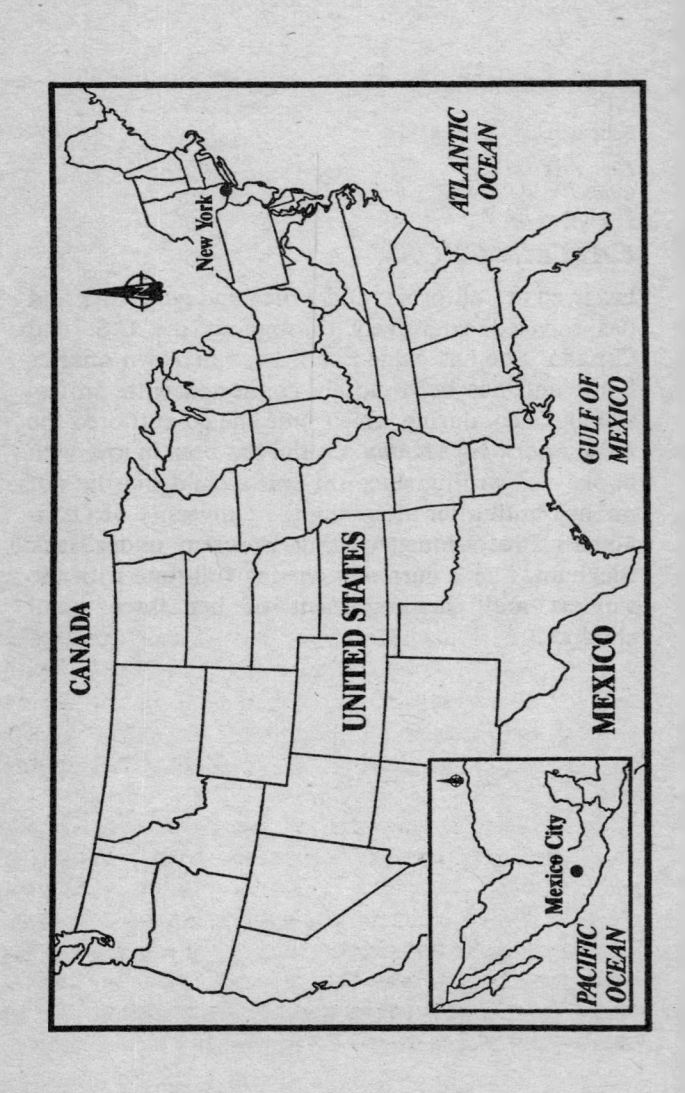

ATLANTIC OCEAN

New York

GULF OF MEXICO

UNITED STATES

MEXICO

Mexico City

PACIFIC OCEAN

Chapter One

He was fascinated the moment he saw her, and Anson Wolfe was not a man whose head was turned easily or often. His life was too grounded in realities.

There was something about her, though, something indefinable. Even in those first moments, before he heard her voice or had any sense of who or what she was, he felt a mystical, gravitational pull toward her, as though she were the earth and he nothing but a helplessly falling body.

He had been leaning against a marble pillar in the palace's immense chandeliered foyer, one hand in his pocket and the other holding the requisite drink, and feeling a bit like David Niven playing the cynical man-about-town. The spectacle flowed around him, but it was hard to see it as real. The gala bore the one-dimensional gloss of a film, or the fantasy perfection of a fairy tale. It had no ties to the world at large—to his world.

But there he was, playing a part, camouflaged in finely tailored evening clothes so that anyone tuning in wouldn't realize he didn't belong in the picture. Anson Wolfe at a full-fledged ball; how ironic.

For lack of something better to do he had been watching the arrivals. Through the open doors he could see the limousines as they drew up. They were always black or white or gray, with a uniformed chauffeur and the kind of back seat large enough to permanently house a family of four. Some had gilt renderings of family crests emblazoned on the doors. He remembered an ad he'd seen in the back of some pulp magazine: "You too can have a family crest! Heraldic Research at reasonable rates. Results guaranteed." He wondered if any of tonight's crests had been mail-ordered.

The men arrived occasionally as singles or in loosely organized groups, but the women were always escorted. Either they hung on the arm of a male relative or they were sandwiched into the family in such a way as to appear surrounded on all sides as they stepped through the massive doorway.

Funny how much he'd forgotten in his years away; the subtle but constant one-upmanship, the feigned boredom, the airs and pretensions. The all-important, unmerciful power of tradition. How had he ever been comfortable in the midst of all this? But then, he hadn't really been in the midst. He'd always been the outsider, and that's probably what had saved his sanity.

The scene had become tiresome. He'd just decided to move to some other setting when she appeared.

The group looked pretty routine at first. They were led by an elderly couple. The man's shoulders sagged a little too much, but the woman's carriage was ramrod stiff.

She looked as if she were on the way to her own coronation.

Following closely behind, like a gaggle of geese, were four middle-aged people. There was a plain, sad-looking woman beside a heavy-jowled, shifty-eyed man, and a pinched, perfectly groomed woman with a vaguely effeminate, disdainful-looking man.

The older couple stood staring straight ahead, waiting for the maids to finish taking wraps. It was the same scene Anson had witnessed over and over—except that something seemed slightly off-key here. The plainer woman kept looking back toward the door nervously, and he realized that the other three middle-aged people were also glancing back and reacting to something with varying degrees of disapproval, disgust and embarrassment.

He could tell now that the older couple, with all their regal bearing, was waiting, as well, though their faces were carefully kept neutral. He straightened and studied the action intently, grateful for something different at last. To his surprise, the milling crowd seemed to be conscious of the unfolding drama, too. A subtle but distinct change occurred in the receiving area, and though everyone around him carried on with conversations, their collective attention was riveted on the door. The entire room was throbbing with expectancy.

Suddenly, a woman in a floor-length cloud of white, silver-tipped fox swept through the doors. Her porcelain skin and dark sable hair were dramatic against the snowy fur. She rushed like a child coming in from play, then she stopped, seemingly oblivious to the hushed, staring crowd. He watched in wonder as she casually reached up and brushed some loose strands of hair away from her face, pulled out one of the diamond combs in her hair and carelessly replaced it to include the straying tendrils. The act was incredibly intimate and sensual.

All movement and sound were suspended around him and the room was too still to breath in. She smiled lightly at her group.

"Oh. Were you waiting for me?" she asked in a too-innocent tone that stopped just short of bitchiness.

The plain woman in the party looked worried and upset. The elderly couple's eyes burned, but their jaws were set and they never wavered in their stance. The rest responded immediately with expressions of mortified disapproval.

Pockets of whispered voices sprang up around Anson, and he drew in his first lungful of air in some moments. Without taking his eyes off her he edged closer, forsaking his safe haven for the broad reaches of the entry colonnade. This was the closest thing to amusement he'd had all evening. He tried to suppress the grin that tugged at the corners of his mouth. He had the unmistakable feeling that this mystery woman's every move was calculated, and that she was manipulating the entire gathering like some master puppeteer pulling strings.

She let the crowd recover slightly, then she threw back her coat, letting the drift of fur fall to the floor. The crowd gasped and a horrified maid dived valiantly for the coat and scooped it up before it had completely settled. The woman ignored the furor and stepped away from the coat as though its fate were beneath her consideration. Diamonds glittered at her ears and throat as she moved, calling attention to the enticing line of her neck.

He chuckled aloud at the sheer nerve of the performance but the sound died in his throat, stilled by the tight, breath-catching awareness of her full presence. It was not just that she was beautiful. She was poised and cool and stunningly desirable.

She wore a simple black dress with a V neckline and long fitted sleeves. It accented her slender waist and then fell to the floor in a fluid line. The dress was cut modestly, but the liquid drape of the silky fabric moved with her body in the most tantalizing way. As she stepped forward the skirt parted in a slit that revealed a length of black-stockinged leg.

Anson's heart pounded like a schoolboy's. He glanced around, embarrassed by his reaction to her, but no one noticed him. All eyes in the room were focused on her. And he realized with a start that the fixed stares were overwhelmingly hostile and frequently touched with envy or lust, as well as outright disapproval. The sheer intensity of the reactions chilled him.

The mystery woman approached her tight-lipped party slowly, leaving no doubt that she was joining them on her own terms. Their anger at her was fierce and uncompromising in its silence. As they regrouped and gathered their dignity for the march into the ballroom, Anson thought he saw a fleeting expression of evil glee in the heavy-jowled man's face. It was a strange and amazing scene, and Anson had the feeling he had just witnessed a skirmish in an ongoing battle of some sort.

He turned, watching their progress across the marble expanse, and he followed them without thinking. Who was she? He quickened his pace and trailed them into the main ballroom. She was surrounded almost instantly by a throng of eager young men. They spirited her away from her disapproving party, put a drink in her hand and vied for her attention. He felt a strange and unreasoning stab of jealousy.

The silliness of it all flowed over him, and Anson forced himself to look away from her. The room was awash in color and music. Hundreds of men and women danced by in a whirl of tuxedos and Paris gowns, but he couldn't seem to resist or ignore her presence. His eyes and thoughts kept straying back to her.

Who was this woman? The question grew in his mind until he could concentrate on nothing else. He couldn't stop watching her. And instead of satisfying him, instead of allowing him to reach that point where he'd had enough and was ready for some other occupation, watching her only left him hungry for more.

Time stood still as the fascination absorbed him. He watched her dance, enjoying the sensual sway of her body and the fluid movements of her long legs. He saw her too-wise, enigmatic smile and the sideways looks she gave to one man after another, obviously turning every knee to jelly. And all around him he noticed others glancing her way and frowning.

Suddenly the mystery woman drew back from her circle of admirers and broke away to move across the room alone. He threaded through the crowd of people, trying to keep her in sight.

"Anson! There you are." The sound of his uncle's voice stopped him. Even though Anson had been away for years, the voice still brought him to attention.

"Uncle Ignacio," he said, inclining his head in the accepted show of respect.

"Are you enjoying the ball, Anson?"

"I'm finding it very interesting, Uncle. Living in New York these past years has made me forget how extremely—" he pushed away the uncomplimentary words that popped into his head "—grand your world here is."

"Your life in New York could be very grand also, Anson, should you choose it to be so."

"I've chosen the life that is most satisfying to me, Uncle," Anson said politely, keeping his anger in check.

"Ah," Ignacio breathed, shaking his balding head. Absently he began to pat his thick chest in search of his cigars. "You and Miguel—" he shook his head again "—may only be cousins but you are like brothers in your thoughts. He has performed splendidly since he came into my firm, but no—it has not satisfied him. He dreams of you and your work with the poor."

Ignacio paused a moment, his brow creasing at this perplexing inconvenience in his life. "What is it with young people today that makes the old ways not good enough?"

With a sound of satisfaction, he located his cigars and pulled several out. He held each one lovingly to his nose, breathing in the scent deeply.

"It seems to me that the bargain you made with Miguel should make you both happy, Uncle." Anson skirted the subject carefully.

"You should know, Anson, from living under my roof all those years, that your Uncle Ignacio is not much of a man for bargains."

"But Miguel said—"

"Yes. I have agreed to this legal aid foolishness, but only so he can purge these ridiculous impulses from his head. When he comes to his senses he will gladly take his place beside me, and the firm can be Obregon and Obregon as it was meant to be."

Ignacio shook his head in the universal gesture of parental dismay. "Miguel has a place as a great and powerful attorney in this country—a man of influence and authority. That place has been assured him since before his birth, and it is his duty to fill that place. He does not belong in the slums scrabbling over chicken ownership and shack rentals."

"And who does belong there, Uncle?" In spite of his vow to himself not to clash with his uncle on this trip, Anson could barely control the anger he felt.

"Men with no other options," Ignacio countered firmly. "Men who were destined by birthright to hold a low place in society. You and Miguel are robbing those men of their places with your clinics and legal aid. You are upsetting the natural order of things. Of course," Ignacio added quickly, "your special circumstances pardon your inclinations somewhat, but my son has no such excuse for his behavior."

Anson took a firm grip on himself before he spoke. "I don't agree, Uncle—as usual."

"Ah, Anson," Ignacio said with a twinkle in his eye. "You temper your words so well now. I believe that indiscreet, hot-headed youth I sent off to college is finally fading. Perhaps it is time now for you to put aside your own childish passions. Remember, I could do much to ease your entry into a first-class law firm."

"I'm not worried about forgetting, Uncle. I'm certain I can rely on you to remind me."

Ignacio chuckled. "Yes, you've changed, Anson. I regret that I've not had much time to spend in your company these past two weeks. And now Miguel tells me that your work is finished and you are leaving us."

"Yes. Tomorrow. I think Miguel is on the right track with his clinic plans now. I've helped him all I can. The rest is up to him. He has a lot of hard work ahead, but he seems determined to succeed."

Ignacio gave a little snort. "Yes, well, we shall see how long he lasts in the filth. We shall see how well he 'succeeds.'"

Anson had to smile. "The same thoughts you expressed about me some years ago, Uncle, if I remember correctly."

Ignacio fastened his intense, heavy-browed eyes on Anson. "But there is a difference here." He paused, never taking his eyes from his nephew. "Miguel has never had the silver spoon from his mouth, while you—you were toughened by pain and suffering while still young."

"Perhaps you're right, Uncle, but I wouldn't sell Miguel short. He may surprise you."

"Enough!" Ignacio declared forcefully. "This is a ball. An entertainment. And I did not force you into your cousin's tuxedo and insist on your attendance so we could discuss serious matters." He smiled and held up the cigars. "A new shipment of the finest Cuban." He held one under his nose again and sniffed appreciatively. "I am meeting Miguel and several colleagues in the smoking room. Will you join us?"

"No thank you, Uncle. I've quit smoking, and besides, I've got a little entertainment of my own going here. I've been watching a rather interesting woman."

Ignacio raised his eyebrows and blinked his eyes. "Indeed? Your aunt will be delighted to hear that. Her fondest wish is to see her sister's son safely married and settled."

Anson laughed. "I wasn't planning on proposing, Uncle. I was just watching the woman. As you say, this is an entertainment...and I've been finding her extremely entertaining."

"May I know who this interesting creature is?"

Anson looked around the room, raising up slightly on the balls of his feet to extend the field of vision his six-foot-three height afforded him. "I'm afraid she's escaped me temporarily. But she was very, ah, noticeable. She's tall and slender and fair-skinned—very dramatic looking—and she was in a black dress."

"A young woman in a black dress? What would a woman in mourning be doing at a ball?" Ignacio's brow wrinkled in question.

"I don't think she was in mourning, Uncle. She acted quite, ah, festive."

"But a black dress on a young woman?"

Anson shrugged. "And she came in unescorted."

Ignacio's eyebrows shot up. "Who would allow such behavior? Where was her husband or her father or her guardian?"

"I don't know. You see then why I was intrigued. I didn't think the social rules regarding women had changed that much since I'd been gone."

"You say she was tall and fair-skinned?"

Anson nodded. "But then most of the old families go back to European stock, don't they? So why should that—"

"But taken together, Nephew." Ignacio spoke as though he'd just solved a puzzle. "She must be a visiting European relative of one of the old families, and they have been lax in guiding her behavior. She obviously does not understand—"

"Oh, I think she understands everything she's doing and just what effect it will have on this gathering. I think she's even enjoying the shock she's causing."

"Wait," Ignacio said, a sudden dawning in his eyes. "Did she join any family group?"

"Yes, and I see them right now. Move to your left and look at that third table in. See them... the elderly gentleman and lady, and the two younger couples?"

Ignacio drew in his breath sharply. "That is Señor Victoriano Velasco and his wife, with their two daughters and sons-in-law. His family is all that is left of one of the oldest and most revered bloodlines in Mexico."

"Well," Anson said, suddenly feeling foolish for having revealed his preoccupation to his uncle, "the lady in question came in with them."

"That woman is the shame of a great family," Ignacio said, a hard look on his face. "She is the widow of their younger son, and she is an evil mockery, a tragic example of what befalls young men who impulsively marry without their family's approval."

Anson absorbed the tirade without comment. He was anxious to hear more, but he knew he had to be careful with his questions or his uncle would mistake simple curiosity for something more.

"What a strange situation," he finally said. "Why don't they just send her back to her family? She's obviously through grieving. Who would criticize them for getting her out of their hair?"

"She has no family, Anson. She's not our kind." Ignacio glanced around, as though worried that someone was eavesdropping. He lowered his voice to a confidential tone. "The son, Paulo Velasco, brought her here from the States, and it appears she was nothing more than an orphaned guttersnipe who married him for his good name."

Anson opened his mouth to speak, then shut it without uttering a sound. What was the use in trying? He would never convince his uncle that there were people in the U.S. who cared nothing about good bloodlines and old names. That there were, in fact, people who considered the very idea ludicrous. It was a sore point with Anson—this society's concept of lineage and bloodline—but why even bring it up? He'd learned long ago that changing his uncle's thinking was like tilting at windmills.

"The Velascos' honor would not be tarnished by casting out such an unsuitable daughter-in-law," Ignacio continued. "Or by furnishing her with an allowance, perhaps, and sending her back to her own country. Her lowly character has been witnessed by all during these past few months while the family has been in residence here in their city home.

"But life is not so simple." Ignacio shook his head sadly. "There is a child involved. Her baby is the family's last male heir, and they tolerate this woman because she is the mother of their only grandson. An unfit mother, but, nonetheless, the mother."

"The plot thickens," Anson said, scanning the room for her again. He saw his cousin's approach from the corner of his eye.

"And what is this! We've been waiting in the smoking room for you two." Miguel's tone was scolding as he approached and reached out to box Anson's arm affectionately.

"Anson is not joining us, *hijo*. He is busy watching that woman who lives with the Velasco family."

"Hmm, Julia Velasco, eh?"

"I'm not ordering, just looking over the menu, Cousin." Anson grinned.

"And Julia Velasco is a lot to look over." Miguel grinned back at him conspiratorially and lowered his voice. "I hear she might be very accommodating. Perhaps I should introduce you. Your American speech and Yankee ways would surely remind her of home."

"No, thanks," Anson said with a laugh. "She sounds like more than I could ever handle. I'm just getting a kick out of watching the little dramas surrounding her. Even in this—" Anson waved his hands to include the whole gathering "—she stands out."

"Maybe she's symbolic," Miguel offered eagerly.

"Oh, yeah," Anson agreed, unable to resist the temptation to tease his younger cousin. Miguel's attempts at being a liberal, crusading intellectual continuously amused him. "You know, you're right, Miguel. She's like a parody, a hedonistic symbol ironically bedeviling a decadent, dissolute and gluttonous society."

Miguel beamed and nodded sagely.

"You talk in riddles," Ignacio said impatiently. "Why must everything be so complicated with you two? I am never certain I understand what you are thinking, or whether you are serious."

"What Anson is thinking, Father—" Miguel's voice was full of satisfied self-righteousness, and the gaze he turned on Anson dripped with admiration and hero worship "—is that even in this garish and hedonistic gathering, Julia Velasco, gold digger turned widow, stands out as a symbol of social decay and her presence as an albatross around this society's neck is a fitting punishment for—"

"Okay, okay." Anson grinned and reached out to put an arm around Miguel's shoulders. He felt a little guilty for putting the quarter in Miguel's slot. "I think we'd better put the soapbox away for the rest of the night, counselor, before the lynch mob forms."

Ignacio shot Anson a grateful look then turned to his son. "You have always placed great value on your cousin's examples, Miguel. Take note of this one; Anson is showing you that a young man must learn to temper his idealism and control his love for his own ideas. Wisdom is born of age, not of excess energy."

Miguel looked pointedly at his cousin with a pouting expression that Anson knew was intended to convey hurt and betrayal. But instead of those emotions, Anson saw only the spoiled displeasure of a very privileged and immature young man. Miguel had a long way to go, but at least he was trying. At least he saw that there were other paths.

"Just take it easy," Anson said lightly. "This is your favorite shindig of the year, remember?"

"And we are off to the smoker," Ignacio declared, linking his arm with his son's and waving the cigars in the air.

"Ah, the Cubans came in!" Miguel's attention was diverted and he lapsed into excited chatter that drifted in with the crowd noise as Anson watched the two men disappear into the swirl of people.

Anson smiled to himself as he watched them go. Miguel wanted so badly to be a crusader, but he enjoyed the comforts and pleasures of wealth and social position enormously. He apparently hadn't realized that his penchant for expensive cigars and sleek automobiles was inconsistent with his crusader image of himself.

Now, Anson thought, turning to scan the room, where is she, this shame of the Velasco family? Julia, he had heard Miguel call her. What trouble was Julia into now? he wondered. He thought back to what his uncle had said. She was from the States, from a family of apparently "no consequence." What a fairy tale all this must have seemed to her. The sudden wealth had spoiled her rotten.

He moved in the direction he'd last seen her, but without success. Maybe she had gone to the powder room? He wandered toward the great hall and took a seat on one of the purple velvet gilt-trimmed benches lining the walls. Women strolled past, discussing what other women had worn to the ball. Men lounged on the numerous benches or leaned against walls. He could see all the comings and goings from the powder room.

Fifteen minutes ticked by, and still there was no sign of her. He watched young couples entering the library with their chaperons close behind. Apparently that was the approved quiet place for courting. He watched the door to the smoking room open and close as males of all ages entered and exited. He saw the servants, women in black dresses with white aprons and men in black suits with white shirts, scurrying in and out of the kitchen entrance with additions to the huge buffet.

Suddenly it all seemed to press in on him. Nothing was amusing or interesting anymore. He had been playing a game with Miguel when he'd spouted off about the Velasco woman and this society, but what he'd said had come disturbingly close to his true feelings.

All this glamour and glitter, all the rules and ceremony and snobbishness weighed heavily on him, and he was tired of pretending otherwise. Just that morning he had been in the slums and seen people living in trees and ditches and seen undernourished children playing around garbage heaps and open sewers. He had seen starving children and sick children and children with flat, hopeless eyes.

But those indigent masses did not exist for the people at this gathering. These sons and daughters of old society thought humanity ended at the edge of their pedigrees. They were too busy worrying about propriety and tradition and designer clothes to consider the plight of the inconsequential poor.

At the end of the hall he saw doors that looked promising, and he headed quickly for them. He needed fresh air and quiet. He stepped out cautiously, uncertain where the exit led. To his relief he found himself on a deserted patio. It was a huge area, dotted with knots of furniture and potted plants and descending in terraced levels to a formal garden. The evening had turned quite chilly, and he doubted he would be disturbed.

Briefly he longed for the comfortable routine of lighting a cigarette, and he had to remind himself of how glad he was that he'd managed to finally quit smoking. Faint sounds from the ball drifted out to him and he walked to a corner, sat down beside a clump of palms and stared off into the velvety blackness, where the light's weak flickering faded. There was neither moonlight nor starlight, and he felt swallowed up by the night and light-years removed from the gathering inside.

The doors opened and closed softly, and he turned his head and strained his eyes, trying to see who the company was.

He almost missed her. The black dress blended with the shadows and she moved quickly, stealthily, as though afraid. Her diamonds flashed in the flickering light. It was Julia Velasco.

She paced, glancing this way and that, and he realized that his position made him invisible to her. If he said something he might startle or frighten her, and besides, what would he say? She probably wanted a breath of fresh air and a moment of privacy just as he himself had, and not an intrusion by a stranger. And she couldn't possibly intend to stay out long—she had to be freezing in that dress.

He decided to simply sit in silence and wait her out. What could he possibly have to say to Julia Velasco?

The door opened and closed again. For a moment he thought it had been the sound of her leaving, but then he saw the man. He nearly groaned out loud. He should have guessed—she was waiting for someone. It was the perfect setting for a clandestine meeting.

Anson glanced around for an avenue of escape, but there was none. There were no other doors to the building on this side. The only way he could discreetly respect their privacy would be to stroll off into the garden for a time, but the garden was wet, so that would mean ruining the dress shoes he'd borrowed from Miguel.

Thankfully their voices were hushed so he didn't have to add eavesdropping to his guilt and discomfort. They moved and she was momentarily bathed in light. She looked very cold in her thin dress, with her arms crossed tightly against her chest. Her body language appeared defensive rather than romantic.

He averted his eyes and slumped down in his chair, feeling uncomfortable in his inadvertent role as spy. Perhaps he could circle around on the concrete and come up the terrace, pretending to be just returning from a stroll in the garden. He could offer a casual "Oh, what a surprise to see someone else out here" nod as he went back into the building. No, they were both acting so furtive that he was certain it would scare them cruelly. There was nothing to do but wait them out and hope for a quick end.

"Not enough!"

Anson's head jerked up at the vicious, demanding tone in the man's shouted words. As his startled glance swept over them he realized that the man was wearing a servant's suit. He was not a guest.

Was the high-rolling widow Velasco dallying with servants?

She said something indistinguishable, and the man laughed darkly. Anson had the troubling sense that she might somehow need help.

"... how bad you want 'em... cost you more... dangerous..."

She screamed, "I have no more money with me!" then turned and started to run back to the door. But the man followed and caught up with her. Anson clenched his jaw and tightly gripped the cold metal arms of his chair to keep from jumping into the middle of the scene. Stay out of it, he cautioned himself silently, although he couldn't put aside the irrational feeling that she needed his help.

The man grabbed her and pulled her into a rough embrace and forced his mouth down on hers. Anson jumped up and started toward them. Julia pushed the man away violently. Anson stopped, uncertain, still screened from their view by the darkness and the plants.

"Here!" she said, ripping a sparkling bracelet from her wrist and thrusting it into the man's hand. "Now give it to me."

The man took a white envelope from his inside jacket pocket and dropped it to the ground in front of her. She bent eagerly to retrieve it and he spit on the ground beside it.

"Filthy bitch," he threw at her as he walked back to the door. He put his hand on the door handle and turned back toward her. "Think I'm not good enough for you, huh? Well, I've heard them talking. I know better." He slammed the door loudly behind him.

Julia straightened, hugging the envelope to her chest. She glanced nervously at the door, then lifted her skirt to her waist, revealing long shapely legs and a lacy garter belt.

Anson's mouth dropped. What next! He covered his eyes with his hand and silently begged for the whole incident to be over quickly. There was total quiet. He scissored his fingers open and peeked, but she was still there! She was frantically trying to figure out a way to conceal the envelope in her undergarments.

Anson had to catch himself to keep from laughing. The clinging silk of her dress and the brevity of her lacy underwear made concealment a real problem. She apparently hadn't thought ahead very well.

She managed to secure her treasure in the top of one stocking on the inside of her thigh. Then she lowered her dress and smoothed it with her hands, as though checking to see if it showed.

He breathed a sigh of relief when she finally went back through the door and left him alone on the quiet, dark patio. He waited a moment, not wanting to pop through the door immediately behind her. He moved to the wall and leaned against it heavily, feeling completely disheartened by the scene he'd just witnessed. The beautiful and foolish Julia was apparently buying into yet another kind of mischief.

Slowly he moved back through the heavy door and into the ornate hallway. His footsteps were muffled in the thick carpeting. She was nowhere in sight, and he hoped he could leave without catching so much as a glimpse of her. He was ashamed of his unintentional spying on her, and he was both saddened and upset by what he'd witnessed.

Julia Velasco was indeed symbolic of everything he hated, everything he'd fought so hard against. She was one of the selfishly spoiled, pointless rich. One of the purposeless beautiful people. And the fact that she hadn't been born to it, that she knew better, made him even angrier.

"Anson!"

He turned at the sound of his name.

"What are you, sleepwalking? You walked right by us without a word!"

Ignacio and Miguel stood just outside the door to the smoking room with two other men. They were all regarding him with puzzled expressions.

"I'm sorry," Anson said, forcing a smile. "I'm afraid my mind was on other things."

"Well, then," Ignacio beamed. "I think it's time we rejoined your aunt and found proper young ladies for you and Miguel to dance with."

Anson shook his head. "Not tonight, Uncle. I'm suddenly very tired and I have to be up early to pack. I was just on my way to say my goodbyes and find a cab to take me back to the house."

He politely warded off all protestations and headed back down the hall to the ballroom, where he hoped to find his aunt and tell her good-night.

Suddenly the powder room door burst open beside him and Julia Velasco rushed out, coming so close to him that he could smell the heady fragrance of her perfume. He stopped to avoid running into her, and she cast him a glance. She had burning eyes that were very dark blue or possibly gray, and skin like English cream. His presence didn't even slow her down. Her glance slid over him, found him nonthreatening, and dismissed him in the blink of an eye.

A shrewd woman, he caught himself thinking—one glance and she knew he was out of her league. But still the closeness, the one brief fraction of a second when her eyes met his, left him shaken and unaccountably disturbed.

"Julia!" a pair of young men called. "We've been looking for you."

She stopped and let them catch up, and he saw her change herself as surely as a chameleon changes at the approach of the hawk. Almost magically her stance became sensual as she tilted her head up and laughed, but it was a sensuality that now seemed to him to be more of a protective device than anything seductive.

"I'm ready to dance," she said in a low, throaty voice, and the men nearly tripped over each other in their efforts to reach her first.

The room felt suffocating and oppressive. Anson couldn't leave fast enough. He couldn't stop to find his aunt—he could barely make himself pause at the door to wait for his coat. He had to get out of there and get away from the social insanity. Above all he had to get as far away from Julia Velasco as he could.

But even after he was outside in the chill, fresh air, even after he'd made his escape and was safe in the back seat of a cab, she haunted him.

Over and over again he visualized her clutching that ill-gotten envelope to her breast as though it contained her salvation. Over and over he saw the burning, joyless, darkness of her eyes and heard the laughter that he knew was as false and empty as the life she led.

Chapter Two

Julia drew in a deep breath and willed herself to be calm. The family was all seated for breakfast by now. It was time to begin. Today was the day. *Today.* The thought sent her stomach into knots.

She stopped in front of the full-length mirror and studied her image. The huge, overstuffed purse looked perfectly innocent. The woman in the mirror did not. The woman looked sharp and feral and capable of anything. She looked spoiled and self-centered and vengeful. But at the same time she projected a calmness; she appeared as unruffled as the glassy surface of a mountain lake at dawn.

Julia reached out and covered the reflection's face with her hand. She hated this woman—the woman wearing her face and body in the mirror. But at the same time she couldn't help but be slightly proud of herself for the convincing image she'd managed to project.

Today. The word kept echoing in her mind.

She squared her shoulders and turned away from the mirror. Her audience was waiting. She had to submerge herself in this role just as she'd learned those years ago in drama class. She had to tuck away the real Julia and keep her hidden. And when she glanced back over her shoulder at the glass there was only the image—sarcastically smiling a rueful, bitchy smile. The real Julia was gone. She was ready.

She stepped out of the bedroom and walked down the hall, glancing briefly toward the nursery. There was no emotion in the glance. It was strictly practical. Had the nurse taken Tonio down already?

She paused a moment at the top of the wide sweeping staircase to prepare herself mentally for her entrance. A maid was cleaning the leaded glass at the landing. The maid's name was Rosa and she had a bad back and a sick husband, but Julia couldn't afford to think about that. She couldn't weaken now. She had to maintain the image. She ignored the maid and continued on.

The house felt so still that she had the eerie feeling of being watched, of having her thoughts listened to. Even the house was against her. How she loathed this pretentious city house with its ornate coldness. She'd often wondered how many generations had spent weeks or months in this house without daring to touch anything or make one change. Tradition. Sameness. Preservation of family history. How sick she was of it all.

But after today...

She breezed into the sun-drenched living room with her purse swinging casually from her shoulder and the hint of a smile playing at the corners of her mouth. This was her last meal at the Velasco table. Pure, tingling joy surged through her at the thought.

"Finally," Leticia said in a frosty tone. "We are leaving promptly for our appointment with the designers, so please eat quickly."

"Oh, am I late?" Julia asked as she slid into the place she always occupied. There were no answers, but she received a number of hostile stares for her efforts.

It was the usual cozy family get-together. Everyone looked slightly tired from the late night at the ball, and frown lines were plentiful. But then, they always were. Only Christina seemed capable of smiling.

At the far end of the formally appointed table sat the señor in his oversize head-of-the-table chair. He didn't fill the chair, either literally or figuratively. It dwarfed him and made him appear slightly lost. He seldom spoke at meals, and frequently looked as though he were hundreds of miles away in his thoughts. When he did speak his words were inserted into the table conversation from out of the blue, and the subject was always stamp collecting or dog racing.

At the opposite end of the table and the opposite end of the spectrum was the señora. She ruled the servants' movements with mere glances, and controlled the very air that the family breathed as they endured their meals. Nothing escaped her attention.

The first meals Julia had eaten around that table were still vivid in her mind: "We don't speak to the help while they're serving, Julia." "Exhibiting hunger is crassly lower class, Julia—we are not field hands." "Laughing out loud at the table is vulgar, Julia."

At first the comments had been prefaced with "I realize you don't know any better, Julia..." Later the preface had been amended to "You should have learned by now..."

Now, Julia sat in silence as a maid served her breakfast.

"So you made it down after all," Teresa remarked snidely as Julia picked at her food. "I would have bet you wouldn't after the amount of liquor you drank last night."

Teresa's eyes were filled with hate. Julia was used to it. Sometimes the hate was mingled with jealousy or sometimes gloating or smugness, but it was always there, lurking in the dark reaches of Teresa's glare.

The hate had arisen after Tonio's birth. Before that the snobbish Teresa had seemed to barely notice Julia's existence. Teresa had been wrapped up in her efforts to attract positive attention from Leticia, both for herself and her ineffectual husband, Mariano, and their five little girls.

But Leticia remained an untouchable presence to her family. She was first and foremost the keeper of the Velasco name, the protector of heritage, the vigilant guard over tradition, and only incidentally a mother or wife.

Julia had quickly seen that Teresa had little value to her mother. Teresa was married to a son of the Diaz family, an old-line aristocratic bunch fallen on difficult financial times. Teresa and Mariano had pointedly chosen to forsake the Diaz camp and make their home with the Velascos, but still Leticia was not pleased. The couple had produced only female offspring. There was not a grandson in the litter, and complications during the fifth birth had resulted in a hysterectomy. Teresa and Mariano had lost all hope of ever producing a Velasco grandson.

Leticia's entire life seemed to revolve around her desire for a male heir. Her reaction to Tonio's birth had been fierce and almost biblical. She had held the tiny boy up as though presenting him to God, and had declared, "The Velasco name lives!"

Julia had still been innocent and unsuspecting at that point, but the words had chilled her and filled her with foreboding. In fear and confusion she had looked away from Leticia and been almost stunned by that first glimpse of the newly hatched hatred in Teresa's eyes.

Now she barely noticed it. It was simply a part of living in the chill bosom of the Velasco family.

"I would have bet you wouldn't make it down at all," Teresa repeated, like a nasty child taunting a playmate.

A maid stooped to move Julia's purse from beside her chair and Julia lunged sideways, slapping the woman's hand off the strap and snapping, "No!" at the same time.

The entire family went silent with shock.

Julia forced herself to regain control. The purse held the beginnings of her new life, but still, she shouldn't have panicked so easily. She had to watch herself.

"We'll be going shortly, so just leave it," she explained curtly to the maid without apology. "And in the interest of speed, please have my sable out and waiting at the door."

Julia turned away, frowned and touched her fingers to her temples in a pantomime of a pounding headache.

"I guess I am a little under the weather this morning," she admitted to the silent group to cover for her behavior.

Teresa and Mariano smirked unabashedly, and Christina's forehead creased in worry. The señor looked vaguely impatient, and the corners of Leticia's mouth turned down in a sharp line of disapproval.

Julia signaled for the maid to take her plate. She was anxious to be done with this and get on with her plans.

She scanned the faces at the table again. No one knew. No one suspected.

But then, Juan wasn't present. And sneaky Juan was the one who was always watching her, always fixing his horrible beady eyes on her the way a big rat would watch smaller rats that he suspected were after his cheese. Did that mean anything? Had he guessed her plans?

No, surely not, because she couldn't imagine him hesitating one instant to denounce her if he thought he had any grounds at all. Besides, the place next to Christina had been empty at breakfast a lot lately, so this morning's absence was nothing unusual.

Christina continued to repeat her husband's excuses of urgent government business that detained him. But no one was fooled. Juan Arista's position in the government was just a token thrown to him at Señor Velasco's request. He had no real power. He was in charge of such things as the wording of park plaques and the continuing publicity of long-faded earthquake relief projects—not exactly the sort of high level politics that ever became urgent.

Juan only played at politics. His real job—if it could be called that—was the supervision of the Velasco business accounts.

Julia had found the differences in the two Velasco sons-in-law interesting at first. Mariano was content to coast along, confident that his lineage was all he ever needed in life. Juan Arista was the opposite. The man had an almost insatiable craving for position and authority and seemed vaguely uncomfortable with any mention of his family background. He wanted desperately to be as important as he imagined himself. And Julia was certain that Juan would have gladly taken the name of Velasco at his wedding and never mentioned the Arista ties again.

Julia no longer considered the men interesting. Mariano was a shallow snob and Juan was despicable. Not only was he unprincipled and unfeeling, he was positively dangerous.

How had Christina phrased her warning? "Be careful, Julia. For some reason my husband is set against you. He repeats stories and he presses my mother. He wants your leaving very much."

And just yesterday Julia had happened to overhear the cowardly sneak's latest whisperings. He had said that if Julia was permitted to gain control of Tonio's trust she would squander the entire fortune without regard for the child's financial future.

"Perhaps if you want to visit your sister in the States again for a time," Christina had suggested. "Perhaps Juan and my mother would relax and enjoy Paulo's baby in your absence, and be calmed in their fears of you."

But Julia knew better. Her absence would not calm Leticia and Juan. "Enjoying Paulo's baby" without the thorn of Julia's presence would only encourage them further.

Julia looked across at her sister-in-law. Dear Christina. Always loyal and concerned. Too many miscarriages and too much unhappiness had left her worn and tired, yet she still had an air of gentleness and depth. Seeing the woman maintaining her dignity next to her husband's conspicuously empty place, Julia felt a stab of regret. If only Christina could come with her...

But Julia couldn't afford such sentiments today. The plan required complete coldness and efficiency to work.

Still, it was hard not to feel something when she met Christina's eyes. If she came across a trapped animal with eyes like that, wouldn't she set it free? But then, she knew Christina wouldn't leave her trap even if she had the chance. The trap was her life. It was all she knew.

Christina would remain the dutiful daughter in spite of the fact that her own mother saw her as subhuman. She was the daughter who hadn't attracted any suitors and who had to have a union arranged by her parents; the daughter who had miscarried over and over and couldn't perform the basic female function of carrying a baby to term; the daughter who now couldn't even keep her husband home nights.

And Christina would remain the long-suffering wife because divorce was unthinkable and scandal was unthinkable, and because she carried a terrible burden of guilt for not being able to give her husband the children she'd been taught were every man's right.

Christina caught Julia's eye and shot her a tiny smile. She looked calm and almost cheerful in the face of her husband's absence. Did she ever wish he would just disappear? Julia wondered. Did she ever have fantasies of shooting him or strangling him or sabotaging his car?

The swinging door was held open briefly as the maids carried the dishes and food back to the kitchen, and Julia caught a glimpse of Teresa's five girls sitting quietly at the children's table. But Tonio's high chair was empty and his nurse was not in sight.

Julia's heart jumped into her throat. "Is everyone ready to go, then?" she asked, as though she were not the one who had delayed the departure.

"Yes," Leticia answered curtly.

"We can't possibly all cram into the limo, can we? I mean with the children and the nurses going, too..." She couldn't afford to call any attention by asking about Tonio directly.

"We're using the Diaz car, as well," Leticia answered.

"Oh, good," Julia said, feigning relief, "I simply couldn't tolerate the baby's crying all the way there."

"The baby isn't coming," Leticia said shortly. "Nurse says he is catching a sniffle and she's keeping him in bed today."

The words jolted Julia from head to foot. Not coming! She stared down at the table a moment, thinking frantically. What now? What now? All her planning, all her hopes...

"I thought," she said offhandedly, "that you had an appointment with some children's designer especially for Tonio and the girls."

Leticia drew in a deep breath, as though irritated at having to explain herself. "The girls will keep the appointment," she said. "Antonio will not." Leticia's eyes narrowed slightly. "Do I hear a sudden interest in the child's wardrobe?" she asked carefully.

Julia shrugged. "Hardly," she said. "I mean, who ever heard of a baby having designer clothes, anyway? And especially when he'll just be rolling around in the country soon." As she spoke she fought to recapture her image as well as her composure. Her mind raced. It had to be today. The plans were all for today, and it could take weeks or even months to duplicate them. If it was even possible to duplicate them at all. It had been incredibly difficult to arrange what she had, to scheme and plot and buy what she needed from that horrible, sleazy man.

She fought down the panic growing inside her.

The family was scheduled to go back to the ranch in two weeks—back to the middle of nowhere. The servants would pack all the personal possessions and the city house would be closed for a period, with the furniture draped and the chandeliers suspended in gauzy bags.

Leticia had cut their city time short this year, but no one was allowed to complain. They would quietly load onto helicopters and be flown hundreds of miles into a land of dirt roads and dry grass, a land devoid of telephones or televisions, taxicabs or airports. A land where the sprawling Velasco hacienda sat like a castle in the middle of a kingdom owned lock, stock and human being by the Velasco family.

She couldn't spend another season at the ranch. She couldn't survive it. Either she would go crazy and give the señora the satisfaction of having her legally committed to an asylum, or she would get so desperate that she'd steal Teresa's cache of sleeping pills and gulp down the lot with the señor's expensive Scotch. Or worse...she might snap under the pressure and accept the señora's offer.

No. It had to be today. One way or another she had to try it today. She had to escape.

She moved in a fog, rising from the table with the others and following the señora to the door. She stood mutely as a maid helped her into the sable coat. The coats were ridiculous in the relatively mild Mexico City weather, but today Julia was glad that she was expected to wear a suffocating fur. She'd chosen the sable because it was the most valuable coat she owned. That, too, had been planned in advance.

The exclusive salon that was hosting the designers was ready for them when they arrived. A uniformed doorman ushered them in and maids whisked away their coats, settled them into brocade chairs and placed filled crystal wineglasses on delicate tables beside each of them. Each woman was presented with a slender gold pen and a small leather-bound notebook to record her choices in. The children were spirited away to another area.

The first designer came out, presented himself and introduced his collection. The modeling began.

Julia's heart felt like a stone in her chest. She'd imagined the place and the afternoon's procedures so differently. She'd thought it would be larger and crowded enough that she could slip out easily while the other women were occupied.

First the baby, and now this unworkably small place. Nothing was going right. Nothing was working. How could she ever sneak out without anyone noticing?

She suddenly felt like a child. She was scared and she needed help and she wanted someone to come along and save her. But there was no one. She was completely alone against the world. The one thing she'd been most afraid of in her whole life was true again—she was alone.

But hadn't that been her fatal weakness then, that needing to be saved? Wasn't that what had prompted her to marry Paul, and wasn't that what had made her hand herself over to the Velascos?

Was she going to live her entire life as some pathetic maiden in distress waiting for a savior to bail her out whenever the going got rough, or was she going to finally grow up and take control? This is a test, she told herself wryly. Are you going to lie down and let the world have its way with you or are you finally going to learn to put up a fight and save yourself?

"That one looked like you, Julia," Christina remarked softly.

"What? Oh, yes."

"Aren't you enjoying the show?" Christina asked. "Don't you feel well?"

The question sparked an idea in Julia's mind.

"I, ah, I am feeling a bit queasy," she whispered.

"Dear, dear," Christina clucked. She reached over to take the little gold pen and notebook from Julia's limp hands. "I'll just keep your notes for you, then."

The second designer appeared and went through his routine, but the models and parade of exquisite clothing were nothing but a blur to Julia. Her thoughts raced. She was no maiden anymore—she was a mother. And childbirth had made her strong. Motherhood had made her tough. And she had an idea that might work—*No!* She had an idea that *would* work.

Nothing was going to stop her. She was going to escape today and she was going to take Tonio with her.

Christina leaned toward her. "You look very pale." Her eyes were full of concern. "This nausea, has it happened before?"

Julia almost laughed out loud. Even Christina fell prey to the family's greatest fear—that she might become pregnant. Though when they thought it might happen was a total mystery to her. She was escorted everywhere and watched constantly. At the ranch she was not even allowed to ride her horse alone or go for a walk without a companion. The chaperon concept was the same in varying degrees for all the women, but for Julia, the errant daughter-in-law, it was enforced almost to the point at which she seemed a prisoner in custody. Only the handcuffs were missing.

"No, Christina. But I'm afraid Teresa is right. I may have had too much to drink last night." Of course she had only finished one of the drinks that had been pressed into her hand. "I hate to ruin anyone's day with this— Mother would be absolutely disgraced by my announcing I had a hangover—but I'm afraid I'm feeling steadily worse."

"Madre de Dios." Christina reverted to Spanish. She wrung her hands and chewed on her bottom lip.

"Are you two paying attention?" Leticia demanded from across the room.

"Oh, yes, Mother." Christina stiffened, dropping her hands to her lap like lead weights. "We're just conferring on styles."

Julia nodded agreement.

Time passed with another designer and more models and offers of coffee and wine refills. The plan grew and jelled in her mind. By the time the modeling concluded she knew exactly what she had to do and how she would do it.

"Luncheon will be served in fifteen minutes, madame." The proprietor's French accent was questionable as he addressed Leticia.

The room suddenly buzzed with activity. As the women stood and began to compare notes, servants appeared in droves, scurrying about with various liquid refreshments and trays of appetizers. The three designers and their secretaries joined the activity, and the proprietor and his assistant hovered watchfully.

"The powder room is through that door and to the left," one of the maids advised each woman discreetly.

Leticia and Teresa immediately headed through the indicated door, and Christina started to follow.

Julia reached out quickly, stopping Christina with a hand on the woman's arm.

"How many did you put down for me?" Julia asked.

Christina turned toward her and fumbled for the little notebook. Her lips moved as she counted to herself. "Fourteen possibilities for you, twelve for me." She smiled. "I hope lunch makes you feel better; we have so much fitting to do this afternoon."

"I hope so, too," Julia agreed. She stalled, chatting aimlessly about the clothes until she saw Leticia and Teresa returning from the powder room. "Well," she said weakly, "shall we go freshen up?"

So far, so good. Her knees shook slightly on her way down the long hall. There were a number of doors, which meant many possibilities. Her scheme was workable.

The first step was accomplished. She had Christina alone in the bathroom. Catching sight of herself in the mirror, Julia almost smiled at her reflection. She certainly looked the part of a person stricken with something. She held one hand up to her head, placed the other on her stomach and leaned weakly against the wall.

"Are you all right?" Christina asked fearfully.

"Perhaps lunch will help," Julia said faintly.

She moved through the louvered door into the poshly appointed toilet cubicle. She paused for a moment, listening to Christina washing her hands, and gathered herself for the unsavory task she'd laid out for herself.

Bending over, she forced herself to retch and gag loudly. Her unsteady stomach made her fear for a moment that she might actually be sick. When she stepped back out of the cubicle and reached for the dampened cloth Christina offered, she felt as shaky as if she had actually been sick.

"I'll take you home," Christina said, her eyes dark with worry. "We can send them our measurements. You belong in bed."

Julia shook her head. That was definitely not what she needed. Being sent home with Christina as a hovering companion and all the servants instructed to take care of her would be an impossible situation.

"No, Christina. Your mother would be furious, and I can't afford to give her something else to be angry over."

"What will you do, then?"

"I'll just have to try to make it through the afternoon without her noticing anything is wrong."

"But how—"

Julia couldn't meet Christina's eyes as she spoke. She was using the woman and it felt awful. "I think we could work something out. I mean, if you would help me."

"Of course! Of course I will help you. But what—" the woman extended her hands helplessly "—what can I possibly do?"

"Just help me cover up, help me keep it from them." Julia discarded the damp towels and moved over to wash her hands at the sink. She couldn't bear to meet Christina's eyes.

"Can you possibly make it through lunch?" Christina asked.

"I think so. And then... perhaps if you insisted we be fitted together. Then... if I needed any help..."

"Oh, yes, yes. Of course," Christina said, solicitously dabbing some of her own makeup on Julia's ghostly face. "Here," she said, holding out a lipstick, "put some of this on now and you'll look much better."

Julia complied meekly and then followed her sister-in-law to the luncheon room. It was going to work. It had to work.

They were barely noticed as they slipped into their places at the ornate French dining table. All the designers were busy flattering the señora and building their orders. Julia pushed her food around on her plate silently and avoided Christina's eyes. *It was going to work*.

The syrupy interchange at Leticia's end of the table dragged on and on until Julia wanted to scream. Instead, she concentrated on her own anger. Juan was treacherous, but his only power came through Leticia. It

"Together?" Leticia arched an eyebrow. "Four people in one fitting room? It will be too cramped to work."

"Oh, no," Christina assured her quickly, "we'll only use one fitter and she can alternate between us."

Leticia frowned and considered her daughter silently a moment.

"I do not understand young women," she said irritably. "I've intentionally arranged it so we have the comfort of separate rooms and individual fitters, and now you two—" she included Julia in her frown "—are insisting on being in a room together with one fitter?"

Christina nodded.

Leticia dismissed them with a wave of her hand and a disapproving look. The absence of a firm no meant that the answer was yes. Julia's heart soared in her chest.

They were shown into a plushly carpeted, square room with mirrored walls, and introduced to a small youngish woman with a tape measure draped around her neck and a cushion full of straight pins fastened to her wrist. The woman, Anna, was clearly not happy at having to fit both women by herself.

"You go first," Julia told Christina. "I'll just sit down over here for a bit." She sank down onto the plump love seat in an exaggerated semifaint, glancing at her watch as she sank. Time was growing short. She had to make her move immediately.

"Señora!" Anna cried. "Are you ill?"

"Yes," Julia admitted hesitantly. "I am...indisposed. I'm afraid that my widowhood overcomes me at times." She leaned her head back and fanned herself.

"But, señora, fitting is very tiring, and you are not well enough for it at this time." The woman moved toward the door and placed her hand on the knob. "I'll send word to the señora—"

"No, no," Christina cut in quickly. "We do not wish the señora to be upset by this. It would ruin the whole afternoon."

"She would probably insist that we all return home immediately," Julia added, "and postpone placing any orders."

Julia could see the fitter's mind anxiously considering all this. The woman was as readable as a child's book. At first she'd been worried that she might somehow be faulted for not summoning immediate attention for a sick customer. Then at Julia's mention of them all leaving and postponing their orders, she became fluttery and mildly hysterical. She was well aware of the importance of these orders and she obviously didn't want to be the one who broke the news of Julia's illness, causing the señora to become upset and leave with her entourage in tow.

"If I could just lie down on a couch someplace quiet for an hour or two, I'm sure I would be much improved," Julia offered.

Christina picked up her alligator purse and reached into it for bills. "Surely there is someplace quiet my sister-in-law can rest without anyone else knowing about it," Christina said softly, pressing the money into the fitter's hand.

The woman glanced down at the money and swallowed so hard that her Adam's apple visibly bobbed. Julia held her breath and clenched her hands into fists, her long nails pressing painfully into the soft flesh of her palm. Come on, she thought. Say yes!

The fitter suddenly broke into a solicitous smile. "Yes, yes. I am certain there is such a place." She put her hand on the knob again. "One moment while I check."

"No one is to know of this," Julia cautioned her as she left, and the woman nodded agreement. "And if possible, please bring my coat—the sable. I'm feeling chilled."

The woman nodded again.

"*Ah, Dios*, Mother will be very angry if she learns we've been sneaking around behind her back like this," Christina said nervously.

Julia nodded weakly. She did know how angry the señora would be when she learned of all this, and she couldn't afford to think about how she was leaving Christina to face Leticia's anger.

Christina leaned over her on the love seat and placed a cool palm against her forehead. The woman's eyes were full of concern.

Impulsively Julia reached up to hug her. Christina pulled back in surprise, fixing Julia with a questioning look.

Julia dropped her arms and looked down. "I'm sorry for all this trouble..."

"Oh. No, no, no. I'm glad to help. I'm glad you trust me in this way."

Julia groaned inwardly. This was awful. Would Christina ever understand or forgive her?

The fitter slipped back in quietly, the rich fur draped over her arm. "Come," she whispered. "I have the place for you to rest." The woman opened the door a crack and checked the hallway, then motioned to Julia with her hand. "It is clear. Follow me."

Christina made a move to accompany them and the fitter waved her back with a whispered "No! If I return alone it will look as if I had to go get something."

Christina nodded. "Sleep," she said to Julia. "I will come to check on you in...?"

"About an hour and a half," Julia said, knowing that asking for any longer would arouse suspicion.

She reached out and touched Christina's arm gently, swallowing against the lump in her throat. As she stepped out into the hall, she suddenly realized she might never see her sister-in-law again.

Adrenaline raced through her veins as she followed the fitter down one empty hall and then another, finally arriving in a quiet office. Julia lay down on the couch immediately. The fitter hesitated a moment, clearly uncertain.

"You can leave now," Julia said firmly. "I will be fine here."

As soon as the woman left, Julia sprang from the couch and ran to the door to listen. Nothing. She opened the door and peered into the hall. Empty.

It was working!

She turned and surveyed the room quickly. It was cheaply furnished and one corner was piled high with boxes. The desk had a light film of dust, as though it was temporarily out of use. She couldn't have hoped for anything more!

Chapter Three

Anson threw the last of his belongings into his battered suitcase and coaxed the locks into place. The bag was overstuffed and poorly arranged, as usual, but he refused to let the servants pack for him.

He straightened his tie in the mirror and combed his sandy curls back off his forehead with his fingers. There were dark circles under his eyes from a restless night. Maybe he would have a chance to sleep on the plane and catch up.

After placing his suitcase and garment bag near the door, he paused a moment to survey the room before stepping out. It was hard to believe he had spent his last two years of high school here. His Aunt Helen had even preserved it with his old mementos still hanging on the walls. But it all felt so foreign to him now.

He took the stairs two at a time, pulling on his suit jacket as he went and throwing a smile at old Raoul, who was polishing the carved banister with tiny careful motions. The others were already seated at the long, gleaming walnut table when he entered the dining room, and they all greeted him with smiling good mornings.

Nothing much had changed in the Obregon household. Meals were still important and there was as much warmth and lively banter as ever. He had to admit that there were times, eating in the silence of his New York apartment, that he missed all this companionship and ceremony and the comfort of family.

"You don't look rested, dear," his aunt scolded in her fragile voice, with its faint North Dakota lilt.

"Maybe he didn't really go home early from the ball." Miguel winked as he passed a heavily laden platter. "Maybe he met some señorita..."

"Miguel!"

"Why, Mother," Miguel said innocently, "I thought you desired Anson's marriage. How can he ever be married if he does not chase a few señoritas?"

"The sort of young woman who would be meeting him on the sly late at night is not marriage material," Helen declared primly.

Anson had to smile. His aunt had lived the life of a Mexican matron so long that she had adopted the attitudes completely and forgotten her upbringing. The "good woman-bad woman" concept was strongly ingrained in upper-crust Mexican society.

"You would be surprised, Mother, at the behavior of some of the modern young women. Even those from good families," Miguel teased.

"Too much is tolerated now!" Helen declared. "There is not enough discipline anymore. Take that Velasco daughter-in-law; the whole city is talking about her disgraceful behavior last night. Baby or no baby, she ought to be put in line."

"I'd like to put her in line," Miguel said with a smirk, wiggling his eyebrows lasciviously. "How about you, Anson?"

"Maybe you should apply for the job." Anson laughed shortly but felt no mirth. The last thing he wanted to do was discuss Julia Velasco or think about her in any way.

"You know the Velascos," she said to Ignacio. "Why don't they just pay the woman off and be done with it? It's obvious she'll never mother that child." She shook her head. "What could the son have been thinking, marrying a tramp like that?"

"I don't think a payoff would work to get rid of her," Miguel reflected, downing half a glass of fresh juice. "She inherited, didn't she? She's probably wealthy."

"Not yet," Ignacio said reluctantly. "It is public knowledge that there is a trust that will revert to her child. However, she does not gain control of the funds for several more years. Until that time she is a beggar."

"Such a shame!" Helen declared. "She'll never take responsibility for that baby. The kindest thing she could do for the child and everyone concerned would be to go back to the States and leave him to be raised in peace and dignity as a Velasco."

"That is clear to all, my dear." Ignacio smiled gently. "And it would be the most desirable outcome, but Señor Velasco is a gentleman and she is the mother of his only grandson. I believe that the señor and señora are waiting for her to set the terms, for her to make the opening move, as they say."

Ignacio gestured with his fork. "Something will happen soon." He nodded knowingly. "It appears that her interest in the child has been steadily declining. Surely she will not be happy to return to the quiet of the ranch after the gaiety she has so enjoyed in the city. When she faces that prospect she will probably make her deal."

"And if she doesn't present her leaving price," Helen said, "I wonder how much more of her behavior the Velascos can put up with?"

"I do not know," Ignacio said with a heavy sigh. "I pity the family. Their patience and kindness has been sorely tried by this woman."

At that moment, a servant appeared with a fresh pot of coffee, breaking the gloomy spell.

"And so, dear—" Helen dabbed at her mouth delicately with a damask napkin as she addressed Anson "—are you and Miguel off now?"

"Yes. If you'll excuse us," Anson said, rising and placing his napkin on the table, "we need to leave shortly."

Anson went upstairs to fetch his luggage. Although he loved his aunt and uncle dearly, and never failed to miss them, he was anxious to be gone. If he stayed much longer he would end up arguing with his uncle and upsetting his aunt.

He simply didn't belong here. He hated the rigidly structured, violently intolerant circles of money and power they were associated with. And he tired easily of their not so subtle efforts to change and redirect his life, of their veiled disapproval of nearly everything he did.

He knew they'd felt the same when he'd been in high school and living under their roof. Only then it had been much milder, more like a constantly present, vague exasperation. Their expectations and outright disappointment had increased with his age.

He knew they sometimes asked themselves where they had gone wrong with their orphaned nephew, and he wished he could somehow make them see that just because he was very, very different from them didn't mean anything was wrong. Each time he came for a visit he hoped that they might have softened, might have decided to like him and accept him just as he was—but, if anything, their disapproval seemed to be growing stronger.

His aunt stood in the courtyard crying into a handkerchief, and Ignacio stood stiffly beside her, with one arm around her shoulders. How he dreaded these goodbyes, Anson thought dispiritedly. They always left him feeling so inexplicably guilty.

Miguel pulled up in his racy new sports car and jumped out to load the luggage.

"We must buy you a nice leather traveling set for Christmas," his aunt said in a quavery voice. "It's not fitting that a successful professional man should travel with those bags. My word! What would the bellmen think if you checked into a nice hotel with such things?"

Anson shrugged. "Probably the same thing the nurses think when you're delivered to the emergency room with dirty underwear."

Miguel straightened from stuffing in the bags and fixed him with a questioning grin.

"Just what is that supposed to mean?" his aunt demanded impatiently. At least she wasn't crying anymore.

Anson laughed. "I don't know. Something just reminded me of one of the things Grandma used to say all the time: 'Don't forget to change your underwear—you never know when you'll be in an accident and have to go to the hospital.'"

Miguel laughed uproariously and slapped his thigh.

"Well, what's so funny about that?" Helen asked indignantly.

"Forget it," Anson said, hugging his aunt tightly. "Leaving is too sad."

"Then stay," Ignacio said expansively. "We could make it Obregon, Obregon and Wolfe."

"Thanks for the thought," Anson said, a lump forming in his throat as his uncle embraced him in a great bear hug.

He moved toward the low-slung car and opened the door, then turned back toward them. "It's good to know I'm always welcome here. But you know what a pigheaded Swede I am about making my own way." He grinned and reached out to slap his uncle's beefy arm. "Why don't all of you just move to New York?"

His aunt responded with an "Oooohhhhh!" and his uncle laughed and shook a thick finger at him.

His goodbyes to Miguel were just as hard, if not more so. Poor Miguel was caught somewhere in the middle. He didn't believe completely in the life his parents revered, yet he wasn't quite willing to really step out on his own and chance anything different, either. Except for the new legal aid clinic he was so valiantly trying to start, he had stuck faithfully to his parents' life plan for him, living his secret dreams vicariously through his crazy cousin.

Anson knew how important he was to Miguel and how much Miguel hated to see him go. Mercifully for both of them, Miguel had an urgent appointment that afternoon and couldn't accompany him into the terminal for lingering goodbyes.

Anson checked in at the proper counter, ridding himself of his luggage and watching with amusement as his tattered pieces joined a pile of designer bags festooned with initials.

Strolling about the airport aimlessly, he watched people and let his mind wander. He had allowed himself far too much time between check-in and takeoff, and now had no way in which to fill it. He headed for the newsstand in hopes of a *New York Times*. No luck. He surveyed the magazines. Stock was low for some reason. Finally he bought a local paper.

He kept moving until he found something to drink, then settled into a chair and worked at relaxing. Perhaps if he concentrated on relaxation now he would be in the right frame of mind to fall asleep as soon as the plane left the ground. He leaned his head back and closed his eyes.

Images raced through his brain. Sleek limousines. The disappointed, disapproving look in his aunt's eyes. The jaded glamour of the ball. The burning unhappiness in Julia Velasco's eyes. He was glad to be leaving.

Restlessly he sat up and opened the paper. Mexico City's myriad problems assaulted him from every story. He leafed through the front section hurriedly, not wanting to delve too deeply into any one account of excess or misery. The name Velasco leaped out at him as he flipped pages, and he automatically turned back.

The focal point of the piece was a large picture of a man presiding over a table heaped with mail. It was the heavy-jowled man he'd seen in the Velasco party—the one whose face had briefly shown that strangely gleeful expression at the height of Julia's entrance scene. He was smiling expansively, but the smile did not touch his eyes.

Anson scanned the story. The man was Juan Arista, a Velasco son-in-law, and the story was a saccharine account of Arista's role in coordinating earthquake relief funds from the U.S. in previous years. No doubt the efforts of a hardworking public relations firm, Anson thought cynically. Somehow he found it hard to believe that the shifty-eyed Arista had ever been struck with a charitable impulse in his life.

Anson twisted the paper into a tight ball and shoved it down the mouth of the nearby trash receptacle. Enough. The world he'd chosen for himself in New York required every ounce of his caring and determination. He couldn't afford to expend energy on worries relating to a city in his past, an overwhelming city, a city he wanted to put behind him. At least in New York he felt he could make a difference.

He wadded his poplin raincoat into a ball and propped it up between the wall and his head. Now he really would relax. He would push Mexico City back into his subconscious where it belonged. He still had plenty of time before boarding and he intended to drift, maybe even doze a little, and be mellow enough by takeoff time to fall asleep before the plane even lifted off the runway.

Julia stood in the center of the deserted office. She had to keep calm and think clearly.

She looked down at her watch. An hour and a half. Ninety minutes before anyone would realize she was gone, and then possibly another thirty minutes while they panicked and tried to decide what to do. Maybe up to an hour more before serious muscle or the police were called in. But there was an even more pressing time element to consider—takeoff time. She was cutting it close. Very, very close.

But then her only chance lay in cutting it so close that they'd never dream she could have made that particular flight.

The room's single window peered at her. Could she possibly? It would be much safer than trying to sneak out through the building as she'd planned.

She rushed to the grimy window and shoved it open. The chill, smoggy air blasted her in the face as she leaned out to survey the surroundings. The window opened onto a narrow, littered alley. There was not a soul about to witness her escape. Her entire body tingled with the energy racing through her veins. This was it.

She pushed the desk chair over to the window. Then she pulled up her skirt and retrieved the envelope from the front of her panty hose, where she'd been wearing it pressed against her stomach. The crackle of paper had been comforting against her skin, constantly reminding her that freedom awaited.

The indignity she'd suffered at the hands of the sleazy character who'd delivered her black market purchase that night at the ball had all been worth it. The envelope held the key to her escape—her airline tickets.

After putting the envelope in her purse where she could reach it quickly, she hefted the purse strap around her neck, pulled on her coat and hiked her skirt up to allow stepping onto the chair.

Carefully, feeling uncoordinated and clumsy, she hung on to the side moldings and slid her legs forward through the opening, finally resting her bottom on the inner sill. She straightened, sitting up in the open window, with her legs dangling out into space. The drop looked farther now. The alley had moved dizzyingly downward.

Suddenly she had the crazy urge to laugh. She could imagine the bizarre picture she made—fashionably dressed woman, skirt hiked up and stockinged legs dangling out of an open alley window. She fought down the giddy feeling, realizing that she was dangerously close to hysteria.

Stop it! she ordered herself, and drew in a deep, forceful breath. She kicked free of her suede pumps and let them fall to the ground. She couldn't risk landing hard on high heels and twisting an ankle.

Twisting an ankle... Her stomach contracted into a knot. What if she fell wrong and broke an arm or leg! What if someone saw her and called the police! What if... Panic gripped her and she froze. Once she dropped from the window that was it. There was no turning back even if she wanted to. They would know. They would know she had been trying to run away.

Visions of barred rooms filled her mind. Who knew what Leticia was capable of? Prisons? Asylums? Leticia's anger might have no bounds. Especially if Julia's purse was opened and her contraband was found. Taking the jewels would be bad enough, but when the baby food was discovered they would know she'd also planned to take Antonio.

She could still change her mind. She could climb back in and tear up the ticket and flush it down the toilet. She could invent some story about looking out of the window with her shoes in her hand and dropping them. She could forget all this and choose other courses, submissively accepting whatever the Velascos had in store for herself and Tonio, or surrendering completely to them and leaving.

The señora's offer blazed through her mind. The nerve of the woman! She had actually offered Julia a large settlement in exchange for Tonio. She'd wanted Julia to sign over all rights to the baby and disappear.

"Time is running out," Leticia had threatened. "The family's offer stands for you to consider, but soon it will be changed and the new terms we offer may not be so pleasant for you."

"Oh, no, Leticia," Julia whispered to herself vehemently. "I'm setting the terms now." She gritted her teeth and slid forward. Time was running out for her. Time was running out for them all.

She turned to face the building so she could hang on to the sill and lower herself slowly before dropping. She hung there for a moment, clinging fearfully. The street still seemed too far below her dangling feet. The rough, dirty wall bit into the skin of her cheek. She could feel her fingers slipping.

She fell.

She landed hard and off balance. Her stocking feet hit the pavement with a slap and she toppled sideways, striking her hip and elbow. Instinctively she reached out with one opened hand to catch herself before her head could smack the ground.

Pain radiated through her. The soles of her feet burned. Her hip was almost frozen with pain. A sharp, electric tingling came from her elbow, creating a numbness from the joint down to the fingertips of that hand. Her scraped and bleeding palm throbbed.

Julia took a deep breath and forced herself to sit up, pulling the purse strap off over her head. Had she broken anything inside it? There was no time to check. She stretched, reaching first one shoe and then the other from her sitting position.

Finally she stood. A wave of dizziness made her reach out to the wall for support. She felt sick and weak. Dazedly, she focused on her watch. The crystal was shattered but the second hand was still moving. She squinted to read the time through the fractured glass. She had to go now.

Still leaning against the wall she put on her shoes. She pulled the purse strap onto her shoulder and started toward the street, slowly at first and then, as the fear built inside her, breaking into a run.

She was breathless and clammy with sweat beneath the heavy coat by the time she settled into the taxi's back seat.

The driver had been startled by her appearance when she'd jumped into the taxi, shouting the address of the Velasco house.

"Is the señora all right?" he asked hesitantly.

"Yes, thank you. I've just had some unsettling news." Her mind raced for a story that would get the desired effect. "I've just learned that my husband has had an accident and I must fly to him. In my haste I ran out of the building, unable to wait for my driver to return—" she glanced down and noticed her ruined hose "—and I'm afraid I fell and ruined some of my clothing."

"Oh, señora, I am very sorry. I—"

"I must pick up my baby," she said, "then go quickly to catch the plane. There is not a moment to lose. My husband—" she covered her eyes with her hands for a moment "—my husband needs me."

"I am at your service, señora!"

"I appreciate that, and I of course will reward your kindness well."

The driver beamed at her in the rearview mirror and gunned the engine. The city raced by in tune to her pounding heart.

"There, around the side," she directed him. "Park over there and I'll just run in the back gate. It's much quicker. And remember, I will be generous if you deliver me to the airport on time."

The driver nodded eagerly.

Julia unlocked the servants' gate and slipped into the side yard. Skirting the fallow garden, she cut through some bushes and raced around to the old delivery door. It was left from the days when every item was delivered by a different individual, before the coming of central suppliers and big trucks, and it was hardly ever used anymore.

Quietly stepping into the tiny receiving area, she listened. There were voices coming from the kitchen. She crept closer to the door and put her ear against it. It was Tonio's nurse's voice! Was the baby in there with her?"

"I can't leave the house," the woman was insisting. "The baby might wake up and I could get into a lot of trouble."

Pause.

"I've already had to lie to be here this afternoon. They wanted me to take the baby for new clothes today."

"How long does the rich *niño* usually nap?" a gruff male voice demanded.

"Several hours."

"How long until the cook comes back?" he demanded in the same gruff tone.

"An hour perhaps."

"And the others are busy cleaning?"

"Yes."

"Then there is no one to notice if you should need air and a walk. Or if that walk should lead to the garden shed."

Silence.

"I am going to the garden shed now. I expect you there quickly." Then, in a softer voice, he added, "I have missed you, Delphina."

Julia heard the slamming of the servants' door as the man left.

What now? Would the nurse go up to check on the baby before leaving? Would she leave and go out to the little building? Would she decide to use the old door and come through the very hallway where she was hiding? Oh, God, what should she do?

Her eyes darted about frantically. The closet! She raced over and shut herself in a large dusty closet, filled with extra cleaning supplies. She left the door open a crack and tried to hear and see. Nothing.

The moments were endless and filled with fear. She had come this far...

A sound. She put an eye to the crack. It was the nurse. Just as Julia had feared, the woman was slipping out through the old entrance—the closest one to the shed. At the door the nurse stopped, glanced around furtively, her tongue darting out to lick her lips, then she was gone, closing the old door softly behind her.

Quickly Julia left the closet, slipped off her heels and left them there. She padded soundlessly down the hall, bypassing the kitchen, and entered the servants' parlor. From there she crept silently up the narrow utility stairs. She heard a faraway peal of laughter and then the hum of a vacuum cleaner. Luckily the servants were forbidden to clean near the nursery when Tonio was napping, so that wing would be clear.

She hurried down the main upstairs hallway. The carpet was dappled with late afternoon sunlight filtering in through a large window. She had an eerie sense of déjà vu.

When she slipped into the nursery she was overwhelmed by a rush of emotion. There was the ornate crib, with its profusion of attached toys and its bright quilt and its unnecessary lace-edged pillows. And snuggled beneath the quilt, knees drawn up and bottom in the air, tiny hands clenched into fists and silky dark hair sticking out in unruly tufts was the baby. Her baby.

Gently, yet with precise movements, she scooped him up into her arms and wrapped the quilt around him, using a corner of it to partially cover his face. His little mouth opened and closed, and beneath his eyelids she could see his eyes move back and forth. He was dreaming. She held him tightly, fighting back the tears that were threatening, and surveyed the room. Was there anything else she should take for him? Anything she hadn't already thought of? There was no time to think about it. diaper bag stood on the changing table, and she grabbed it as she left.

Again, the hall was deserted. Julia slipped out of the nursery, pulling the door shut softly and clutching her precious bundle tightly to her breast. Thank God he was a sound sleeper. She went back the same way, down the utility stairs and through the old delivery door, pausing only to retrieve her shoes. The garden shed stood between her and the gate. Damn! She hadn't thought of that. Were Delphina and her visitor in there right now?

She crouched and ran along the line of a hedge to the shed. The baby stirred slightly. *Don't wake up,* she prayed silently. *Not now. Please don't wake up.*

She edged along one side of the shed. Were they inside? Would they hear her? The gate was so close. She readjusted her purse and the diaper bag and shifted the baby for a better grip. Then she half squatted, half bent and moved awkwardly beneath the level of the shed's window. Leaves crackled beneath her feet, and the muscles in her back and thighs burned with her efforts at stealth.

Giggles and soft scuffling movements sounded from inside the little building. The couple was inside, but apparently they weren't noticing anything.

At the corner of the shed Julia stood up straight again. Gathering herself, she drew in a shaky breath, straightened her shoulders, then moved with confidence and purpose out through the gate and into the back seat of the taxi.

The driver turned, surprised by her sudden appearance and instantly apologetic for not having jumped out to open her door in time. He beamed down at the sleeping baby, made a little cooing noise in his throat and opened his mouth to speak.

Julia cut him off sharply before he could utter a word.

"The airport," she said. "Fast." She pulled the equivalent of fifty dollars from her wallet and showed it to him. "This is yours if I make my plane."

His eyes popped out and a film of sweat glistened on his upper lip. *"Sí, señora. Sí.* I understand. Great haste."

Anson was groggy as he walked onto the plane and found his seat. Damn, he thought, it was an aisle one. He would be constantly jostled and wakened during the flight by passengers en route to the bathrooms or flight attendants with their serving carts. He hadn't remembered to specify seating at check-in and the clerk had probably thought she was doing him a favor, placing him on the aisle where he would have the chance to occasionally stretch out his too-tall-for-an-airline-seat form.

"Excuse me," he said, trying to catch the attention of one of the attendants.

The nearest uniformed woman raised her carefully penciled eyebrows. They were colored to match her artificially red hair.

"If the plane's not full, could I possibly be moved to a window seat?"

The woman looked at him sternly, as though he had suggested breaking some rule.

"I just—" he shrugged apologetically "—can't sleep well on the aisle."

"I'll see what I can do, sir," she said formally. "But I can't move anyone until all passengers are on board and the doors are closed."

"Thank you. I appreciate it," he returned gratefully, amused at the ability of the woman to make him feel as though she were doing him a favor rather than simply performing her job.

He sat down, his raincoat and briefcase on his lap, irritated at the prospect of staying alert and ready to move for an indefinite period of time. Though he had been toward the end of the boarding line, passengers were still straggling on, bumping into him as they fumbled awkwardly down the aisle with their carryons and *piñatas* and souvenir straw purses.

The activity gradually trickled down and stopped. He glanced at his watch—surely it was time for takeoff. The watch was stopped at twelve, and a crisscross of fine lines radiated from the center of the crystal. Damn, he'd broken another one! He'd checked the clocks in the terminal whenever he'd wanted the time, so he hadn't even noticed.

He destroyed watches so reliably that he had long ago vowed to never spend more than twenty-five dollars on one of the things. Why couldn't they make indestructible watches, anyway?

The flight attendants began readying for their seat belt and oxygen demonstrations. Surely everyone was on board by now, so why couldn't he change his seat. As if in answer to his thoughts the red-haired attendant appeared and advised him that she had done him the favor of locating another seat. He gathered himself for moving. Suddenly there was a commotion in the front and the attendant frowned. "One moment, sir. They seem to be allowing late boarders on."

He sagged back into his seat and she marched down the aisle toward the activity. She returned quickly with the news that he was a lucky man. The late passenger did not have the ticket for the window seat she was moving him to—the only window seat left, she stressed.

He stood, suppressing a grin at her officiousness, hefted his coat over his shoulder and picked up his briefcase. He cast a brief glance toward the front of the aircraft. There was a bustle of activity as several attendants helped the latecomer settle in, stowing what looked like a diaper bag in the overhead bin. The passenger, a slender, stylishly dressed woman holding a bundle he presumed was a baby, had her back to him and was conversing with an attendant. Suddenly the woman turned, maneuvering into the row and dropping into a middle seat.

Just as Anson took a step into the aisle he stopped dead and stared in stunned disbelief. In that one fleeting instant the woman looked incredibly like Julia Velasco!

Now he could see nothing but a sea of heads and backs of seats, and he had the compelling urge to walk up the aisle and stare at the woman—to see her close up—to reassure himself that it wasn't Julia Velasco.

"Sir," the attendant said, clearing her throat impatiently. "Have you changed your mind about moving?"

"Oh, um, yes—I mean no. I'm ready."

Reluctantly he followed her down the aisle toward the rear and buckled himself into his new window seat. It was in the smoking section, but that was a small price to pay for hours of uninterrupted sleep.

He wadded up his coat and stowed it in the overhead bin. It looked forlorn between a carefully folded Burberry and a chic leather jacket. He stepped over two scowling men and settled himself, shoving his battered briefcase with one side of the handle held on by a bent paper clip, under the seat. Had he really seen Julia Velasco, or was the woman haunting his subconscious to the point that he was imagining her face on someone else?

Of course it wasn't Julia, he told himself. What a crazy notion. His exhaustion was making his eyes play tricks on him. He yawned and leaned back, absently gazing out the window at the airport activity.

He was so tired. Tired from his sleepless night. Tired from his work with Miguel's impractical clinic ideas. Tired from his verbal fencing with his aunt and uncle. And most of all, tired of Mexico City, with its hopeless poverty and its bored aristocrats, with its flagrant greed and corruption and discrimination, and with its Julia Velascos. He much preferred a clean, crime-free, well-run, people-oriented city like New York. He smiled to himself at the absurdity.

Still, he could have sworn... *You are persistent, Counselor,* he chided himself silently. But he knew that he wouldn't be satisfied until he was able to get a close look at the woman.

What if it *was* Julia Velasco? The question drifted in his mind, floating into his dreams as his eyes grew heavy and he sank into a deep, troubled sleep.

The baby still hadn't roused. Julia held him tightly, her heart pounding in her chest, her breathing not yet recovered from running through the airport and begging the airline people to open the door and allow her on board the plane. Such a close call—she still couldn't relax. Not until the jet was airborne. Not until she was off Mexican soil and headed toward Texas.

The engines rumbled and then the plane shook gently with the force of the powerful jets. Slowly, the plane taxied until it made a wide swinging turn and stopped. Suddenly the engines revved and the entire craft shuddered and lurched forward, picking up speed until it was racing down the concrete and finally lifted off the end of the runway with a resounding roar.

The pilot ascended almost vertically, putting everything on a tilt and making the pressure build in Julia's ears. The baby stirred and made a face, then opened his eyes and let out an angry wail. The pilot banked gently and eased up on his climb and the attendants unbuckled their harnesses and hurried to their stations.

"Shh," Julia crooned, rocking the baby gently in her arms.

"It's his ears," a sympathetic attendant said, pausing to lean over and pat Tonio's back. "Does he have anything to suck on?"

Julia looked at her blankly.

"Sucking helps to clear their ears. You know, like chewing gum." The young woman's Southern accent was so un-Mexican—so comforting.

"Oh." Julia smiled. Thank you."

The baby had stopped crying on his own, though. He had resorted to his favorite comforter, his thumb and index finger, and he had them planted firmly in his mouth and was sucking like mad. His teary eyes were round and frightened.

"He'll be just dandy now," the woman drawled with a sunny smile. "Do you have a bottle needs heatin' or anything?"

"No, he drinks from a cup. But some juice would be nice whenever you get the chance."

"Sure." The woman smiled again and reached out to pat Tonio's head. "Anything for a cutie pie."

The attendant moved down the aisle, and all at once Julia sagged. She felt as if all her bones had been turned to jelly. Her eyelids drooped, her head felt too heavy to hold up. The only strength she had left was in her arms—just enough to cradle her child.

She lifted him slightly, brushing her face against his silky head, breathing his wonderful baby smell, hearing the faint sucking noises. His body quivered in a little sob, left over from the frantic wailing, and she clutched him to her with a sudden ferociousness, pulling his blankets up to shield them both from view. Tears flowed down her face as she wept soundlessly, her cheek pressed against the top of his delicate head.

They had made it. No one had found them or recognized them. No one had caught them or sounded the alarm. By the time the family pieced it all together and traced her, she would have disappeared in the anonymity of New York City. No one could stop her now.

"We did it, Tonio," she whispered through trembling lips. "We did it."

Chapter Four

He would never know now.

Anson had slept through landing and had been one of the last passengers off the crowded plane, so he had missed seeing the woman. She was most likely in a cab and halfway to a Neiman-Marcus by now. Or on a connecting flight to Omaha, Nebraska. It wasn't that he hadn't tried, either. He'd been so obsessed with knowing that he'd walked and looked and even checked the luggage-claiming areas. But he hadn't caught so much as a glimpse of her. She was obviously gone, so he could relax and forget about it.

He felt a vague sense of relief as he headed toward the gate for his connecting New York flight. The matter was over and he could put it out of his mind completely. No more thoughts of Julia Velasco. He could banish the woman from his mind.

* * *

Running away. Why did that suddenly feel so much like a defeat to Julia rather than a victory?

Sitting in the plastic, Houston airport chair with a fussy baby—bone-weary, fearful and fighting an almost overwhelming sense of desolation— Julia wondered if her entire life would consist of one retreat after another. Would she never develop the strength to stand and fight? Had Paul been right about her all along?

Why, at twenty-five years of age, did she again feel as buffeted and vulnerable as she had at fifteen? Why couldn't she seem to shake this quaking need for someone bigger and stronger and smarter to come along and save her from life?

And running away again. Was that the only solution she'd ever be capable of? The only action she'd ever have the nerve to take?

She saw, looking back at her childhood, how easily she'd slipped into these patterns. Of course it was probably normal for an orphan to feel alone and to search for some benevolent protector. And the terrible foster care situations had spawned the urges to take flight.

What a shock that first experience had been. Quite a change for the Lehman girls, who had always been the lights of their devoted parents' lives.

No more pink-curtained bedrooms full of dolls. No more lazy days with neighborhood playmates. No more affection or encouragement. No more music lessons for Beth or extracurricular sports for Julia. The Lehman girls were the worst kind of orphans—a pair of kids past the age of "cute," with no relatives or friends willing or able to take them in.

They were shuffled from situation to situation. Some were decent, some were not. Julia ran away halfheartedly from two of the bad ones, but was easily recaptured. Schools changed in dizzying progression and Beth retreated into a tough, sullen shell and Julia grew vague and timid. The former captain of the girls' basketball team became a silent, frightened little mouse. She stopped trying in class, convinced that she was no longer capable of finding the answers or doing the work. The only thing that survived had been her interest in drama. She'd managed to act some, hanging around and waiting for the parts no one wanted. Playing someone else had been a good escape... almost like running away.

Finally, at fifteen, she'd been placed in a home so terrible and abusive that she knew she wouldn't survive if she stayed. She planned and saved and boarded a midnight bus. And never looked back.

Her only regret had been leaving Beth behind. Beth had been two years older, with a job and a boyfriend and high school graduation on the horizon. Beth would have only set herself back by leaving, so Julia had known without asking that Beth wouldn't go with her. And she'd been so afraid of being caught—so afraid that she hadn't even trusted Beth with the information. She'd left her sister just as she'd left Christina—without a goodbye. The guilt still gnawed at her sometimes, in spite of Beth's repeated assurances that all was long forgiven.

She'd ended up finally in San Diego, California, her savings nearly spent on bus fares and sandwiches. She took a job washing dishes and spent her sixteenth birthday crammed into a two-mattress flophouse room with five frightened illegal aliens. She picked up Spanish fast during those months with the young Mexican girls.

Things did not go well, and she was continually afraid. Men on the street harassed her and tried to lure her into prostitution. Street peddlers tried to con her into the drug scene. She couldn't earn enough to live decently. She went to old movies when she could spare the change, and dreamed of a knight who would carry her off to his castle.

And the knight came.

She'd been sick for a long time and the illegal girls had become frightened. The *gringa* hadn't the strength to get up off the mattress. Julia still didn't know if it was concern that had prompted them to call for help or fear that they would all be in trouble if she died. At any rate, the girls had gone for a young doctor who always helped the illegals.

She'd been lying on the mattress for days, in and out of feverish dreams, at the point where dying didn't sound so bad, when suddenly the most beautiful and gentle man appeared. She'd thought it another dream.

He'd bent over her, eyes full of concern, voice calm and soothing, and she'd handed over her life. It was a funny way of thinking about it, but it was the only way she could possibly describe it. Paul, the idealistic young intern, had taken her over, molded her, guided her and finally married her.

How long ago that all seemed. How much she had grown and changed... yet, here she was again, the frightened child seeking escape.

Her life seemed stuck in the same patterns that had developed in her childhood. Sometimes she wondered if she didn't have some inherent weakness, some genetic link to the hunted rather than the hunters. But she was twenty-five years old now. A grown woman. She had a child. If she was ever going to find the strength to stand tall and make her own way in life, wasn't it about time? Hadn't she come far enough to put those immature responses behind her and take her place in the world as an adult?

"What kind of a person am I?" she said out loud, and Tonio stopped his movements and studied her with an intensity that made her smile. She ruffled his hair then smoothed it with her palm. He was so perfect. He was worth more than Leticia had offered.

The PA system crackled into life and a feminine, professional voice addressed the waiting passengers. "Attention please. Flight ninety-three, direct service to New York's La Guardia Airport, will have a delayed departure. Thank you for your patience, and we will keep you informed regarding the new boarding time."

A surge of fear gripped Julia. Could the delay have anything to do with her? Were they coming after her? Had they somehow delayed the flight in order to catch her?

No, it couldn't be possible. She shook her head and tried to calm herself with logic. If the family had been wise to her in the beginning they would have stopped her before she left Mexican soil. That meant it had been a surprise to them. They would have had to start from scratch in tracing her and she had been careful about using an assumed name and not advising the airline in advance that she was traveling with a baby.

They couldn't possibly have traced her movements so quickly—even Leticia's black powers had their limits. Still, it would be hard to relax until she was back in the air and on her way to New York.

New York. The name was like magic to her. Not that she had a history of fondness for the city. Actually, she'd only been there once in her life and the visit had been brief. The thing she remembered most about New York was its size, its ability to swallow people. And that's what she wanted—to be swallowed, to be unfindable.

The baby began to fuss and fret and Julia drew in a long breath and leaned over to fish in the diaper bag for his rubber squeak chicken.

"We're safe in this airport," she repeated to herself over and over. "No one knows we're here, and no one here knows who we are."

Anson arrived at the gate just in time to catch the tail end of an announcement. The flight was delayed. More time to kill.

He looked around for an empty seat. His eyes scanned the rows of chairs and stopped. It was her! The woman with the baby! And it *was* Julia Velasco—he would swear to it.

He moved closer. Was it possible that some other woman could look this much like her? Granted, there was a difference. This woman looked somewhat tired and frayed around the edges, and the glamour and glitter he'd seen were missing. But the sable hair was just as lustrous. The creamy skin was just as beautiful. And the gray eyes caused the same jolt inside him. No, It had to be her.

The chairs were arranged in long back-to-back rows, and there was an empty spot directly behind her. He crossed to it and sat down, self-consciously running his fingers through his hair and immediately feeling silly for wondering about his appearance.

She was holding the baby upright in her lap and the child was leaning over her shoulder, hanging toward the empty chair. He had a death grip on a rubber chicken and he was chewing intently on both the chicken and his own pudgy fingers. He brightened immediately at Anson's appearance and gave the chicken a break, dropping it from his mouth while he fixed Anson with a curious stare.

Anson turned the back of his head to the baby a moment while he mulled over his opening line. He knew almost nothing about babies, but he assumed the gumming of the chicken meant teething. Would it sound stupid to say, "I see he's teething"? Did only roving grandmothers say things like that?

Suddenly, the hair on the back of Anson's head was locked in a little hand. It was as good an opening as any.

"Hey there, big boy. Not so hard."

"Oh, I'm terribly sorry," the woman said, turning in her seat. "I didn't realize..."

The baby's wet little hand was now firmly entwined in a clump of Anson's hair, and the mother's turning and pulling the baby toward her did nothing to help matters. Anson's head was roughly yanked backward, and he wondered which would give first—the hair or his neck.

"Oh, dear. Oh, I'm so sorry..." the woman muttered over and over as she worked at disengaging the baby's grip. A few strands felt as though they were being sacrificed.

"There," she announced.

Anson massaged the spot on his scalp while turning toward her in his seat. "What a grip, huh?"

The baby chuckled gleefully as the mother pried his little fist open, picking a few plucked hairs from between the wet little fingers. She gathered the harvest on her upraised palm and she held her hand out, looking down at the accumulated strands as though wondering how to return them, then looked up at Anson in dismay.

"You can keep it," he said. "I've got plenty more."

The corners of her mouth curved up slightly—not quite a smile, but almost. Her eyes were deep and unreadable and they looked as though she'd been crying recently.

She leaned over and brushed the hair into an ashtray, again holding the baby upright and facing toward Anson. This time he kept his head out of reach. The yellow chicken fell into Anson's lap as she straightened.

Anson overcame his distaste and picked up the slobbery chicken. He held it out toward the baby.

"Here you go, big boy," Anson said, but the child ignored the rubber bird. Anson squeaked it a few times, but the baby kept his big dark eyes fastened on Anson's face as though hypnotized.

"I think he likes me," Anson said.

"Come," the mother said softly, "turn around here and leave the poor man alone."

"No. That's all right. Really," Anson insisted. "I love kids."

She smiled and Anson was completely unprepared. It wasn't what he would have expected from her at all. It was a gentle smile, almost shy, and it touched her eyes in the nicest way.

"What's your name, fella?" he again held out the wet chicken.

"His name's Antonio," she said.

Anson felt a curious stab of disappointment. He'd heard the Velasco baby's name mentioned. It was Antonio. This really was Julia Velasco beyond any doubt. For a moment he had almost hoped...

Julia was silent but watchful as he continued to play with the baby. Questions raced through his mind. If she was such an unfit and uninterested mother, what was she doing traveling alone with the baby? Why hadn't she brought a nurse or maid along to help take care of him?

He couldn't imagine the Velasco family allowing her to go on a long trip alone. He couldn't imagine someone as spoiled as she was wanting to tackle the trip alone.

Even without the baby he would have expected the Velascos to insist she travel with a companion. What was going on?

Anson made periodic comments, trying to engage her in conversation. She was polite, but wary. She seemed very nervous, and anxious to board the plane.

"Antonio. A Spanish name?"

Silence.

"I just came from Mexico City," he offered. He was shocked at the naked fear that filled her eyes.

"Mexico City?" she asked in a horror-stricken voice.

He fished in his pocket until he came up with a business card. People's Aid Association was in large print and below it, in smaller letters, Anson Wolfe, and below that, Director. Across the bottom ran the New York City address and phone.

She took the card with a trembling hand and studied it carefully.

"I was in Mexico consulting on a clinic that people have hopes of being just like ours," he said as she stared down at the card. He somehow sensed that it wouldn't be wise to mention his ties to the Obregon family or the true extent of his knowledge and experience in Mexico City.

She calmed visibly and started to hand the card back to him.

"Keep it," he told her. "You're going to New York. Who knows? You might need help with something."

The baby lunged for the card and she bent to drop it into her purse. Then she straightened and regarded him suspiciously.

"What kind of aid?" she asked finally. The question's tone would have been at home in a murder investigation.

"Mostly legal. At least, that's the way it started out. But people need so much more. Advice about all kinds of things—help finding places to live, job counseling." He shrugged. "We don't do nearly enough, but we try. And it's free."

She relaxed again and nodded as though she approved of what he'd said. "Yes," she said, staring out into space with a faraway look in her eyes. "A nonprofit legal clinic. Mexico City could use that."

He wasn't sure whether she was being sincere or subtly sarcastic. Her strangeness, her sudden fear and suspicion, added to the questions he had.

Bits of information he'd heard about Julia Velasco darted about in his mind. A disgrace. An unfit mother. A guttersnipe before she'd snagged her rich husband. A trust she couldn't touch for years. A baby that was the only grandson and male heir of the Velasco family.

The baby cooed at him and reached out to reclaim his chicken.

"Until the trust matures she is a beggar," his uncle had said. "She'll never take responsibility for that baby," his aunt had said. "Her interest in the child has been steadily declining. She will set the terms. Something will happen soon... The señor and señora are waiting for her to make the opening move."

A heavy weight settled in Anson's stomach. He was afraid he might have just stumbled on to Julia Velasco's opening move.

* * *

Julia was so nervous that she thought she might scream for them to get the boarding started. What in the world was taking so long?

The man sitting behind her was charming, and she appreciated his entertaining the baby, but she was so edgy she could hardly concentrate on his polite conversation. Only when he'd said Mexico City and frightened her to death had she really listened to him.

She wished she could just turn to him and in all honesty explain that it had nothing to do with him personally, but she just wasn't up to socializing right now. Her endless role playing made her yearn for a little forthrightness, but she was sure he'd take it wrong, and he'd been so kind about the hair pulling... She didn't want to hurt his feelings.

The baby began to squirm in her lap and make little unhappy snorting sounds. He jammed half his fist into his mouth and sucked noisily.

"Oh, no," Julia muttered under her breath. It was time for him to eat again and boarding hadn't even begun yet.

She hesitated a moment, wondering if he could be stalled, but true to form he suddenly spit out his fist, turned bright red and let out a loud, angry wail. If there was one thing Tonio would not tolerate it was hunger.

"Shh, shh," she crooned and reached for the diaper bag. She fished around with one hand and held the stiff, angry little body with the other. He was screaming so hard now that she was afraid he might have trouble breathing.

She grabbed the first jar her fingers touched in the bag and tried to hold on to him while opening the tightly sealed cap.

"Here, let me get that," the man behind her said, reaching to take the jar from her hand.

The lid opened with a loud pop. "Mmm, pulverized apricots. You're gonna love these, buddy."

Tonio paused in his crying to give the man a suspicious but curious glare.

"Oh, no!" Julia cried. "I don't have a spoon! I was going to feed him on the plane so I didn't bring—"

"Hold it," the man said, jumping from his seat. "Watch my stuff," he called over his shoulder as he loped away from her toward the main terminal.

She tried to cuddle the screaming baby, but he only wailed harder and bent his stiffened body away from her. How could she have neglected to bring a spoon? How could she have been so stupid as to not realize he would get hungry? How could she be so insensitive and ignorant that she didn't know how to keep her own child satisfied?

She could feel the stares and whispered words of the people around her, and she had the panicky feeling that perhaps she wasn't capable of taking care of him. From the moment of his birth, the Velasco doctors and the Velasco nurses and Leticia had made all the decisions regarding her son. Julia had never been considered even adequate as a mother.

What if they were right? What if she harmed Tonio in some way? What if . . . ?

A heavy blackness pressed in on her. Maybe the whole idea had been wrong from the start. How could she ever live with herself if her plan would hurt the baby somehow?

Tonio exhausted himself with his screaming and lapsed into heartbreaking sobs. He sank weakly against her chest and looked up at her with mournful, tear-rimmed eyes.

An elderly woman who had been eyeing her from a few seats away stood and gathered her things. She stalked toward Julia on sturdy shoes, her wrinkled mouth turned down.

Julia cringed. She knew what the woman was thinking. She knew that the woman had watched her and seen through her confident facade. The woman was seeing the truth—that she didn't know how to keep Tonio happy—that she was frightened and unsure as a mother—that she was possibly even unfit as a mother.

Afraid of meeting the woman's eyes, Julia bowed her head, certain that the woman would reprimand her or accuse her as she passed. The sturdy shoes stopped in front of her. The woman expelled a disapproving "Hummph," making Julia wince and raise her eyes hesitantly to take her punishment.

"In my day we were much stricter with them, dearie. The mother made the rules then, not the child." The woman shook her head. "I feel sorry for you young mothers today." Shaking her head again, she moved on.

Julia could have laughed out loud. The woman hadn't been accusing, she'd been sympathetic. She'd seen Tonio as a little tyrant and Julia the hapless victim.

Were all the stares sympathetic? Julia risked a tentative look around. No one seemed to be paying any attention at all to her. Maybe it would work out. Maybe she was doing all right with the baby.

Still, she felt a new and even stronger sense of helplessness. There was so much she didn't know about child care. There were so many things that could go wrong. How would she know if she was taking good enough care of him? She couldn't even risk calling Beth, to tap into her sister's motherhood experience, as she was afraid the Velascos would have Beth's house watched and her phone tapped.

What would she do all alone in New York if Tonio got sick? What would she do if he hurt himself? Or what if something happened to her—who would look after the baby? She had a sudden horrible vision of herself unconscious or paralyzed from some stupid household accident, and the baby starving to death in his crib before someone ever discovered them.

She reached down with one hand and fished the business card from her bag. Anson Wolfe, it read. She wasn't ready for a man in her life. She wasn't ready for romance. But maybe she did need a friend in New York. And maybe Anson Wolfe was just the right kind of friend to have.

A comforting warmth filled her when she saw him returning. He was almost running, his long legs covering the ground in giant strides, and he was grinning, seemingly oblivious to the frowns and stares he was attracting. She felt herself relax, felt a tiny smile tug at the corners of her mouth. Somehow the sight of him running toward her, tie and tweedy sport coat flapping loosely, worn, white sneakers peaking out from under stylish cord slacks, and plastic spoon held high like some kind of Olympic torch, made her feel very safe and secure indeed.

The boarding announcement sounded and people all around them scurried forward, rushing for a place in line. Anson kept his seat and watched the apricots disappear into the eager little mouth.

"There's no hurry," he assured Julia. "These big jets take forever to load, so you've got plenty of time."

Still, she was agitated and obviously anxious to join the line of people. Her patience with the baby was undermined by her shaking hands and nervous eyes. He studied her, noticing for the first time that her expensive suit was somewhat soiled and her stockings torn.

"What now?" he kept asking himself. What was he supposed to do? He thought he knew what she was up to, but what in the hell was he going to do about it?

Julia fed Tonio impatiently. The baby wiggled and grabbed for the spoon. The apricots had made him feel much better and now he was playful as he downed the peas. He was, of course, oblivious to the fact that people were swarming onto the plane ahead of them and that they had already missed their chance to claim the early boarding privilege that traveling with a baby afforded. Now she would have to wrestle the baby and the heavy bags onto the plane amid the jostling of other passengers.

The food was almost gone. She urged him to take the last bites, but he was nearly impossible to hurry.

"Kind of stubborn little guy," the man remarked.

He was hovering close to her and had made no move to join the boarding line.

"Thank you again for the spoon," she said. It was all she could seem to come up with.

He shrugged and grinned slightly, as though to say it was nothing, and when she looked straight at him he appeared suddenly nervous or flustered for some reason. He used one hand to rake his hair away from his forehead, cleared his throat and looked pointedly around as though to prove he had something on his mind.

As soon as his hand left his head, the hair fell forward again. It was beautiful hair—thick and just curly enough, and it was a striking mix of sandy brown and silver gray. It looked as uncontrived and natural as the rest of him. In fact, she would have believed it immediately if she was told that he had never studied himself in a mirror or given himself to any sort of style consciousness. His poise and presence seemed to radiate from a strong inner core rather than a belief that he'd turned himself out artfully that morning.

She found herself smiling at him for no reason, and her own smile embarrassed her and she felt the most ridiculous flush rising to her cheeks. What in the world was wrong with her? Right in the middle of escaping to New York she was sitting here blushing at some man like a teenager!

She dropped the empty jar into the trash, wiped Tonio's face and stood to gather her things.

"Anything I can carry for you?"

His eyes were the most wonderful clear blue. The kind of blue that almost doesn't look real. She told herself that he probably had on tinted contacts. Shaking her head in answer to his offer, she hefted the bulky bags to her shoulders. Still he hovered.

"It would be no trouble," he insisted. "I don't have much of my own to carry."

Why not? She did intend to call his number in New York. She did intend to have him as a friend. But still, she was vaguely uneasy as she handed over a bag to him.

She joined the end of the line and ignored him as she concentrated on maneuvering through the jetway and then the crowded, narrow aisle with her remaining bag and a wriggling, energetic Tonio. Anson followed her closely, making small friendly gestures to entertain Tonio as they went.

About halfway down the plane she stopped, looking up at the numbers and then down at her ticket to make certain the empty window seat was hers. It was a match.

"Excuse me," she said, and the two women already seated in the aisle and middle seat frowned up at her. "I need to get in, please."

"Here," he insisted, pulling the bag on her shoulder. "Let me hold those while you slide in."

"Are you two together?" demanded the heavyset woman in the middle seat. Before there was time for an answer she was standing and loudly announcing that the airline was stupid and incompetent for not seating couples together.

"But we're not—" Julia tried to explain.

"It's okay—" the man said.

"No," the woman insisted. "We're switching seats." She pushed the other seated passenger, forcing that woman to stand and causing a general commotion.

"What's the problem here, folks?" asked a cheery, frosted blonde in an attendant's uniform.

Julia opened her mouth to speak, but the loud woman cut her off. "This couple," the woman insisted in a scolding tone, "should be seated together so the father can help with the baby."

"Well, then—" the attendant smiled at the woman "—that's very kind of you to offer to move. Would you like to just switch seats?"

There was no point in trying to explain and creating a further scene, so Julia settled mutely into her window seat. Apparently Anson was of the same opinion because he just shrugged and exchanged seat numbers and sat down beside her in the middle position.

His closeness made her uneasy. His broad shoulder brushed hers. His elbow shared her armrest. She concentrated on the preflight activity and the takeoff and the scene through the window and the baby's ear troubles as they climbed. But when all that was finished and the plane had leveled off and Tonio was asleep, there was nothing left to shield her from the uneasiness.

Tonio shifted, snuggling against her, his mouth working noisily at his fingers even in sleep. She bent to kiss his head and then pulled the blanket around him.

"Hey, we were fated to pair up," Anson said with a chuckle.

The words startled her. The deep, primitive part of her—the part that whispered warnings about ladders and black cats and moonlit graveyards—still had a strong suspicion that fate was out there working.

"Your watch," he explained, pointing to the expensive timepiece she wore on her right wrist. He moved his left hand, holding his own watch up next to hers. The pattern of cracks webbing the crystals was similar.

"Only I see yours is still running," he remarked wryly.

She laughed more than she should have. The laughter was mostly relief. Fate hadn't joined them together, after all.

"I know the little guy's name," he said, "but you haven't told me yours."

"Oh, you're right." She ducked her head and fiddled with the baby's blanket. "It's Julia," she said, unable to meet his steady blue gaze. "Julia Regis."

The combination sounded so strange to her. Regis had been the last name of a beloved drama teacher.

"Going to New York for a visit?" he asked.

The question sounded harmless enough, but her pulse began to race. She knew that refusing to answer or being too evasive would only cause unnecessary suspicion. Any normal person would be willing to answer that sort of question. Again, she couldn't meet his eyes.

"No." She cleared her throat. "I'm going to try living there." The sentence sounded too bare. What else would be normal to say under the circumstances? "I, ah, I'm divorced and I guess I just needed the typical change of scene, you know?"

He nodded as though he understood, but she could feel his eyes studying her. Did he sense her lying?

"Do you have a place yet?" he probed. "Finding a place in New York can be tough."

She shook her head. "Did you have a hard time?" she asked.

"Yes," he admitted. "But it was harder for me because I wanted to be in a specific area—near my office. I'll warn you: it did take a while and I wore out several realtors."

Nodding, she said, "I was afraid it would, but I didn't want to do it long distance. I mean, without seeing the apartment, I wouldn't know what I was getting into, would I? And how would I even know if the real estate agent was trustworthy? I didn't have anyone local to check anything out for me and—"

She stopped herself and shrugged. She needed to slow her words down and sound more sane. "So I have the names of several nice residential hotels where I can live while I hunt for something permanent."

Had she said enough? Had she said too much? Would he be satisfied now and leave her alone?

She lowered her seat and leaned back, hoping to discourage any further conversation. She needed to be very careful about what she said to him, needed to get her stories and her facts straight in her mind before she talked to him anymore. His sharpness and perception were apparent in his intelligent features. She did an imitation of a tiny yawn and closed her eyes, pretending sleepiness.

Next stop, New York. The thought sent a thrill through her. There was no one to stand in her way now. She was beginning a new life. She was free. Free of everything. Free to make her own rules and live on her own terms. Free to be the real Julia... whoever that was.

Anson shifted again in his cramped middle seat. His legs didn't begin to fit. His shoulders were too wide and there was no good place to put his elbows. But that wasn't what was bothering him.

In the years he'd been in law he had grown secure in his ability to reduce situations to a clear-cut right or wrong. But try as he might, he could not arrive at a definite answer now. Julia Velasco was running away. He was certain of that. But she was an adult and a free agent, so shouldn't she have the right to come and go at her own discretion? And as to the child, it was her baby, was it not?

Still, he felt as though he were witnessing a crime in progress. But what should he do? What could he do?

If there was only an errant daughter-in-law to consider, it would be easy to just mind his own business and forget the whole thing. But it wasn't just the woman—there was the baby to think about. There was the baby's welfare to think about. There were the grandparents to think about. There was a moral question involved that transcended legal technicalities.

But the law was not based on emotion or moral right. And legally Julia had committed no crime. He suspected that she intended to eventually "sell" the child to his grandparents. But that was only a supposition based on gossip and not something he could prove even to himself. So what was he going to accuse her of? Not wanting to live with her in-laws? What a laugh that would get him. He could think of no action to take at all.

Confronting Julia herself with his knowledge would accomplish nothing. Calling his uncle for advice felt too much like an admittance of helplessness; and if Ignacio followed his loyalties he would probably just insist that Anson notify the Velascos, anyway. And calling the Velascos was absolutely repugnant to him. Who knew what that bunch was capable of in defense of their sacred family honor? If they managed to get their daughter-in-law back into Mexico they would be allowed to enact whatever terrible retribution they chose with little outside interference. He would never even consider being a snitch for them.

So what was the answer? There seemed to be none. Yet he couldn't just turn his back, either. What if something bad happened? What if the baby ended up being harmed in some way? Neglected? How could he live with that possibility?

So here he was, a black-and-white man trapped in a situation where everything was a dirty shade of gray. Who was worse: the spoiled, misguided Julia, who saw the baby as something akin to a winning lottery ticket, or the arrogant, grim-faced Velasco family who saw the child as nothing more than a continuation of their precious bloodline?

In his own mind neither party was fit to have custody of the child. But then he couldn't let his own personal prejudices further complicate the mess.

He couldn't assign guilt to her based on the meager facts that he had, but there was something he could do. He could keep an eye on Julia. He could try to keep something bad from happening. He could watch out for

Tonio and call in a child welfare group if he had to. He would do whatever was necessary to protect the baby, and maybe, just maybe he could protect Julia Velasco from herself in the process.

He turned toward her. Her obvious exhaustion made her look almost fragile, and the child held so tightly in her arms gave her the air of a Madonna. The words he'd planned caught in his throat.

He reached out and gently straightened the baby's blanket. The touch startled her, but when she saw that it was only him touching the blanket, a ghost of a smile crossed her mouth and flickered in her haunted eyes. It tore inexplicably at his heart.

"You're both going to be worn out when we land," he said softly, almost to himself.

She nodded and closed her eyes again.

"I could suggest a hotel, maybe get you settled. I mean, if you didn't already have definite plans."

She opened her eyes and stared at him a moment with a searching intensity that made him nearly weak with guilt. Then suddenly her gaze softened and she sighed, as though surrendering in some way.

"Yes, I would appreciate that." Her voice was low, but unmistakably practical. "I need a decent place." She glanced down at the child. "But one that's not too expensive. Perhaps offering weekly rates." She looked suddenly unsure. "Is that possible, do you think?"

With that last question he knew he had her. She was willing to trust his judgment. He had passed with her. He had convinced her. The rest would be easy.

"I think it's possible," he answered. "I have some ideas I think will work."

He leaned back against his seat and thought about which place would be best for her and Tonio. There was a suitable one convenient to his office that would make checking on her a breeze.

She trusted him. That was what he'd wanted, wasn't it? That was what he needed in order to carry out his plans.

So why the hell did it make him feel so awful?

Chapter Five

Julia had thought the worst was behind her. But it wasn't.

She woke up that first morning in a strange hotel room, and looked around her at the impersonal furniture and the anonymous walls, and she was gripped by an anxiety so fierce and consuming that it eclipsed all else. What would she do if they came? They could come into the room and take the baby and kill her and there was nothing to stop them. She still wasn't safe.

She was certain something was wrong. Her plan had gone too well. Her escape had been too successful. As Paul had always been so quick to point out, she seldom did anything completely right. So she couldn't believe she had triumphed so easily over the mighty forces of the Velascos, or that she had actually tricked Leticia.

As the days passed, she imagined they had only let her think she'd escaped. They were toying with her. They were out there watching the hotel. They were waiting, biding their time before they moved against her, like a cat with a cornered mouse.

Her sleep was filled with nightmares—horrible scenes in which Tonio was wrenched from her arms and used as a pawn in hideous games that always ended with the baby being dropped off a mountain or turned to dust. She kept a light on all night and spent desperate hours clenching damp sheets to her chin and staring at the door and the windows for the slightest sign of movement.

She was terrified of leaving her room. She called room service for food, and she tried to keep even that to a minimum because every time she opened the door for the waiter her heart pounded at the possibility of someone else hiding in the hall and waiting for her to undo the bolt.

She watched the old television and played with Tonio. She listened for noises. She kept the shades drawn so *they* couldn't see her. The hotel was filled with elderly people who insisted on the central steam heat being set at maximum, but she wouldn't even crack open the window for a breath of cool air. The room might be stifling, but if she unlocked the window *they* might climb in.

To keep cool she padded around barefoot in her slip and kept Tonio in his diaper, just as though it were midsummer. For relief she locked the bathroom door and took long, cooling baths while Tonio hung over the edge of the tub and watched or sat with her in the tub and splashed.

She had two absolute rules. She never let the baby out of her sight and she never, ever took a shower. Who knew what might happen while she was behind that curtain with the water roaring?

The first day Anson called, she told him she was fine and just resting and getting settled.

The second day he called and the third and the fourth she continued with that theme and added a story about spending her time on the phone with realtors. But he wanted to drop by the hotel and visit, and he grew increasingly more insistent and less willing to accept her evasions and negative responses.

Finally, on the fifth day, he wouldn't take no for an answer. Frantically she straightened the room and dressed in the blouse and skirt to her suit and zipped Tonio into some coveralls.

She felt stiff and formal as she opened the door to his knock. Who was this man, anyway? What did she really know about him?

Anson stepped inside. He looked at her too long. He looked at Tonio too long. He complained about the stuffiness. He wanted to take them to lunch.

"I'm really not hungry and—"

"Okay," he said, "you can have coffee or something while my buddy and I eat."

Tonio had climbed happily into Anson's arms.

"I don't think—"

"No more excuses. We won't listen to any more, will we, big guy?" Anson tweaked the baby's belly and Tonio dissolved into a fit of laughter. "We're going down to the coffee shop, Mom. You can come or not."

Julia rushed after them, wringing her hands and gnawing on her lower lip. The elevator ride was a nightmare. Every strange face looked sinister. And she had to create a scene with a waitress in order to get a table in a corner away from the windows. She told Anson she had a sinus condition that made her eyes sensitive to light at times. She was afraid he didn't believe her.

Lunch was strained. Only Tonio enjoyed himself, banging on his high-chair tray and responding to the finger games Anson played with him.

Anson made careful comments about how tired she looked and how she'd lost weight. Again she blamed it on some vague sinus difficulties. Anson said that the baby looked fine and she agreed, adding that, thank heavens, he hadn't developed any sinus problems.

After lunch Anson walked them back up to the room and she invited him in because she was afraid to go into the empty room alone. He played with the baby and she watched silently. Anson wanted to know where she'd been—what sights she'd seen. Again she pleaded illness, saying she hadn't felt well enough to explore yet.

He'd suggested she rest more, then asked if he could get them anything. Hesitantly she suggested diapers. The next day he arrived with a case of disposable diapers and an assortment of baby food. He played with Tonio, looked around the room and left.

From then on he came once a day without fail. He didn't ask if it was all right. He just came. And he brought something each time. He brought shampoo and bubble bath and grocery bags filled with fruit and crackers and cheese. He brought magazines and books. He brought a pull toy and a talking telephone with eyes that winked.

She thanked him and insisted on paying him something. He accepted for all but the toys, which he claimed were gifts. He began talking about taking her to a doctor, so she pretended she felt better. She told him she and Tonio had started going out for walks in the mornings. She told him she'd begun contacting realtors. He seemed to believe her.

But of course she was lying. Nothing could have convinced her to leave that room. She sent her suit and blouse out to the hotel cleaning service when needed. She rinsed out her underwear and Tonio's clothes in the sink, using the flowery-scented bars of soap the hotel provided.

She didn't let anyone into the room anymore except Anson. Her room service meals and her clean linens and supplies were all left outside her door in the hall, where she could stealthily scoop them up when she was certain no one was looking.

The old television broke and she didn't report it because she didn't want to let anyone in to repair or replace it. That was when she started devouring the newspapers Anson left, and reading every single article. That was when she stumbled onto the tiny paragraph that finally set her free.

The story was on a back page, with two more articles about some Third World countries in the midst of revolution. It was about the rioting and unrest in an area in Mexico. She read it mechanically, skimming over the grim details of the bombing and destruction of a huge plant that was the area's primary source of revenue.

Suddenly the words jumped out at her.

> Juan Arista, company spokesman and well-known politician, refused to speculate on the possibility of a reopening. An offer to buy the facility and all rights to production in the area were announced publicly by Mariano Diaz, newly installed head of Diaz, International, but informed sources say the Diaz proposal will not be considered.

Julia read the words over and over until she had them

memorized. Then she dropped the pages to the floor and stared at the wall.

That was the main Velasco plant they were talking about. And somehow Juan Arista had maneuvered his way into being the family's spokesman when in the past the señor had always spoken for the family interests.

And Diaz! There was a juicy bit of news. There had been bad blood between the Velasco and Diaz families ever since the marriage between Teresa and Mariano. The union that was supposed to act as an alliance between the two old lines had instead driven a wedge between them when the Velascos had discovered that the Diaz enterprises were not financially sound. The wedding had proceeded, but the Velascos had pulled out of the business merger at the last minute.

The Diaz camp had accused the Velascos of being dishonorable frauds who were out to ruin and discredit their rivals. The Velasco interests accused the Diaz side of concealing the truth and cheating in order to lure the Velasco money into saving them.

Both families had competed for the loyalties of the new couple. Being practical, Teresa and Mariano had of course cast their lot with the more wealthy and promising side and moved in with the Velascos. The Diaz family had never stopped trying to convince their son to return, though, and it looked to Julia as if the Diaz side had finally won.

Mariano had gone back to the enemy camp. And Julia was certain that Teresa and the girls had gone with him. The Velasco business had sustained a crippling blow and the Velasco family was splitting apart.

Life was continuing on in Mexico. The whole country hadn't mobilized behind the Velascos in an effort to reclaim the missing heir. And the Velascos had other pressing problems. They had a host of troubles to deal with. They hadn't dropped everything to give all their energy to finding her.

She walked to the window, opened it for the first time and leaned out to look around. How silly it had been to think anyone could have climbed ten stories of smooth stone to break in through her window! She looked down and saw the crowds filling the sidewalks, some hurrying to destinations, some strolling leisurely, and she realized that no one down there knew or cared who the crazy woman leaning out the window in her slip was.

This was New York, and the city had swallowed her, hidden her, given her true anonymity. The prison she was in now was of her own making. And she saw with sudden clarity that the only danger she'd faced had been from her own imagination.

In a rush she dressed Tonio and herself and hurried downstairs to the street. The polished brass of the old revolving door, the noise and bustle of the street, the smell of chestnuts roasting in the vendors' open carts, the chill air on her cheeks all had the most incredible joy and significance to her. She really was free.

She spent the rest of the day racing about. She sold all her jewelry, though she decided to keep her coat till spring, and rented a safe-deposit box to store her cash and papers in. She bought herself jeans and leather sneakers and sweatshirts with the New York skyline stenciled across the front. She bought Tonio warm quilted snowsuits with feet and hoods and matching mittens that made him look like a fat little bunny. She bought an elaborate, endlessly adjustable stroller.

And she thought about Anson. Was he calling her room and puzzling over the unanswered ringing? Was he wondering where she was?

She resisted every impulse to call him during the day. She wanted to flex her muscles a bit and revel in her newfound confidence first. Then maybe this time when she saw him, things would be different. She wouldn't feel so insecure and hesitant in his presence.

By late afternoon Julia was feeling strong and renewed, and she gave in to her eagerness to see him. She read the address on his business card to a cab driver and crossed her fingers in the hope that he hadn't gone home yet.

She was no longer the paranoid fool he'd been toting care packages to. She was no longer the edgy puddle of fear he'd been seeing every day. She was back on her own two feet and ready to stand toe-to-toe with the world—as well as counselor Anson Wolfe—and she couldn't wait to show him.

She talked her way past his assistants and walked into his office unannounced.

"Surprise," she called confidently.

But the moment she walked into his office and saw his surroundings for the first time, saw him behind the huge desk with its impossible stacks of files and memos...

The moment he raised his eyes from the paper he was studying so intently, looking beautifully serious and impressive with his loosened tie and the sleeves of his white, white shirt rolled up...

The moment the total surprise registered in the lines of his face and he reached up with a strong graceful hand to take off his metal-framed reading glasses—he wasn't wearing contacts and his eyes were really that blue...

The moment she heard his voice searching for words and saw the questions mixed with delight mixed with a charming hesitancy...

She lost it all. Her confidence and composure dissolved.

"I, ah, I was out and I just—"

"You look great," he began, standing and moving around to the front of the desk. "Do you want to sit down or—how 'bout coffee...?"

She shook her head.

"Tea?"

"No, really, I—it's Tonio's nap time. I have to go. I just wanted to—"

"Oh. Well, if you have to..."

"Yes. I can't stay. Maybe, ah..." Her throat was suddenly so dry that she had to keep clearing it to speak. "Maybe I'll talk to you tomorrow?"

"Oh, sure. Sure." He ran his fingers through his hair.

She began backing the stroller out through the door.

"Well, ah..." He followed her as though unwilling to say goodbye. "Do you have something to do tomorrow? I mean, do you have any special plans?"

She shook her head.

"I could suggest some museums or something. Maybe fix you up with some kind of sight-seeing itinerary?"

"Yes," she said. "I love museums."

"You do?" He brightened. "So do I! You won't believe how many wonderful museums there are in this city. I never get enough of them."

"Maybe you could come, too?" she blurted out, then was immediately embarrassed. "I mean, maybe sometime when you're not busy, you might want to..." Her hastily added words trailed off into nothing.

A shadow passed over his eyes, and he looked suddenly tired and serious. "I don't have much time for museums," he said in a distant, professional tone. "Just drop by tomorrow morning and I'll give you a map and some suggestions."

Julia swallowed hard and yanked the stroller the rest of the way out of his office. She waved her goodbye, not trusting her voice. How foolish she'd been. Anson Wolfe was a dedicated man who was devoted to helping people. He had seen she needed help and he had been giving it. He didn't want or need her for a friend.

She felt rejected and hurt, and angry with herself for having those feelings. She'd presumed too much. It was all her own fault. She vowed not to make that same mistake again.

Anson sat in his office, his sneaker-clad feet propped up on his desk and his hands clasped behind his head. He stared absently at the dust motes playing in the shafts of morning sunlight filtering through his blinds. He couldn't seem to concentrate on anything.

She would come by this morning. The map he'd marked for her and the museum guide he'd composed were sitting on the corner of his desk, waiting for her to pick them up. He'd called to tell her they were ready and to be sure to stop by. He hadn't meant to call. He hadn't wanted to call. But he couldn't seem to stop himself. He had to be certain she was coming.

But he didn't really want to see her, did he? She had made him so nervous, popping in like that with such a dazzling smile and a glow in her eyes. Would she be the same today? Or would she be back to the huddled, haunted creature he'd been watching these past few weeks—the wan, frightened woman clinging to safety?

The frightened woman had been easier to deal with. He had been able to protect her and watch over her and feel like a benevolent big brother. It had been very safe. And it had been simple. Now what was he dealing with? How was he going to keep tabs on her if she'd really found her wings?

"Ms. Regis is here," one of the secretaries called from outside his door.

"Send her in," he said, jerking his feet down from the desk and straightening his tie. He picked up a file and pretended to read.

She breezed into his office with a bright smile. Her hair was pulled back into a ponytail and her eyes were shining as brightly as the baby's. She was dressed in jeans and sneakers and that preposterously rich-looking sable coat, and she was pushing Tonio in the new stroller.

Something funny happened in his chest, and he felt almost helpless for a moment.

"I hope you didn't go to very much trouble with the map," she said. Her voice was pleasant but neutral.

"Oh, no. I enjoyed it. I'm just a frustrated New York tour guide, I guess."

She smiled, but she could have given the same smile to a stranger. There was a distant air to her.

"What are you most interested in?" he asked, picking up the map from his desk, but not offering it to her. He was afraid she would leave the moment she got her hands on it.

"Everything!" She laughed. "I'll have to force myself to take it slow and not run from one to another."

He worked at smiling, but it didn't feel as if it came out quite right. Reluctantly he handed the map to her.

"The Modern is my favorite," he said. "Museum of Modern Art. I like to take a sandwich and eat in the sculpture garden sometimes."

"That sounds lovely. I think that's where I'll go today, then."

"I haven't been for a while."

"That's too bad." she smiled. It was a pregoodbye smile.

"It's big—almost overwhelming the first time. I mean, before you know your way around."

"I'm sure I'll be fine," she said, obviously impatient to be gone.

So what was wrong with tagging along to a museum? Anson asked himself. Why shouldn't he? It was perfectly innocent.

He hadn't taken the time to do much that he liked lately. In fact, he couldn't remember taking any time off—except for Mexico—since before the split with Laurel over a year before. He owed himself some museum time.

And how else was he supposed to keep a watch over her and the baby? If she was going to be running all over town now, it was going to be hard to keep on top of things unless he was willing to do a little running, too.

"I could go along with you—I mean, if you didn't mind. Talking about it has given me this urge to go, and it would be fun to show you the building."

She shrugged. "Don't you have to stay here?"

"I'm the boss," he said a trifle sheepishly. "I get to make the rules."

"Well." Julia looked down a moment. "If you're going anyway, I guess it makes sense to go together."

"Perfect sense," he said, jumping up to grab his tweed sport coat from the rack.

That was the beginning. Then there was the Met and the Whitney and the Natural History, and for the first time since he'd opened the office he found himself spending more time on leisure than on work. But it wasn't exactly leisure, of course. His time with her did have a serious purpose behind it. Only sometimes it was hard to remember that when he was laughing with her over Tonio's antics or sharing an awe-filled moment with her in front of a work of art.

Mexico City and the Velascos and that glamorous, spoiled woman he'd seen at the ball all seemed so far away now, almost as though they'd been part of a bad dream. Could it really be true that this was the same woman? No. It wasn't true. This Julia and the one he'd seen and heard about in Mexico were two completely different people. And both people couldn't be real. So one of the Julias was a fake, a phony, a clever act, and as difficult as it might be to face, the logical choice was the newest woman—the New York Julia.

He called his aunt and uncle in Mexico. The Obregons were surprised to hear from him, as he generally didn't call them much. He visited and tried to come up with plausible questions he needed his uncle to answer so the call wouldn't seem too suspicious. Then, just in passing, he mentioned the Velascos. And he got an earful.

Julia's disappearing act was apparently still hot gossip in Mexico City. His aunt carried on about how everyone should have been more careful. After all, she pointed out, the woman had conned that poor young doctor into marrying her and then squandered the first part of his inheritance so quickly that he'd had to put his medical clinic up for sale to make ends meet. And look at the way she'd wormed her way into the Velasco household and talked them into buying her those jewels and furs—she had probably planned on stealing them all along.

Anson's blood ran cold as he listened to the accusations and the plight of the poor grandparents who had no idea whether their little grandson was alive or dead. They were living in torment, Helen said, waiting to hear the price Julia wanted for the baby and praying that she didn't harm him in the meantime.

It was difficult for Anson to hold back from saying anything, from defending Julia. There were a lot of things she might have been, but she wasn't a danger to her child. He wanted to say that maybe there was more to the situation than the Obregons knew, and maybe the Velascos weren't so innocent. But he didn't dare say a word because he knew Ignacio would feel compelled to turn her in.

He ended the call in frustration and disgust, but after he'd hung up and had a chance to sort things out, he realized his upset was not really due to the fact that he couldn't stick up for Julia with the Obregons. He was disgusted with himself. The call had painted vividly the Julia he'd been managing to ignore or discount. He'd been tripping around the city enjoying himself with her when all the time he knew what she was really made of. He'd allowed himself to be completely taken in by those dark gray eyes and that heady smile.

His entire life was based around facts, yet he'd blithely pushed aside everything he knew about her. He knew that she'd taken the baby and made a sneaky exit from Mexico. He knew that everything she'd told him about her background was a lie. He knew that she'd brought enough jewels with her to sell for a tidy sum, and he didn't doubt that the Velascos had paid for those gems and had legal claim to them.

Sneaking, lying and stealing. Those were the facts. And even with the most liberal interpretation of right and wrong, she didn't come out looking too good.

He doubted that she intended to "sell" the baby back to the Velascos, but he didn't even know that for sure.

Maybe her enjoyment of Tonio was just another part of her New York act—if it was an act.

How had he gotten into this so deeply? he wondered. He couldn't sleep, he couldn't relax, he couldn't concentrate. What he didn't know tortured him, and what he did know made him feel even worse. He was angry and fed up with himself for the tangle of emotions he was feeling, and he experienced frightening twists of confusion.

Finally he decided that the only solution was to stay away from her for a week. So the next day, when she showed up at his office with the baby for yet another day of sight-seeing, he told her curtly that he'd been neglecting his office too much and she'd have to learn to make her own way. He heard the catch in her voice and saw the brief flicker of hurt in her eyes, and he felt awful. He spent the week slamming around the office and was accused of being a grouch by all his co-workers.

Gradually the impact of the phone call faded, and once again he began to shut out the reality of that other Julia—the Mexico City Julia. Once again Anson came to the conclusion that sight-seeing with her was perfectly innocent. There was Chinatown to explore and the Seaport, and of course he couldn't pass up Tonio's first trip on the Staten Island ferry.

Sight-seeing was harmless. Complete strangers could sight-see together. And he was always careful to keep it light and impersonal, and to cut the day short when evening fell, because being together after dark was somehow different. Always he managed things so they were never alone together. He wouldn't go up to the new apartment she was just moving into and he'd never invite her to his place. A formal chaperon couldn't have kept it any more innocent.

Yet there were times when she brushed against him or looked into his eyes when things didn't feel innocent at all. There were times when being with her in the middle of a public place scared him half to death.

And who knew how long his self-deception might have continued if it hadn't been for the tree lighting.

Anson opened the paper one morning and saw a notice for the annual switching on of the lights festooning the enormous Christmas tree in Rockefeller Center. It was one of his favorite Christmas traditions.

He drummed his fingers on his desk and thought about Christmas and about Tonio and about how much the baby would like the lights. The tree lighting was after dark. But then, this was a special circumstance. Christmas spirit should be shared and common decency dictated sharing this beloved New York tradition with newcomers to the city.

He reached for the phone.

Julia answered the phone eagerly. Except for the occasional solicitor, Anson was her only caller.

"Do you and Tonio have plans for this evening?" he asked without preamble.

"No," she answered carefully, hopefully.

"There's something tonight—" she could hear the studied casualness in his voice "—kind of a traditional thing. I go every year and I thought you might—"

"What time?" she cut in quickly, then mentally kicked herself for sounding so unabashedly eager.

"It's outside," he cautioned. "And it'll probably be cold."

"That's fine." She peered down into Tonio's bright face. "We like outside things, don't we, Tonio?"

"Aren't you going to ask me what it is?" Anson asked.

"No," she said simply, again wishing she didn't sound so damned eager.

"Okay," he said, laughing. "Meet me at Rockefeller Center by the skating rink around five."

Julia grinned at Tonio as she hung up the phone.

She felt giddy and high, as though she'd had too much wine. The buzz lasted all day and was still with her as she dressed herself and the baby for the cold night outing. Tonight felt different. Not only was Anson seeing her in the evening, but he was the one who had made the plan and invited her.

Knowing that she was acting as silly as a high school kid on her way to a date, she tried to reason with herself. This wasn't a date; Anson was just her friend—her very dear and special friend. And her excitement was due solely to the fact that this invitation made her feel as if he truly and completely liked her in return.

She'd never felt certain of that before now. She'd always had the disquieting sense of something hidden and festering just beneath the surface of their polite yet friendly relationship. She was never sure that he really wanted to be with her, and sometimes she thought she caught him studying her with something close to disapproval or suspicion.

She'd tried to ignore it, and she'd chided herself for expecting too much from him and being too sensitive. She ignored the lurking, dark glances just as she ignored the way his blue eyes sometimes made her want to bolt and run, and the way an electric tension sprang up between them sometimes and she had to cover up with a joke or sudden attentiveness to the baby.

Sometimes she wondered if he had some obscure reason for not wanting her as a close friend. Did he have a policy against becoming friends with people he'd helped, or a negative feeling about non-New Yorkers, or a thing against females as friends?

He was a careful man. He didn't share his inner self easily. Whatever bond they'd forged was based on shared enjoyment and time passed together rather than a baring of souls. How often she had wanted to open up to him and pour out the truth! How often she'd wanted to go deeper and further with him!

But she couldn't risk it, and he seemed to be equally careful about protecting his privacy. What were his secrets, and could they possibly be as dark or threatening as her own?

That evening, she walked slowly along the promenade leading to Rockefeller Center's skating rink, absorbing the sounds and colors of the season. The air was crisp and the sky was a clear aquamarine blue. The sweet harmonic notes of a carol filled the air, and she pushed the stroller toward the small knot of singers. They were young, possibly high school students, and their eyes sparkled and their faces were flushed from exuberance and the cold. Each of them wore a dark coat with a bright-red knitted scarf and tam.

How sharp and clear her life seemed now. It was as though the world had just come into focus around her. She felt a sense of confidence now in her abilities as a mother and she was developing a new understanding of what it meant to be independent and capable. She was finally getting a chance to learn just who and what Julia Lehman-Velasco was.

Julia knelt beside the stroller. "You're going to love Christmas, Tonio," she said, but the baby ignored her.

He was absolutely still, his brow creased in concentration and his gaze fastened on the singers.

Julia laughed softly. Anson would be coming soon, and life felt very, very good.

Chapter Six

Anson passed the huge Christmas tree and the outdoor rink with its ice nearly obscured by skaters, and turned into the promenade. He'd said five o'clock. He glanced down at his new watch, only $19.95 and guaranteed to withstand a dive off the cliffs at Acapulco. The trouble was it didn't keep very accurate time, so he wasn't sure if he was early or late.

The strains of a Christmas song filtered to him, and he started through the crowd toward the source. He saw the tops of the carolers' red hats and moved in closer.

There she was, across from him, at the edge of the circle of listeners, her eyes glowing and a smile pulling at the corners of her mouth as she watched the singers. Anson felt a sudden rush, a helpless feeling as though he were being carried along by something beyond his control.

He waved to catch her attention, and she smiled and waved back, then threaded through the crowd toward him.

"Hungry?" he asked. Food always made him feel safe with her.

"As a matter of fact, I am," she said, sounding surprised to realize that fact.

Julia fell into step beside him for the two-block walk to the pizza parlor. She liked the way he adjusted his long stride to match hers. And she liked the way he was so watchful and concerned, pointing out slick ice or reaching down to help guide the stroller up and down curbs.

"I have to admit," she said, over her second slice of olive-and-sausage pizza, "that I cheated. I read the paper and I know what tonight's surprise is."

He laughed.

The most wonderful tiny crinkles formed in the corners of his eyes, and there were lines framing the corners of his mouth, as well. She had the urge to reach out and trace them with her fingertips before they disappeared. She loved to watch him laugh.

They hurried back to get a good spot for the ceremony. The crowd grew, and she folded the stroller and held Tonio in her arms. People pressed in on them from all sides, pushing them closer, until finally they were touching as they stood side by side.

Anson reached over and took Tonio from her with strong, gentle hands. She looked at the two of them so close beside her in the dark, and then she watched the splendor and ceremony. She felt a total peace, a oneness with time and the universe and all that was good in human nature.

When it was over, he looked down at her with a warmth so powerful that it radiated through her entire body.

"Would you come to dinner tomorrow night?" she asked softly. "And help me christen my new apartment?"

"Yes," he said, without hesitation, and there was a voice down inside her whispering something about fate that had nothing to do with broken watches.

Anson dropped his glasses onto a stack of papers on his desk, pushed his tie up into place and stood to reach for his coat.

"That's it for today," he announced to the two assistants who were huddled over their own stacks of paper.

Both looked mildly surprised but were quick to abandon their work, as well.

"Got something on tonight?" Kathy asked innocently, but her grin gave her away.

Elmer, her co-worker, chuckled and reached over to neatly fold Anson's glasses and snap them into their case.

"What's all this grinning?" Anson shot at the two of them. He was enormously fond of both young people and had selected them personally from the dozens of law school students who had applied.

"She's just jealous," Elmer teased. "She was hoping you'd suddenly lust after her."

Kathy laughed. "It's true! It's true! But promise not to tell my fiancé."

"You two are crazy," Anson accused as he pulled on his heavy overcoat. "Maybe you both need vacations."

"Nah," Elmer said. "We'd lose touch with earth if we didn't have these walls to look at every day. Besides," he added with a devilish grin, "I kind of like soaps."

"Soaps! What—"

"Oh, you know, all the office gossip about the boss's love life and—"

"Elmer!" Kathy squealed.

"Well," Anson declared in his most professional tone of insult, "I don't think..."

"Ah, come on," Kathy soothed, "don't take it wrong. We're just glad to see you finally having a good time and, you know, really dating and all."

"Dating? Am I dating?"

"Yes," Kathy said knowingly. "Seeing a very attractive woman, even though accompanied by a baby, as often as you see Julia, is dating."

"Says who?" Anson muttered and stalked out without waiting for an answer.

He stormed down the subway stairs and ended up on the wrong train. Dating? Who in the hell said he was dating?

Angrily he abandoned the subway at Forty-second Street in favor of walking. It had been years since he'd taken a wrong train.

He shoved his hands into his coat pockets and marched down the sidewalk like a man with a mission. The streets were crowded with office workers toting briefcases and Christmas shoppers weighted with bundles. Buildings were decorated festively, and street-corner Santas were ringing their bells. Gradually he slowed his pace and calmed down.

Why had he let a little teasing and a wrong train irritate him so much? But he knew the answer even before the question formed in his mind. Julia.

Everything was turned upside down.

He'd never meant to like her. He'd never meant to become...

What...? Friendly...? Involved? Hell, he didn't even know what it was he hadn't meant or what it was that had happened.

He'd only spent time with her to watch over her and the baby. He'd only gone places with her because she happened to be going places he enjoyed. He'd only invited her to the tree lighting in a burst of Christmas spirit.

Of course that was all a lie. He had been lying to himself just as surely as Julia had lied to him when she said she was a divorcée named Regis. And he'd come face-to-face with the existence of his own deceit last night.

The searing strength of the lie had finally come home to him when she stood so close to him in the dark. He'd felt her body warm beside him, watched her face shine with delight as the lights on the huge tree were turned on and listened to her voice as she whispered to the baby about Christmas. Once he'd faced the lie, there was nothing left to hide behind. There was nothing to shield him from the truth.

And the truth was that he wanted to be with her—that he had wanted to be with her all along.

There was no point in pretending otherwise or fighting it any longer. When she'd shyly asked him to come to dinner and be the first company in her new home, he'd never even considered saying no.

So did that mean he was dating her?

He zigzagged to go around a slow-moving couple with arms locked around each other's waist and heads tilted together until they touched. Now *that* was dating. He certainly hadn't done that with Julia. He hadn't even touched her, not in that way, at least. And he wanted to. Sometimes he wanted to so badly....

There were times when she looked at him sideways out of those dark gray eyes, or when she smiled that rare, dazzling, heady smile that he felt he might ignite and burn on the spot from wanting to reach out and touch her.

Oh, God, what had he gotten himself into? How could he feel this way about a woman he suspected of so much? How could he feel this way about a woman he wasn't even sure was real?

And if this New York Julia was just an act, wasn't he falling for a woman who didn't even exist? Was the way she looked at him a lie? Were her smiles at him only pretense? How could he ever know what to believe about her? How could he ever know what was real?

He wanted to be with her.

That one overriding, irrefutable constant seemed to erase or dim all the rest. Nothing else mattered much—even the fear that he was being manipulated and used just like all those poor slobs he had witnessed drooling over her at the ball.

If she wasn't real, then her feelings for him couldn't be real. She might be leading him on and playing up to him simply because he was useful. Using men was apparently Julia's most polished skill, so why shouldn't she have formed a very practical attachment to him? What had he expected when he had literally put himself at her disposal on the plane? She had probably seen the possibilities immediately. Anson Wolfe: protector, errand runner, companion, legal adviser, possible cover and general guide to the Big Apple had laid himself at her feet and begged her to tromp on him.

But then...maybe not. Maybe this wonderful, vibrant Julia was the real woman and that haunted beauty in Mexico City was an illusion. Maybe the stories were all wrong and the Velascos were wrong and his aunt and uncle were wrong and he himself had been wrong about the things he'd seen and heard.

He turned the corner toward Macy's and the Herald Square window where they'd planned to meet. A steel band was doing "Rudolph the Red-Nosed Reindeer" and there was a mime dressed as an elf performing inside the window.

He spotted her, holding Tonio up so the baby's eyes were level with her own. Her cheeks were flushed pink from the cold, and she was laughing. All his negative thoughts, all his doubts and fears and worries dissolved into nothing at the sight of her. He was filled with a sweet aching to be near her that eclipsed all else. If this was dating... what the hell. He would date Julia Velasco until she no longer had a use for him, and he would worry later about regrets.

Julia sat down on the plastic bench and set the brake on the stroller. Anson always insisted on carrying Tonio whenever they rode the subway. That was fine with her. The baby loved it.

Settling back, she smiled at the serious conversation the two of them were having. Anson was warning Tonio of the dangers of the third rail and the baby was listening as though he understood every word.

People filed in around them, taking seats or stationing themselves near poles or handholds. She felt a great generosity, a warmth toward every other human being, and she felt happy and contented with herself. Tonight was the night Anson was coming to her apartment.

She felt like a grown-up. The thought nearly made her laugh. But it was true. She finally felt like a grown-up and it was terrific.

Paul wouldn't love her at all now if he were alive. That was sad, but she knew it was true. He had never wanted her to grow up and he had fought it and held her back in every way possible.

At the time, she'd seen Paul as confident and secure, but she saw now that he had constantly needed someone helpless and lost, someone like she had been, in order to feed his own self-esteem.

Would she ever understand it all?

Had she only loved Paul out of gratitude? Maybe. She certainly had never loved him as an equal or as an adult, because when she'd tried he had pulled away, and their fragile relationship had been destroyed. He had wanted her as a child or not at all.

She looked over at Anson. What did he want or need from a woman? Had he ever been in love? Had he ever been hurt? Probably. Did he have any regrets? Had he learned anything?

Did men learn and grow like women, or were they just static—fully formed at puberty? Paul had certainly refused to change or even consider another viewpoint. He had been unflinching in his attitudes and beliefs.

She remembered how much she'd worshiped him. How awed she'd been by his capabilities and complete control, how much she'd admired his absolute certainty. But now she saw that it had all been a sham. His control had been based on fear. His total confidence had been a cover-up for the insecurities that ate away at him from the inside. His absolute certainty was just a defense against the possibility of being wrong. He had been terrified of being proved wrong. Or admitting fear. Or of losing control.

Julia drew in a deep breath and closed her eyes a moment. If she could just understand everything she knew it would help sort out her life. If she could see the truths about Paul and face the facts about her unhappy marriage, maybe she could finally weed out the leftover insecurities Paul had nurtured in her. Forget the anger and betrayal she still felt toward him.

Paul had been her teacher and guide. Then he'd suddenly thrown away all the things he'd taught her were important. He'd plunged into an endless downward spiral of drugs and gambling and women. He'd put his medical clinic up for sale to finance his excesses and he'd rendered their marriage vows meaningless.

Paul had left her nothing to believe in. He'd taught her not to believe in herself and then he'd shown her his own ways weren't to be trusted. Only the tiny life growing inside her had kept her going.

She had escaped from the Velascos and come to New York. She had grown and learned and made a start at being an adult. But she'd done it all for Tonio. She had made every significant move for her child. Now she needed to learn the world for her own sake.

She never wanted to slip into helplessness again. She never wanted to spend her life waiting for a savior again. She wanted to be independent and self-sufficient and strong. Yes, she wanted to be a good example for her son—but she also wanted to be strong for her own sake.

Most of all, she wanted to like herself. She wanted to know who she was and be happy with that. And she wanted people like Anson to respect her just as she respected them.

"What do you think, big boy? Think this train will ever get going?" Anson's dialogue with Tonio cut into her thoughts.

Tonio chortled something to Anson in response, and Julia laughed at them.

Another surge of people boarded. Julia watched as five elderly people dressed in the clothes of their old country squeezed through the doors along with a big hulking man whose pasty skin was covered with a scraggly growth of whiskers. The big man was obviously angry as he pushed his way onto a crowded bench. The elderly group huddled around a pole.

"Damned pushy creeps!" the big man yelled with a Bronx accent underscored by some European influence. "Why don't you learn how to behave! If you can't learn some manners you oughta get out!"

The small group all stared down at the floor silently, and the entire carload of people was quiet and uncomfortable.

"Somebody oughta beat some manners into ya!" he shouted viciously. "Ya hear me!"

Anger mounted inside Julia.

"Listen to me!" the man demanded loudly. "Look at me when I talk to ya!"

"You're being very rude," Julia said evenly.

The man turned and stared at her in disbelief.

"What?"

"I said you're being very rude." Julia's heart was thudding loudly, but it wasn't from fear of the man so much as fear of anything akin to public speaking. Everyone in the car was staring at her now.

"Who the hell you think you're talkin' to, lady?"

"I'm talking to you. And I'm telling you that you're being rude. You're bullying those people and you're upsetting everyone in this car."

"But they stepped on my foot," he announced, like a child justifying himself.

"That's no excuse for the way you're acting."

The man's face turned from childlike to ugly and mean. "Just shut up, ya dumb broad! Shut your stupid mouth and—"

"Wait a minute there," Anson cautioned, standing up.

The man stood up and walked over menacingly to tower directly over Anson. "What'd you say?" he challenged, glaring down at Anson.

Julia stood up quickly and Anson handed Tonio to her. She plunked the baby into his stroller and moved up close beside Anson. He reached out to push her back, but she held firm.

"What's the matter? Cat got your tongue?" the man said with a twisted grin.

Julia prayed for a stop. Why did they have to be on an express?

"You're the one who needs to learn some manners," Anson told him. "You can't treat people like that. Now why don't you just sit down and—"

"I'll show *you* about learnin' manners," the other man threatened, and Julia clutched her bag frantically. If he jumped on Anson, she'd whack him over the head with her purse.

Suddenly there were more people standing. They crowded in on both sides of Anson and Julia, collectively glaring at the big troublemaker.

The big man gave up slowly. First his face fell, then his shoulders. His taut arms settled loosely at his sides, and finally he sagged into a seat, muttering about how a guy couldn't even speak his mind in public anymore.

The train roared into the station, and Anson grabbed the handles of the stroller and wrestled it through the door without releasing the brake. Julia hurried off behind him and reached down to free the wheels as soon as he came to a stop on the platform.

"I just realized my knees are shaking," she told him.

"Geez!" he exclaimed. "I wouldn't have known it in there."

"Well, I was too mad to be scared," she explained.

Anson grinned and shook his head. "You're a tougher New Yorker than I am."

"You did okay," she said with a laugh.

"That's only because you couldn't tell what I was thinking," he said, blowing a deep breath out through his mouth in an expression of relief.

"And what were you thinking?" she asked. "That the stupid woman needed help? That you had to step in and save me from my mistakes?"

"No," he admitted quickly, sounding as though he was vaguely puzzled by her implication. "I was thinking that even if there was a stop and the doors opened in time, I wouldn't be able to run fast enough pushing the baby stroller."

Julia laughed until she had tears in her eyes. As she fell into step beside him she reached over to link her arm with his. It felt perfectly natural.

"Now we'll see if your mom's as good a cook as your buddy Anson, huh, Tonio?" Anson said to the baby, who was craning his neck to peer up at him from the stroller. "What do you think she's fixin', huh, big guy?"

"It's a surprise," Julia said lightly, and she had the heady feeling that the whole rest of her life might be one big, wonderful surprise.

Chapter Seven

After she turned the oven off, Julia untied the cotton towel she was using as an apron. She was so nervous that her hands were trembling. She desperately wanted this to go well. Not only was it her maiden cooking effort in her new apartment, it was also the first time she had ever had a chance to do something really nice for Anson.

She couldn't blow this. She had the feeling that if one thing went wrong tonight she'd never get him back into her apartment again. He was so hard to figure out sometimes....

She pulled the salads from the refrigerator, losing herself in thought as she worked. Anson had made it a point to tell her not to expect any evenings at his apartment. She uncorked the wine. Was his skittishness simply because he was afraid she might expect him to reciprocate and ask her to his place?

"How are you two doing out there?" she called into the living room.

"Fine," Anson called back softly. "He just crashed."

Perfect. Everything was going just as she'd planned. The fish was just right, tender and fragrant with fresh spices just the way everyone loved it in Mexico City. The exotic salad was the product of the almost overwhelming choice of greens and vegetables that the greengrocer had had to offer. The saffron rice had been a successful experiment and the kiwi tarts from Balducci's were perfect.

Now, on top of all that, Tonio had fallen asleep. Dinner was going to be just as quiet as she'd hoped.

She peeked out into the living area of her four-room furnished sublet and felt a powerful surge of emotions. This was her place, for eight months, anyway, and it was beautiful. It was on the third floor of an old mansion, and the rooms were rich and dark with original oak woodwork and stained glass and marble. There was even a fireplace with a carved wooden mantel, polished and worn from years of people leaning against it. Only the tiny, windowless kitchen was stark and modern, added when the house was divided up, she supposed, and stuck into a space that had probably once been a closet.

She loved this place, her place, the first real place of her own in her life. Looking out into the living room and seeing the huge polished coffee table set informally for dinner, Tonio asleep on the thick rug in front of the fire and Anson lying beside him, she felt a peace and completeness she hadn't known was possible. She watched Anson gently pat the baby's back with hypnotic slowness as he stared into the fire.

"Would you mind taking him into the bedroom and putting him down?" she asked. "Dinner's ready."

Anson looked up at her as though coming back from some deep reverie, jerked his hand away from the sleeping child as though he'd been caught at something and then looked down at Tonio with something akin to terror.

"Pick him up while he's asleep?" he asked incredulously.

"Don't worry." She smiled. "Once he's asleep it would take an earthquake to wake him." Her choice of earthquake made her once again aware of how Mexicanized her associations had become.

Gingerly Anson gathered the limp little form into his arms, glancing up at her as though to question whether he was doing it right. She smiled to reassure him and returned to the kitchen.

But there was a tightness in her chest and a burning in her eyes. There was something about seeing Anson cradling her child, something about the gentleness in those strong hands and the tenderness in those warm, questioning eyes.

She forced herself to take several deep breaths and drink a big glass of water. Careful, she cautioned herself fearfully, there are some very dangerous thoughts creeping in here.

After regaining her control, she carried the food to the table, lit the candle and watched Anson's reaction with proud pleasure.

"This is wonderful," he said. "I never expected..."

"I hope you don't mind sitting on the floor. There's no dining table and I—"

"No, no. This is fine." He positioned his lanky frame at the coffee table across from her. "Looks to me like this is where they ate. I mean, it's an enormous table and where else—"

"Yes," she agreed quickly. "Where else?"

"There's not room in the kitchen—"

"Or the bedroom," she cut in.

"Why would they have taken their dining table with them if they had one?"

"Why?" she repeated.

They both burst into laughter at once.

"Why am I so nervous?" He grinned.

"I don't know. Why am I?"

"Probably because the food is getting cold." He smiled and picked up his filled wineglass. "To your new home," he said, lifting his glass. "May it be a happy one."

She picked up her own glass and touched it to his. The wine was liquid gold in the firelight and a joyous lightness coursed through her as though the wine was already flowing in her veins.

In a contented haze she lifted the glass to her lips and raised her eyes. Her heart nearly stopped. She couldn't drink the wine. She couldn't move. The planes and angles of his face were chiseled with shadows from the flickering flames and his eyes were so incredibly blue. And he was looking at her. Looking at her with a depth and intensity that pierced clear to her soul.

What was this woman? The question echoed in Anson's brain. He wanted to delve down into her most secret places. He wanted to know her most private and intimate self. He wanted to pry her open and take the truth by force. Was this woman real?

In a heart-stopping moment he searched with his eyes for the truth. He begged with his eyes for the truth, then ruthlessly demanded it. All in a moment of time that was both fleeting and infinite. But all he could find in that dark, expressive gaze of hers was a touching fusion of fear and hope and vulnerability.

He withdrew, suddenly shaky and self-conscious, afraid of his own emotional intensity. He fought for self-control.

"The fish looks interesting. Is it a Mexican dish?" he remarked, clearing his throat.

"Yes," she answered simply, and began transferring portions of food to her plate.

They ate in silence, both painfully conscious of the fine threads of tension strung between them.

"It's delicious," he said, indicating the fish.

She nodded absently. "My sister liked it, too. I'm afraid it's one of the few good Mexican dishes I learned to cook in all those years."

He kept his head down to conceal his surprise. This was the first time she'd come close to admitting she'd lived in Mexico.

"I mean, all those years of visits," she added lamely.

Her words inflamed him. He could see tiny bits of truth showing through her shield of evasions and lies. She had never mentioned a sister. He was seized by an almost uncontrollable need to press her for answers.

"You have a sister, then. Any other siblings?" He tried to sound casual and kept his eyes on his food as he spoke.

"No. It was just Beth and me. She lives in Illinois now. And you?"

"What?" He was inexplicably startled by her returning a question.

"Siblings?"

"No. I've got a cousin who's like a brother, though." Careful, he cautioned himself. It wouldn't be wise to reveal his connection to the Obregons.

She nodded as though she saw that as good. "And how about parents?"

Funny how only people who'd lost one or both parents would phrase that in such a vague way. People with parents took so much for granted. They just assumed that everyone had them, and their questions were always about what your parents do or where they live.

He knew her parents were dead, but again, he had to be careful. That was something she hadn't actually told him, so he had to pretend not to know yet.

"My parents were killed when I was about fourteen," he said, careful as always to keep the statement neutral. "We had a big wheat farm in North Dakota where there's lots of open country. My dad bought a small plane to get around in, and we used a tractor blade to smooth a strip and built a hangar out in the pasture. They crashed trying to get home during a storm. I found the wreckage the next day." He let out the breath he'd been unconsciously holding. "It was the first time I hadn't gone along."

He was amazed at his monologue. He'd never volunteered that information to anyone.

She seemed both shocked and upset by his story, and for a moment he was afraid she might cry.

"I'm so sorry," she said, obviously fighting for composure. "I—" She cleared her throat. "I lost my parents too. A car accident. It was—" she drew in a rugged breath, and shrugged as though helpless for words "—devastating."

There was a momentary lull in the conversation as each of them was lost in the past. "So what happened to you?" she asked finally.

"Relatives," he answered carefully. "And you?"

"Foster care," she replied bitterly.

SILHOUETTE GIVES YOU SIX REASONS TO CELEBRATE!

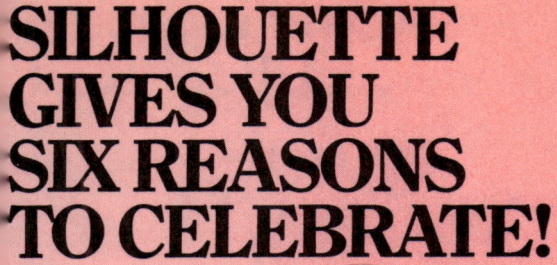

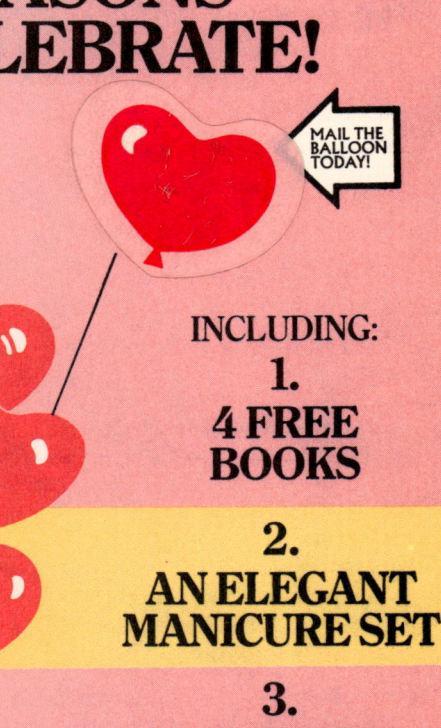

MAIL THE BALLOON TODAY!

INCLUDING:

**1.
4 FREE BOOKS**

**2.
AN ELEGANT MANICURE SET**

**3.
A SURPRISE BONUS**

AND MORE!

TAKE A LOOK...

Yes, become a Silhouette subscriber and the celebrati‹ goes on forever.

To begin with, we'll send you

- **4 new Silhouette Special Edition novels—FREE**
- **an elegant, purse-size manicure set—FREE**
- **and an exciting mystery bonus—FREE**

And that's not all! Special extras— Three more reasons to celebrate.

4. Money-Saving Home Delivery. That's right! When you subscribe to Silhouette Special Edition, the excitement, romance and faraway adventures of these novels can be yours for previewing in the convenience of your own home. Here's how it works. Every month, we'll deliver six new books right to your door. If you decide to keep them, they'll be yours for only $1.95 each. That's 55¢ less per book than what you pay in stores. And there's **no charge for shipping and handling.**

5. Free Monthly Newsletter. It's the indispensable insider's look at our most popular writers and their upcoming novels. Now you can have a behind-the-scenes look at the fascinating world of Silhouette! It's an added bonus you'll look forward to every month!

6. More Surprise Gifts. Because our home subscribers are our most valued readers, we'll be sending you additional free gifts from time to time—as a token of our appreciation.

This beautiful manicure set will be a useful and elegant item to carry in your handbag. Its rich burgundy case is a perfect expression of your style and good taste. And it's yours free in this amazing Silhouette celebration!

SILHOUETTE SPECIAL EDITION®
FREE OFFER CARD

4 FREE BOOKS

ELEGANT MANICURE SET —FREE

FREE MYSTERY BONUS

FREE HOME DELIVERY

FREE FACT-FILLED NEWSLETTER

MORE SURPRISE GIFTS THROUGHOUT THE YEAR—FREE

PLACE YOUR BALLOON STICKER HERE!

Yes! please send me four Silhouette Special Edition novels **FREE**, along with my manicure set and my free mystery gift as explained on the opposite page.

CBS057

NAME _____
(PLEASE PRINT)

ADDRESS _____ APT. ____

CITY _____ STATE _____

ZIP _____

Terms and prices subject to change.
Your enrollment is subject to acceptance by Silhouette Books.

SILHOUETTE "NO RISK GUARANTEE"
- There is no obligation to buy—the free books and gifts remain yours to keep.
- You pay the lowest price possible—and receive books before they're available in stores.
- You may end your subscription anytime—just let us know.

PRINTED IN U.S.A.

Remember! To receive your four free books, manicure set and surprise mystery bonus, return the postpaid card below. But don't delay!

DETACH AND MAIL CARD TODAY

If card has been removed, write to: Silhouette Books
120 Brighton Road, P.O. Box 5084, Clifton, NJ 07015-9956

BUSINESS REPLY MAIL
FIRST CLASS   PERMIT NO. 194   CLIFTON, N.J.

Postage will be paid by addressee

SILHOUETTE BOOKS
120 Brighton Road
P.O. Box 5084
Clifton, NJ 07015-9956

NO POSTAGE
NECESSARY
IF MAILED
IN THE
UNITED STATES

There was another period of silence in which he ate just to be doing something. She seemed to be eating just as halfheartedly.

"And you said you're divorced..." He hated himself but he couldn't help it. He had to chip at her lies.

She nodded.

He could feel her pulling back, retreating. Still he couldn't stop. "And your ex? Tonio's father? Doesn't he help you at all?"

"No," she said shortly. "A person should only rely on herself. Everything else is an illusion."

Her eyes were haunted and distant now, and she became yet another Julia, a stranger to him. She was not the warm New York woman he'd come to know, nor was she the spoiled and frivolous beauty he'd glimpsed at the ball, nor the calculating and evil creature that the Velascos painted. The firelight no longer warmed her features. She looked pale and icy and completely unreachable, as though she had tapped into some cold, inner strength.

"Why are you asking me these questions?" she asked with a steely evenness.

He could feel himself crumbling, becoming as transparent as glass. He could feel his own agonizing truth bubbling up inside him, and he came close to telling her everything. Only the fear stopped him. The fear that tore through his body like a sharp knife and twisted his stomach into a knot.

What if the truth made her hate him?

He took a drink of wine to buy some time.

"I'm just interested in you. You're interested in me, too, aren't you?" he managed weakly. His efforts at deceit suddenly made him ill.

She studied him a moment, then nodded, visibly relaxing as she did. Wordlessly she carried the dishes to the kitchen, and he followed her with his hands full, as well.

"Coffee?" she asked. He nodded.

He tried to help as she arranged the coffee things and brought out little fruit tarts for dessert. He felt clumsy and dull and more unhappy with himself than he had in years. He ate and drank mechanically without tasting or enjoying.

When they were both finished, she leaned back and stared silently into the fire. Her dark hair and creamy skin were bathed in a glow from the flickering light, and a painfully sweet longing spread through him, catching him by surprise with its intensity and force. It had been ages since he'd felt this kind of need for a woman—the kind of need that went light-years beyond the mechanics of physical release. He wanted this one special woman so badly at this moment that all else in the world lost meaning or reality.

She turned to look at him and her eyes were warm again, trusting. The look brought him back to earth. He couldn't possibly make love to her...seduce her...take advantage of her...whatever it would have been.

She didn't really want him, and if she allowed him to take her it would probably be only a practical measure to control him a bit longer. Besides, what kind of a person was he if he took advantage of the circumstances and forced himself on her? And God knew, deeper involvement with her was a dangerous thing, and...and... His thoughts careened this way and that, like computer circuitry gone haywire.

"I'm not very good company," he said, intending it to be a prelude to leaving.

Slowly, with the most unstudied but sensual movement, she leaned toward him and placed her hand on his.

"You're the only company I want," she said simply.

And he knew, with searing clarity, that there was only one reason he hadn't tried to make love to her. It wasn't any good unless she wanted him, too. Unless he believed that she needed him as much as he needed her. He couldn't bear the thought that this was part of some act or that it was false in any way. He had to believe this was real . . . even if nothing else was.

Julia pulled her hand back quickly from his and stared into the fire. Her fingers burned from the contact with his skin. Her heart raced in her chest and her mind raced after feelings, trying to pin them down, make sense of them. What did she want?

Did she see this man as a friend or as a lover? Was it possible to have one person as both? This was all so new and untried for her. She'd married Paul before she'd even learned how to date!

Now here she was alone with a man; a kind, sensitive man; a man with the bluest eyes she'd ever seen—and she was suddenly weak inside, feeling as frightened and uncertain as a teenager. She had no experience to fall back on.

Oh, God, she wanted him. But did she dare trust that desire? And if she gave in to those feelings, would that destroy their friendship?

She was afraid to meet his eyes, afraid to let her skin touch his again, afraid to face the ache that was building inside her.

Sex had never been very important in her relationship with Paul. In fact, Paul had always encouraged her in thinking that the sex was for the man. He hadn't expected her to initiate it, or even to enjoy it very much. She had been pitifully ignorant about lovemaking, and so she had accepted Paul's teachings and attitudes without question.

Later, of course, when she'd begun to change, she had questioned it all. But by that time, though, everything was crumbling, anyway. Paul had been unhappy with her in a hundred different ways. And the Paul that she had worshiped, the dedicated, idealistic young doctor, had somehow been lost along the way.

She had understood by then that he was a troubled man and that the ties and emotions that bound him to her were tangled and warped, and increasingly fragile. But that understanding hadn't seemed to help. She couldn't begin to make him face his own need for help. Paul Velasco would never admit need. Or fear. Or even pain.

They had come close to each other briefly after he'd learned he was dying. That brief period of closeness was the only real sharing she remembered from their entire time together. Tonio had been conceived during that time. But the time had been too short to heal the hurts and disappointments, too short to fill all the empty spaces between them, too short to open up and learn to truly love each other.

So the pain still lingered inside her, festering and welling up at times to eat at her. Had she failed Paul in some way? Had everything been her fault?

Anger flared inside her. This was something for her—just her and she was letting it be clouded by ghosts from the past and fears from the present. Wasn't this exactly what she needed to learn about for herself? Why was she letting it be ruined?

Every dream she'd ever dreamed was here at her fingertips. Every vague yearning, every ill-defined longing had all been gathered up and poured into this moment, into wanting this man. If she didn't reach for this now she would never learn to reach out for anything in life.

She looked away from the fire, careful not to linger on his face.

"We never sit on these," she said, indicating the two overstuffed tuxedo couches that faced each other at the edge of the wide hearth rug and flanked the heavy table. "We always end up on the rug."

She was trying to fill the silence with something. She was hoping to keep him from leaving.

"If you tried to put him on the couch he'd just fall off," Anson said, and she knew immediately what he meant. She was continually surprised at his awareness of everything to do with the baby.

"Yes, he would."

"He likes the rug. I could tell tonight it's his favorite spot in the apartment."

She smiled, almost laughed. Anson was always so serious in interpreting Tonio's likes and dislikes.

"The rug is too thick," she told him. "The little toys get caught in it and he gets mad."

Anson smiled and shook his head.

Silence filled the room again. It settled in heavily and made the space between them loom larger. She braved looking into his eyes. She tried to read them, tried to see herself in them.

He shifted slightly, worrying her with his uneasiness.

"Let's move away from this table and sit closer to the fire," she suggested, trying to sound casual.

Without waiting for his reaction, she got up, walked to the very center of the huge oval rug and sat down. She was afraid to look back, afraid that if she gave him an opening he would begin his going-home speech again. She'd already headed it off once.

She stared into the fire, breath held, listening for his movement behind her. The fire crackled. The seconds slowed to a crawl. The sound of her own heartbeats filled her ears. Would he leave now or would he stay with her? She had nothing left to hold him but herself.

Suddenly he was there, standing over her. She looked up at him, feeling naked, exposed. Could he read her thoughts? She could feel the blood racing in her veins and feel her entire body throbbing, heating, soaring with need and fear. She had never experienced such vulnerability.

Slowly he sank to his knees beside her, holding her with his eyes. The room spun around her crazily. He reached down and captured one of her hands. His fingers burned her skin. Without taking his eyes from hers he pulled her hand toward his mouth, turning it gently. His lips were light as they brushed her palm. His eyes held hers in a smoldering lock. She thought she might die.

"I don't know if this is right," he said, and the anguish and need in his voice pierced through her.

Was it possible that he was uncertain and fearful, too? She was filled with a rush of tenderness, and she leaned toward him, resting her fingertips against his lips.

"Don't talk," she whispered. "Don't think."

He closed his eyes and leaned his head back, drawing in a deep breath as though to gather strength, and the gesture cut through her like a knife, wounding and frightening her. She threw her arms around his waist and hugged him tightly, pressing her face into the hard contours of his belly and squeezing her eyes shut against the threatening tears.

"Please don't think," she said, and her muffled voice sounded torn and ragged.

His strong hands gripped her shoulders, pulling her clinging arms loose and making her feel suddenly weak and helpless. He was holding back. He was pushing her away.

Her arms fell limply to her sides and she kept her head down, unable to open her eyes, afraid to look at him and wishing he couldn't see her. She wasn't strong enough to overcome his reservations in addition to her own. She couldn't fight both battles.

She saw the reasons for it all with bitter clarity. There was too much unsaid, there were too many gaping crevices between them. And as long as she couldn't give him total honesty there would always be those dangerous empty spots separating them. She would never be able to reach across all those spaces to touch him, to really connect with him. It just wouldn't work. How had she ever believed otherwise?

The pain of that knowledge spread like an acid inside her, devouring her. And she felt as if it might consume her from the inside, leaving her a hollow shell.

The fire crackled in the silent room and her pulse beat dully in her ears.

"This is insane," she heard him whisper. It was almost as though he was talking to himself.

He gripped her shoulders tightly. He seemed to want to hear something from her, but she had no idea what. She bowed her head and waited.

"I've never been in love before," he said suddenly, and the words gripped her with their power.

Gently he pulled her up to her knees to face him. She was limp, unresisting and unresponsive. He brushed her hair back from her forehead and tilted her chin so her face was raised to him. Slowly she opened her eyes. His expression was shadowy and sad and filled with endless pain and sweetness. It tore into her, ripping through her mind and laying her emotions bare.

He reached out to cup her cheeks in his hands and he bent, brushing his lips lightly against her mouth. She stiffened and pulled back a little, searching his eyes.

The world dissolved around her, falling away, leaving only the two of them. When he gathered her roughly into his arms, pressing her tight against him, she responded eagerly, winding her arms around his neck and twining her fingers in his hair as his mouth took hers.

There was nothing else but him and what she wanted to give to him, take from him, share with him. Reality was the smell of his hair and the taste of his skin and the feel of his hard chest against her nipples straining beneath the thin silk of her camisole. Truth was the consuming darkness of his eyes locked on hers and the sweet throbbing heat of their bodies joining. The world was their oneness.

She woke, still tangled in his arms and suffused with a liquid contentment, and lay quietly, studying him in the firelight. He was so beautiful. So amazingly perfect. She devoured his sleeping form with her eyes, anxious to know and memorize every inch of him.

His smooth high forehead, the angles of his cheeks, the firm line of his jaw—she visually traced it all in the golden light. She could barely keep herself from reaching out to touch him. The crisp hair on his chest was enticing and the width of his shoulders and casual strength of his arms beckoned her to touch.

She knew, if she stayed close, she wouldn't be able to help herself; she was bound to wake him. So she carefully eased away from him, gently freeing herself. He didn't stir. She took one last loving look, then went quietly from the room.

She stood naked in front of her bedroom mirror, disappointed at her reflection. Her hair was tousled and her skin was flushed, but otherwise there was little proof of their lovemaking. How could her lips look normal when they felt so bruised? She ran her hands over her breasts. How could her nipples, still tender from the sweet pull of his mouth, not show some evidence? She wanted to see some visible reminder of the soaring joy she'd felt when he'd filled her with love.

Her disappointment gave way to amazement at the thought. *Love.* He had filled her with love. She had felt it in his every touch and look and movement. She had heard it when he whispered her name.

She examined herself with an interest she'd never felt before. What did he see in her? She grew critical with the woman in the glass. Were her breasts the right size? Had he seen the faint silvery lines of childbirth on her skin? Was her stomach as flat as it should be? Could he possibly see her as beautiful? She wished she could make herself more beautiful for him. She wished she could make herself more desirable to him than any other woman he'd ever known.

Peering at her reflection closely, she wondered who he saw when he looked at her. Did he see the Julia who was Paul's widow? Did he see the Julia who was Antonio's mother? Did he see the runaway, cowardly Julia? Did he see the lying Julia?

When he looked at her with eyes so filled with love, who was he looking at? She looked at the image in the mirror and wondered if she herself knew who the woman was. Was this woman looking back at her now the real Julia? Or did she still have more growing and changing to do before the woman hidden so long inside her emerged?

Lillian Hellman had called herself an unfinished woman. What if that summed up herself, as well? How could she offer herself to Anson when she didn't even know if she was finished yet.

So what in the hell did she have to offer Anson? An option on the finished woman, whenever she was done?

She could hear herself trying to explain to him.

I love you Anson, only I'm not exactly sure what that means because love is sort of turned around and messed up in my mind, and I can't promise you anything because I may still be evolving into something and who knows what I'll come out like in the end. And besides, I'm not really who you think I am because I'm in hiding and most of what I've told you is lies.

A tear formed in the corner of her eye and slid down her cheek.

They had managed to reach out and touch each other briefly, but that didn't solve anything. It didn't make all the problems go away. It didn't erase the lies or evasions.

If anything, it only made the situation worse. How much deeper the wounds would cut him when he learned the truth about her. And how false their lovemaking would seem to him when he finally discovered her own unreality.

She looked at the woman in the mirror as though viewing her from a great, unbridgeable distance.

"This doesn't stand a chance, does it?" she whispered aloud.

Anson stirred and then sat up, startled and disoriented. It took him some moments to realize where he was.

The fire had died down and he was cold. He reached for his clothes and began pulling them on in a foggy haze. He was going to be a wreck for his meeting tomorrow morning. Or was that this morning?

He sank onto a couch with his shirt half-buttoned. There was a faint bar of light beneath Julia's bedroom door. Was she checking on Tonio? He let his head fall back against the couch.

There was no going back now. No pretending. The feelings he'd fought to keep locked inside were all free. And they were frightening in their intensity.

He thought of Laurel. He thought of how he'd never lost control with Laurel—never had one impractical, totally emotional moment in fourteen months of living together. He'd thought all that romantic nonsense was phony, and that people's silly and unrealistic notions of love were a product of too much television or too many novels.

How wrong he'd been.

Tonight he had ached with need and uncertainty. He had experienced passion in all its fearsome, unrestrained magnificence. And now he was feeling enough fear and elation to last the rest of his life.

He stared at the bedroom door and imagined her walking through it with a shotgun in her hands. She'd point the shotgun straight at him and squeeze the trigger.

A dark, unreasoning sense of impending doom assailed him. He had opened himself up, given himself totally to a woman he had doubts about. A woman who might be unscrupulous and deceitful and fighting for her own survival. If the Mexico City Julia walked through that door and into the room she wouldn't hesitate to destroy him if it suited her ends.

She had wanted him. Her eyes had burned with wanting him. But could he trust that? He had seen how polished she was at playing different roles, so how was he to trust what was real?

All he could be certain of were his own feelings. He had never felt like this about a woman. He had never wanted a woman so much. The word marriage had never voluntarily entered his thoughts, and now here he was ready to propose!

The bedroom door opened and she stepped out, wrapped in a long soft robe. His heart jumped around inside him crazily. He tried to smile. He wanted her to smile back at him in reassurance. But as soon as she got close enough for him to see her face, he knew that there would be no smiles passed between them.

Something was wrong. Her eyes held sadness and regret and not a shred of hope.

He swallowed hard. She didn't even need the shotgun. She could destroy him efficiently without it.

Julia went straight to the fire and added another log. Tiny flames sprang up around it from the dying embers. She turned toward him. "This shouldn't have happened."

"But it did," he countered.

"We can't pretend it didn't happen and just go back, can we?" she asked in a childish plea.

"No."

She nodded and hugged herself, rubbing her arms as though she were suddenly cold.

"I'm not who you think I am," she said flatly.

He kept silent.

"You see," she said with a shrug and a faintly apologetic, faintly cynical smile, "I'm not even sure who I am."

"That's garbage," Anson said, hating himself instantly for the remark.

She moved over to the couch opposite him and sat down gingerly, perching on the very edge as though poised for flight. "I owe you so many explanations, but I—" She drew in a deep breath and looked away from him toward the fire. "I had a husband who wanted me to be a child. I tried to be what he wanted for so long that I never found out who I really was."

She twisted her robe in her fingers and continued to stare into the building flames. "Then I was supposed to become a mother, only before I figured that out my in-laws decided I wasn't good enough at it. They saw me in a totally different way and —" she cleared her throat "—for various reasons I eventually had to...become what they saw...in order to get to the point where I could—"

Her voice had a catch in it, and she kept having to pause and clear her throat to continue, "—have the freedom to find out if I was anybody at all. I mean—" she turned toward him with a heartbreakingly uncertain expression "—what if I am only what other people see? What if there is no real Julia?"

Anson wanted to take her in his arms and stroke her hair and tell her that the Julia he loved was real. He wanted to make everything else go away. But he didn't know how to begin. He didn't know how to approach the moment without revealing that he knew exactly what she was afraid about, that he'd known all along. He was afraid she'd hate him if she knew.

She had come very close to honesty just now. Was that trust, or just the willingness of the executioner to reveal some grains of truth before the final moment?

Was this the beginning of something—an opening up—a prelude to baring souls? Or was this the end of everything?

She stood and walked back to the fire. Her decision was made. He could tell by the way she moved. She already knew what she was going to do—she was just working up to it. And he realized that nothing he said would make any difference at this point. All he could do was wait to find out what the verdict was.

She jabbed the fire with a long brass poker, then she turned toward him, the poker still held in one hand. He tried to read her face. Her eyes were shadowed.

"It was a lovely evening, wasn't it?" she asked suddenly.

"Yes," he answered hesitantly.

"So there should be nothing to regret, then, should there?" She smiled a thin, false smile. "In a way, I guess it's a very nice ending—"

"Ending? Is that what this is!" Anson jumped up from the couch. The hurt inside him exploded and grew into a bright, blinding glare. "Is that all any of this has meant to you?" he demanded.

She recoiled as though from a blow, and her reaction was perversely satisfying. He wanted to strike out and hurt her as badly as she was hurting him.

"You've been using me, haven't you?"

"Using you! Using you?"

"You couldn't make it without someone in New York to hold your hand. You were too spoiled and childish to face being on your own, so you hooked me into the picture."

"I didn't need you!" she ground out angrily. "I never needed you. I don't need anyone! I can make it just fine on my own."

He laughed bitterly. "You aren't real. You're like a hollow, empty doll. There's nothing inside you. And I don't think you even know it."

Tears glistened on her cheeks, but otherwise she was as silent and still as stone.

"So now I understand all this." He laughed and the sound echoed flatly in the room. "This whole seduction bit. This was the kiss-off, right? The thanks-for-everything, it's-been-nice-knowing-you scene. Now you don't have to feel guilty for using me because you paid me off with a good dinner and a rousing little performance on the rug, right?"

He shook his head in wonder. "God, what a fool I've been. What a stupid, blind fool."

"I'm sorry," she sobbed. "I'm so sorry—I—" Her voice broke and her shoulders sagged. The poker thudded onto the rug as though she'd lost the strength to hang on to it.

He couldn't listen to another word. Couldn't survive another wound. "Save it!" he ordered, jerking his coat from the rack. "I don't believe a word that comes out of your mouth, so don't waste your energy."

Anson slammed out into the cold street. He walked till dawn. His breath trailed after him in vaporous streams as he circled, around and around the deserted blocks, always coming back to her street and her building. The light stayed on in her bedroom window.

Chapter Eight

The day was gray. Most days were gray. But then, Christmas was gone now and there were no more lights or tinsel. What did she expect from January?

Julia sank down sideways onto the cushioned window seat, tucking her bare feet under the afghan and hugging her legs so she could rest her chin on her knees. It was her favorite position these days, now that the constant presence of melting slush on the streets made stroller pushing nearly impossible, and the bitterly cold air aggravated Tonio's seemingly perpetual case of the sniffles.

She watched the light snow fall without feeling the least bit restless or trapped. It had been weeks since she'd ventured out for anything more than the essentials of life or an occasional fifteen minutes of sun in the park across the street, yet she felt entirely content to perch in her bay window and read, or watch the street below or simply daydream. Mostly daydream. For even if she did sit down with a book or with the intention of watching the world, her thoughts always drifted away at some point.

Would this madness never stop? It seemed to be growing worse instead of better. It seemed to be strengthening and expanding, threatening to overwhelm and control her. Was this love or insanity? Or was there a difference?

She stretched out her legs and leaned back, adjusting the loose pillows behind her back. She tilted her head sideways and closed her eyes, letting her forehead rest against the cold glass. *Anson.*

Thoughts of him were always there, held at bay only by acts of sheer willpower. Even so, the thoughts would creep in if she wasn't careful. If she let her mind wander for a fraction of a second she would be seeing his eyes instead of the page in front of her, or hearing his laugh instead of the music on the radio.

He was inside her, filling her with joyful memories and intense physical pain, making her stomach jump and her heart race. She couldn't escape him, not even in sleep. Sleep meant dreams, and her dreams were always of him—Anson as passionate lover, Anson as caring friend, Anson as deserter or betrayer or foe, Anson dead, Anson missing, Anson, Anson, Anson.

She missed him. She wanted him. She needed him in her life. Sometimes Tonio would crawl to the door and just sit, looking at it, and she wondered if he was waiting for Anson to come back, too.

Why? Why had everything happened this way? Why had she met him so soon, before she was ready to love anyone?

She had picked up the phone so many times and started to dial his number, but his parting words kept lashing out to stop her. "You're not real. You're like a hollow, empty doll. I don't believe a word that comes out of your mouth..."

Whatever chance she'd had with him she'd destroyed, and she had to learn to live with that.

Losing him had been good for her in some ironic way. She had been devastated and lost. She had confronted dark, naked truths about herself and her life. And then she had sunk into numbness and apathy.

But she had survived. She had faced it all without running away, and she had survived. For the first time in her life she felt absolutely sure about herself. There were a lot of things she still didn't understand. Things about Paul and her relationship with him. Things about Leticia and the Velascos. Things stretching back to her parents' funeral. But those things didn't matter to her anymore.

What mattered was the present. What mattered was the life she was living now. And she didn't wonder who the real Julia was anymore. She knew. And she realized that in continually asking herself who the real Julia was, she'd still been waiting for some outside force to define her. She'd still been waiting for someone else to tell her the answers, when the answers were inside her.

Funny, it was all so clear now.

She reached down and picked up the brochure that had fallen to the floor. There were so many intriguing classes offered. She'd gone in to talk to a counselor already about the possibilities. And she'd found a wonderful co-op for child care during classes. The questions in her life now were exciting: what was she most interested in? what did she want to be in terms of an occupation?

At least, most of the questions in her life were exciting. There were still a few that were not. She hadn't figured out how to handle her "Velasco problem." She wanted to stand up to Leticia and have it out with the family once and for all, because she was not going to spend the rest of her life in hiding.

Julia had carefully considered every angle. She was fully prepared to renounce all claims to any Velasco inheritances. She didn't want their money, and she was perfectly willing for the family to retain ties with their grandson, just as an ordinary family would, as long as they respected and recognized her position as the mother. She certainly didn't want to deprive her son of relatives. And she very much hoped Tonio could have a close relationship with his Aunt Christina.

And, of course, there was the big question haunting her, looming over her. Was it possible to have another chance with Anson? If she was strong enough now to stand up and fight the Velascos, might she also be strong enough to fight for the man she loved?

But she couldn't even consider trying yet. She had to wait until the showdown with the Velascos was over and the dust in her life had settled. She had to wait until she could offer Anson complete honesty. There was no chance for them as long as she still had to deceive him about herself.

So she had gotten the name of an attorney, a man in the state department, whom she was going to call. And she was going to have him advise her and set up a meeting with Leticia for her on neutral ground. And she was ready to go to war.

Dusk blanketed the canyon of her street in shadow as the sun sank behind an irregular line of tall buildings. Lamps snapped on and the scene three stories below became a pattern of light and dark, varying from the blaze of the corner delicatessens to the deep black pool of the midblock park. The squat, old-fashioned, iron pole lamp in the park was the constant victim of rock-throwing adolescents and seldom added its yellow glow to the area. Suddenly it was dark. Night fell quickly in the winter.

She made no move to turn on her own lights. Tonio was sound asleep, still under the lulling influence of the pediatric cough syrup, and she was enjoying the quiet. The coughing and stuffiness had kept him fussy and irritable all day.

A woman rounded the corner by the Italian deli, a big German shepherd on a leash pulled her along in jerky stops and starts determined by his interest in various surfaces or spots on the sidewalk. Julia smiled as she watched the excited animal and its patient mistress. New York dog owners with their fashionable breed consciousness and their fetish for extremes in size, either extremely large or unbelievably small and their leashes and doggie sweaters and pooper scoopers had always amused her.

The shepherd strained at the leash, insisting on a course straight toward the small, dark park. The woman held back unsuccessfully, then seemed to give up, immediately launching into a frantic fumbling act that resulted in the sudden and startling illumination of a high-powered flashlight. The white beam cut through the darkness, slicing this way and that as the woman shifted her purse and steadied her grip on both the leash and the light.

Julia followed the wandering beam's path, enchanted by the starkly lit vignettes briefly exposed by the sudden direction of the spotlight—a drift of snow that sparkled like some mythical cache of diamonds, a pair of lovers in a doorway who pulled apart and stared sheepishly into the light, the man in the dark coat and hat who covered his face with his hands and ducked behind some bushes when the light caught him leaning against a tree in the park.

The man! Julia sat bolt upright and pressed her face against the glass. The woman and her light were past the park now and the man was again swallowed by the darkness. She jumped up, adrenaline racing through her veins, and started for the door, then Tonio's room, then to the phone. What should she do?

Gradually the panic subsided into a general, but intense, fear. She checked the locks on the door, closed all the drapes and picked up her phone to make certain the dial tone was still there. The familiar buzz was comforting, but it didn't give her an answer as to whom she could call.

Even if they believed that a man was watching her, the police would offer only temporary help. One pass in a squad car to ask if she was all right and they would go on to more pressing business.

Her sister and brother-in-law in Illinois certainly couldn't help her. She was terrifyingly alone. There was no one in New York who cared about her and Tonio except...

"Calm down," she ordered herself, and restricted her pacing to the rug in front of the fireplace.

The apartment that had been such heaven to her now felt like a hopeless trap. How had they found her? Surely not through the forwarding mail service. That had seemed so foolproof and reliable. She had written short letters to both Beth and Christina—letters of explanation, reassurance and, especially for Christina, apology. But she had used a reputable cash mail service that guaranteed untraceable delivery.

How could the Velascos possibly have located her? More important, how could she have grown so complacent that she no longer kept her senses alert?

How had she been so dumb as not to feel the danger or even suspect anything the first few times she'd seen the man? Julia couldn't even remember now how many times she'd been aware of him—several times in the drugstore or deli, she thought, and once on the sidewalk in front of her building and, of course, yesterday in the park. Maybe more. She couldn't be sure.

She'd just assumed he was a new addition to the neighborhood, and though he had seemed a little odd, perhaps a little too watchful, life in New York consisted of learning to share public space with all manner of odd human beings. So she had sensed no danger. Even in the crowded park when the man, always in his dark hat and coat, had been sitting alone, hunched down on the wooden bench, and some children had accidentally hit him with their ball and he had yelled angrily at them in Spanish, she hadn't sensed danger. Spanish was a language frequently heard in her neighborhood. She had been so stupid and secure and wrapped up in her thoughts of Anson that she hadn't stopped to realize the man was watching and following her.

Refusing to recognize what was happening, she'd passed over him. Until now. Until she saw him standing in the dark—no, hiding in the dark—right across from her apartment, and she suddenly knew, with a swift and gut-level certainty, what he was there for.

She picked up the phone again. There was too much at stake. She had to ask for help.

Anson unlocked the door to his tiny studio apartment and wearily tossed his bag and coat onto the folded futon that served as a couch. The all-night flight from California had whipped him.

He opened the refrigerator and pulled out a carton of orange juice. It was the only choice. Everything else looked moldy or petrified. He tipped up the carton, drained it and tossed it into the overflowing trash as though it were a basketball. The shot caused the precarious balance of crumpled sacks and old newspapers and previously emptied juice cartons to topple sideways onto an important stack of contracts on the floor beside the kitchen table.

"How'd these papers get here?" he demanded, stooping to rescue the stack. He stood and looked around the L-shaped living, dining, sleeping area. "How did any of these papers get here?"

It didn't matter how many briefcases full of papers he carted back to the office, there were always more stacks breeding and multiplying on his floor and in his chairs and on every spare inch of table surface.

How could he have ever brought Julia here? How could he have ever fit her and the baby into his life at all? He'd had no business even considering it. What did he know about husbanding or parenting or even being responsible enough to throw the damned cheese out when it grew fur.

He'd been so stupid that last night. He'd been so set on his own version of things that he hadn't given her much chance to explain. What had she been thinking? He'd probably never know now. He'd probably never know what went wrong.

How pigheaded! Something went wrong, so he'd just immediately assumed the worst about her. God, he was stupid. All he knew was the law, and sometimes he felt as if he was even inadequate at that.

He moved a stack of legal magazines and sank down on the end of the folded futon. Picking up his notebook, he read his small, uneven scrawl.

San Diego Summation:
Doctors on staff at hospital recall Paul Velasco's fierceness and intensity. Aloof. No close friends. Julia vaguely remembered as Paul's charity case. Mixed-up child who rarely spoke. His surprise decision to marry the girl was a shock to all. Couple left for Mexico City soon after.

Impressions—Velasco not well liked but admired for his apparent dedication. Recalled as young man with a troubled past and chip on shoulder. Prudish and proper. Couldn't relate to mature women.

Anson sat back to stare at the wall. Paul Velasco was well remembered and the picture had been drawn clearly for him. Poor Julia. She'd never had a chance. An orphan at twelve. An unhappy runaway at fifteen and a bride at sixteen. Maybe if Paul had been the right kind of man... But then, the right kind of man would not have taken advantage of or married a mixed-up sixteen-year-old.

He began flipping pages. He had pried into so many aspects of her life in his obsessive search for answers.

The cold details of Julia's foster care ordeals were chilling. And he couldn't help but think "What if?" What if he had not had loving relatives to take him in when his parents had been killed? What would have happened to him?

The thought made him newly appreciate the love and support the Obregons had lavished on him. And it made him approach whatever Julia had done in later years with a great tolerance and sympathy.

Mexico City. The remainder of his spiral notebook was filled with information from Mexico City. He'd been astounded at the similarities between the medical clinic Paul had started and the legal clinic he himself ran in New York. Paul's heart had apparently been in the right place when he'd founded the free clinic. Or so it appeared.

He drummed his fingers on the pad and considered everything he now knew. With what he'd learned about Paul, it was very probable that even his clinic, indeed his entire career in medicine, had been aimed at negating his family background.

Anson, though, still had the nagging feeling that something important was missing in his understanding of the Velascos and their son. Even the startling story of the older brother—killed in some mysterious accident at home while Paul was in his teens—had not shed any light on Paul's estrangement from his family or his obsessive life-style.

The Velascos appeared to be a typical old-line Mexican family; rich beyond belief and able to trace their roots to the earliest blue-blooded Spaniards in the country. They seemed to be no better or worse than the other families of their type in Mexico.

Juan Arista, a son-in-law, looked like a shady character who might be worth further digging. Especially now that the elderly Velasco had retreated into semiretirement, apparently disgusted over developments at his family's oldest plant and at his daughter Teresa's defection to the Diaz family camp. The old man had handed over a lot of authority to Arista in this move.

But that would take more looking into. Meanwhile, Anson had the story of a man bringing his child bride to

Mexico and founding a medical clinic on the edge of a slum in Mexico City. All his sources had agreed on that beginning. Then things got fuzzy and people's versions began to conflict.

Some painted Paul as a good Samaritan and a devoted husband. Some painted him as a worthless playboy squandering his inheritance in every way possible. Some saw him as bitterly estranged from his family, and others saw him as a young man simply acting out a few normal rebellious urges against his parents.

As to Julia, no one seemed to know her very well. She was conceited, shy, reclusive, domineering, lonely, scheming or simply immature, depending on which version Anson wanted to look back at. She was alternately reported to be adored by her husband, abused by her husband, neglected by her husband, revered by her husband, controlled by her husband and spoiled rotten by her husband. Anson could take his pick of stories and come up with any Julia he chose.

He had not been able to come up with hard figures on the inheritance Paul had supposedly had when he'd married. He didn't know how much there had actually been or what had happened to it. Anson did learn, though, that Paul had had another trust that he couldn't touch for several more years unless his family supported him in waiving the time constrictions. He had apparently not contacted his family or asked them to do this. He had been broke, though, and had made arrangements to sell the clinic for a large sum to a developer who had planned an office tower.

The sale had not gone through at the time of Paul's death, and Julia had inherited full title to the clinic. She had canceled the sale and leased the facility out to a group of young doctors for a token fee.

Those were facts he could verify.

After that, things got cloudy again. The Velascos were mostly seen as saints who had taken their poor, widowed daughter-in-law in. The only concrete testimony he'd heard against them was the story a nurse told. She said she'd quit working for the Velascos' doctor after she'd been ordered to hold Julia down shortly after childbirth so the doctor could forcefully give Julia a shot to dry up her milk. It seemed Julia had wanted to nurse the baby but Leticia Velasco had considered nursing lower class and wouldn't allow it.

From there the story was increasingly garbled.

One version had Julia hating her baby and her motherly responsibilities, and plotting and scheming against her in-laws from the beginning. Another less-told story had Julia as a pitiful victim, systematically driven insane by her maniacal in-laws. Everyone agreed, however, that she had at some point become a social disgrace and an unfit mother.

Anson closed the notebook, leaned his head back wearily against the wall and closed his eyes. There was only one thing he was absolutely certain of after all his research—he believed in Julia. Whatever her motives, whatever her reasoning, he believed in her. He'd been a fool to ever doubt her. He'd been a fool to find her guilty without a trial.

She had been through a lot in her life, more than he'd ever imagined. And she had come out of it shining. She had come out of it as a beautiful, wonderful, caring person. He would stake his life on that. And there was no one on earth who could convince him that she didn't love her child, that she hadn't been devoted to that baby from the moment of his birth. She'd never intended to sell Tonio. She'd sell her soul first.

Somehow it barely mattered now that he didn't know or understand everything about her, because he felt as if the truth had been there for him to *feel* all along. And that's what he'd fallen in love with, that truth welling up from inside her. No amount of lies or acts or evasions could disguise that truth for anyone who really knew her. The essential truth of her inner beauty and spirit was always there, whatever she was pretending to be or whatever lie she was living.

Her inner beauty had been the answer to her hypnotic appeal all along. Although he knew he had lost her, that didn't keep him from loving her. It didn't keep him from wanting to help her. He needed to make up to her for all the doubts he'd had. It was important to him to prove to her somehow that he believed, and that he finally realized the Julia he loved had been the real Julia all along.

The pain of losing her would probably never go away. But he could ease that pain by doing something positive. He could try to help her. He was certain, if he kept digging, he would find something that she could use to fight the Velascos. He could help her free herself of their tyranny and cruelty.

Of course, he wanted to do more than that. He wanted to gather her up and protect her and shield her and shower her with so much love and happiness that all the pain and heartbreak from her past would be erased. But he had blown his chance to do that.

He scrubbed at his face roughly with his hands and drew in a deep, despairing breath. What had he ever had to offer her, anyway? Certainly not money. And even his one talent—the law—didn't seem like much now. He couldn't even come up with an answer to the legal question of how to protect her and the baby from the Velascos.

He dreaded the hate she'd feel toward him when she learned about his original motives—about how he'd mistrusted and suspected her. But he was going to have to tell her. When he figured out the plan and approached her with it, he would have to face her with everything. His conscience would allow no less. It was time for total honesty. She deserved the truth as much as she deserved his trust.

He closed the notebook and wearily rubbed his eyes. His head fell back against the cushions. Julia, Julia, Julia. Would the regrets and pain and guilt ever go away?

He was just falling into sleep when the phone rang.

Tonio was trying to walk, but the fear knotting her stomach wouldn't allow her to enjoy the fact. Julia paced back and forth, barely noticing the baby's delighted edging around the coffee table. It had taken all night to get Anson on the phone.

She peered carefully around the edge of the curtain. The street was busy with commuters en route to work, and the man was nowhere in sight. He was out there, though. She could almost feel him watching.

She didn't know what she expected Anson to do. What could he do?

Poor Anson. He was no doubt thoroughly confused by her frantic call. Hearing his voice had made her lose all control. The voice that she had wanted to hear for more than a month had caused such a rush of emotion in her, stirred up so much longing and need that her cry for help had become nearly incoherent. After he'd gotten some of the story out of her, he had told her not to worry, that he was on his way. And that was all that was important.

She was calm now, but she felt almost sick inside. She couldn't possibly involve him in this without telling him the whole story. As soon as he walked in the door she would have to tell him the truth. And that thought scared her almost as much as the presence of the man outside. She dreaded seeing the disgust in his eyes when he learned about all the awful things she'd done and all the lies she'd told him.

There was only one consolation. Telling him would destroy all remnants of her old life. All the illusions and false images would be permanently shattered. The rest of her life would be based on truth.

There was a buzz and she heard Anson's voice over the downstairs intercom. She pushed the button to unlock the building's front door. Eagerly she ran to her own door and waited for him to climb the three flights of stairs. She waited, listening from just inside her door, hesitant to unlock it until she knew he was there.

Behind her Tonio gurgled and chuckled, making his endless upright rounds, clinging to the edge of the coffee table. All the fear and apprehension were still there, but a sense of peace descended on her as she waited. The moment of truth was here and she was strong enough to face it.

There was a strange noise in the hall outside her door. She pressed her ear to the wood.

"Anson?" she called hopefully.

More noise. She heard sounds of scuffling and then a dull thud.

The sudden thought that Anson needed her caused her to fling open the door. Her heart plummeted and the scene around her took on a sudden clarity and brilliance. There was a yawning, broken spot in the wall's plaster across from her door, and the sharp smell of sweat and damp wool overcoats. The sound of the baby playing blissfully behind her seemed an unfitting background for the bright blood on Anson's head. The darkly ominous gleam of the metal gun pointed at her face.

"Julia!" Anson cried, his voice a strangled blend of pain and apology.

Chapter Nine

"Just be nice, lady, and nobody's gonna get hurt, understand?"

A short squat man waved the gun at her. Another man held a gun pressed against Anson's side—he was the watcher, the dark-coated man from the park.

Julia felt frozen to the spot, unable to move. She'd never seen a real gun close up, and her mind seemed unable to grasp the meaning of the whole scene.

"Understand?" the squat man demanded with a thick Brooklyn accent.

She nodded woodenly.

The dark man grabbed Anson's briefcase and threw it toward the door. She watched as Anson was made to take off his coat and submit to a thorough frisking.

She saw the blood trickling from the cut on Anson's forehead and watched him stagger into the apartment, apparently still dazed from the blow they had dealt him in the hall. The two men entered behind him and slammed the door shut. They gagged, then handcuffed Anson to the ornate antique telephone table that was bolted to the wall.

Julia felt detached from the scene, an impartial observer. It wasn't really happening to her.

The dark-coated man produced some official-looking papers from an inside pocket. He sat down on one of the couches and leaned over the coffee table, unfolding the papers and smoothing them out flat on the polished wood.

Tonio watched everything with thoughtful lines creasing his forehead.

The short man shoved her over toward the coffee table and ordered her to sit on the floor. She barely felt it when she banged her knee against the wood.

The two men stared at each other.

"You didn't tell me to bring no pen, Berto," the squat man whined.

Dark Coat glared at him then jumped up and stalked to the telephone. He roughly jerked the stick-on pen free from its little curly cord, then stalked back and thrust the pen into Julia's hand. She hoped it wrote. It had been a cheap pen and it had skipped from the beginning.

"Here. Sign here," he ordered, pointing a dirty, nail-bitten finger at a black line near the bottom.

It was some sort of adoption agreement written in Spanish legalese. Tonio's name was on it, and she caught a mention of Juan Arista's name before it was snatched away from her and folded up.

The squat man roughly cuffed her hands to the heavy table's legs. He wadded a handkerchief into a ball and forced it into her mouth—it made her feel like gagging for a moment—then he tied another one tightly around the outside, to keep her from spitting out the ball.

The cloth tasted new and stiff. How funny, she thought, they must have gone handkerchief shopping just before they came here.

Tonio, who had been watching everything in mute fascination, crawled over to her with wide, questioning eyes. He loved it whenever she sat on the floor.

"Mama, mama, mama, mama," he muttered in singsong.

He pulled himself up, clinging to her arm, and plucked curiously at the gag. Then he eased himself into the space between the table and her body, rested his head against her chest and began noisily sucking his thumb.

Tears flooded her eyes, spilling down her cheeks and wetting the gag.

The dark-coated man went to the phone and dialed a number. He spoke in heavily accented English, and asked if the airplane was ready. He wanted to know if the nurse was there waiting. He announced that he and the child would arrive within the hour.

Both men tucked their guns in under their coats and visibly relaxed. The squat one bent over and tried to be friendly to Tonio. The child ignored him and snuggled tighter against Julia's chest.

"Search. Gather the *niño*'s supplies," the dark-coated man ordered. "Find blankets and diapers and... and—" the man fumbled with his English "—the little foods in jars. I go down to the street and find a taxi."

"Ah, Berto," the squat man complained. "I don't know nothin' about babies."

Berto glared at him menacingly, then left. The squat man began poking around the apartment, muttering to himself angrily. Julia wished her gag was off so she could just tell him where to find things. Where Tonio's favorite blanket was; which food he should eat for lunch and which for dinner; how to give him milk from a cup.

Her eyes, following the squat man around the room, suddenly discovered Anson. She was vaguely puzzled by the fact that he was still there, fastened to the telephone stand. He looked better now, less dazed and pain racked. His eyes were alert and watchful, but when they met hers across the room his expression changed to worry. Why was he looking at her like that?

She felt Tonio's body movements and heard his little noises before she smelled the smell. Oh, no. How was she supposed to change his diaper with handcuffs on?

"Okay, okay," the squat man was reassuring himself as he came from the bedroom with the diaper bag and an armful of blankets.

He piled them on a chair and bent over to peer at Tonio.

"We're all set, buddy. Come on out here now for Vinnie."

Tonio, of course, didn't budge.

Vinnie knelt down and gingerly worked at extricating Tonio from his grip on Julia. The baby hung on with fierce determination. Vinnie pried the little fingers and pulled the stiff little body.

A terrible cutting pain began in Julia's stomach and traveled through her chest.

"C'mon, buddy," Vinnie coaxed. "You're gonna go live with your grandpa and grandma and have ponies and Cadillacs and silk suits. You're gonna high-roll it down there."

Tonio started to whimper as Vinnie succeeded in finally pulling him free and lifting him. The whimper escalated into a frightened wail and Vinnie looked increasingly distressed.

"Hey, hey, now. I ain't that bad," Vinnie said, making an awkward attempt at cuddling Tonio against his thick chest.

He held the baby with one beefy arm around the child's shoulders and the other against Tonio's diapered bottom. Tonio squirmed and Vinnie held him tighter, putting pressure against the diaper. When the man realized what was oozing out from the diaper and dripping down his arm and covering the front of his slacks he let out a scream.

He dropped Tonio onto the couch like a sack of hornets and began frantically searching his pockets. He produced the key to the handcuffs and quickly freed Julia.

"I ain't no nursemaid," he muttered angrily as he yanked the cuffs from her wrists and slapped them down on the table. "Take care of him," he ordered Julia. "You're the mother!"

Julia jumped up, tugging the gag down and spitting out the wad inside her mouth. "Shush, shush," she soothed, "Mama's here. Mama's going to fix you right up."

She pulled a clean diaper and a plastic dispenser of moistened wipes from the diaper bag.

"Lemme have some of those," Vinnie snarled, and grabbed at the wipes. He wrinkled up his nose as he cleaned his skin and clothes.

Carefully, methodically, Julia unfolded the waterproof pad and slipped it under Tonio. The baby was lying quietly on the couch now, sucking his thumb and watching her with wet eyes.

"It's time for his nap," she said. Her voice sounded funny to her.

"Yeah, he'll get plenty of chance to sleep on the plane," Vinnie snapped.

Julia's hands went limp and she turned her head to watch him scrubbing at the spots on his pants.

"Why are you doing this?" she asked, but her voice sounded flat and lacked any question.

"Money," he said with a little chuckle.

"You must be good to have found us."

"Well..." He stopped his scrubbing and looked up. "I ain't no dummy." He puffed out his chest a little. "I got more cookies in the jar than that wise-ass Mex hood downstairs. Neither of us guys had to be too smart with loverboy there leadin' us to the jackpot."

He grinned and jerked his head in Anson's direction. "He yakked a trail all the way from Mexico City to New York." Chuckling, he tossed off a military salute to Anson. "Right, counselor?"

Julia frowned. What had she just heard? She couldn't seem to make any sense of anything.

"Hey, get back on the job, lady," Vinnie ordered.

Julia turned back toward the baby and began the unsavory task of removing the messy diaper.

Vinnie turned slightly green, stood up, fidgeted with his collar and demanded, "What's takin' him so long, anyway?"

"You can't get a cab on this street," Julia said matter-of-factly.

Vinnie stalked to the window to look down at the street. Julia didn't hesitate. She didn't think. She stood, picked up the oversize pottery jug on the end table, walked up silently behind the muttering Vinnie and smashed it over his head.

She stood there staring as he made a half-turn from the window, a look of total surprise on his face, and then crumpled to the floor. He looked so strange lying there surrounded by shards of broken pottery. Distractedly, she wondered if breaking the jug would cause her to lose the sublet.

Anson struggled furiously against the cuffs and made low, desperate noises in the back of his throat.

She had downed the guy but now she was just standing there! He kicked the wall and banged his hands against the table, and squeaked and growled frantically. Finally she turned and looked at him.

She was acting as if she were sleepwalking and he was afraid she was suffering from shock. He nodded his head at her and used his body to beckon her. She walked toward him slowly, a quizzical expression on her face.

"Mmmm, uhhhhh, mmmmmm," he croaked urgently through his gag.

She cocked her head as though wondering about him, then slowly reached out and tugged at his gag. He nodded vigorously and she pulled it all the way down and removed the wadding in his mouth.

"Julia," he said sharply. "Think, Julia. The other one will be back. This one will wake up. We have to save Tonio."

Tonio's name caused her to draw her breath in sharply. She looked back at the couch. The baby had fallen asleep right where she'd left him.

The man on the floor moaned.

The sound caused her to jump and appear suddenly frightened. She raced over to him and fumbled in his clothes, pulling out the gun. She handled the weapon gingerly.

"Good, good! Now unlock me. He left the key there on the table when he took off your handcuffs."

As soon as he was free Anson pulled the limp Vinnie over to the telephone table and handcuffed him into the same position he'd just been in himself.

"We've got to get out of here," he said, "before the other guy comes back."

Julia held the gun out to him.

"Hell, no. I don't want that. I'd probably shoot myself."

She dropped it on the table silently and quickly wrapped the baby in a blanket and gathered him into her arms. Anson parted the curtain to check the street. Berto was still on the sidewalk.

"Let's go." He grabbed both their coats, his briefcase and the diaper bag on the way to the door.

"My purse," Julia called, and he scooped it off a chair as they ran.

They took the stairs as quietly and quickly as they could. The entryway was empty. Anson held up his hand for her to wait. He crept forward and peered through the outer glass doors. Berto was on his way back!

"He's coming." They exchanged desperate glances.

"Over here," she called, running around to the side of the stairs and pulling open a chipped metal door.

He followed her into the darkness and nearly gagged at the stench.

"It's the garbage room," she whispered.

Anson left the door open a crack and listened. The outside doors opened and closed. The inside door opened and closed. Berto had apparently wedged the doors open. His light footfalls sounded on the stairs and then faded.

They ran out of the building and down the sidewalk. The freezing air cut through Anson's clothes and burned his lungs. He glanced over at Julia and wished he could stop and put her coat on her. They ran two blocks and then three, turning corners, trying other streets, but there were still no cabs.

"Damn!" Anson stopped, gasping for air.

Julia stopped beside him, shivering and panting, clinging tightly to the bundled baby. Quickly Anson pulled her coat on her and shrugged into his own. He looked up and down the block, then met her eyes. What he saw there scared him.

"Come on," he said, tugging her sleeve, and they both broke into a trot.

Block after block they ran. There were cabs passing on the street now, but they were all occupied. Finally he stopped on the terraced granite steps leading into Union Square from Fourteenth Street. He had been responsible for them finding her! How could he have been so stupid? Someone in Mexico City had reported his questions to the Velascos and they'd traced her through him. Instead of helping her he had given her away. And now he was responsible for keeping her safe. And he was terrified of failing her again.

Anxiously he scanned the park. The ice encrusted benches were deserted. Across to the west an old man in a red cape was feeding crumbs to the pigeons. Everyone else was hurrying, chins tucked into mufflers and hands in pockets, toward somewhere warmer. There was no help here.

"God, what I'd give for a policeman," he said out loud.

The city bustled around him. Cars streamed by on the streets surrounding the square, and pedestrians scurried along the walkways. The bronze of George Washington on horseback loomed over him in accusing silence. He felt as helplessly alone as if he'd been stranded on the tundra faced with a hungry pack of wolves.

"They're here," Julia cried. He followed the direction of her gaze and saw them.

One was coming from the east and one from the south and they were converging on the Fourteenth Street intersection. Both men appeared to spot them at the same time, and they yelled and waved at each other as they broke into a run.

Anson locked Julia's arm in his tightly and dragged her with him. Around George, over the low stone wall, across the dry grass with its crunchy coating of new snow, down the steps to the Fifteenth Street subway entrance under its ornate glass dome, and down the broad concrete steps to the tunnels below.

There was a short line at the token booth. He let go of her arm to fish in his pockets. His heart pounded and he silently prayed, *please, please, let me have two left.*

"Got 'em!"

As they cleared the turnstiles he saw Berto and Vinnie pounding down the stairs in pursuit. Both looked grim and determined.

Again he clamped on to Julia's arm and ran. Past the camera store and the snack shops, down the broad, gently sloping concrete floor. He looked back through the welded rods that separated the sections and saw Vinnie and Berto standing in line and cursing at each other for their lack of tokens. Maybe later, he promised himself, like maybe years later, this would all be funny.

There was a rumbling in the bowels of the station and they made for the stairs the uptown side. Running, dodging in and out of the crowd, bumping into people, they careened down the stairs.

The platform was only sparsely occupied—there was no crowd to hide in. He stood, holding Julia close to him, and peered down the track. The sound of the approaching train grew to a deafening roar, and Anson could see the reflection of light. He looked up. There, like two animals peering through the bars of their cage, were Berto and Vinnie standing on the overhead walkway and looking down. They were only one flight of stairs away.

The train, a numbered express, rumbled in and screeched to a stop. Anson pushed Julia into the car ahead of him. He stood at the doors, waiting for them to come, hoping the doors would close in time, but ready to jump back out and prevent them from boarding if the doors didn't close. If he could keep them off the train, at least Julia would have a chance.

He watched them come around and down. The train made a sighing noise. The men were on the platform. He tensed, ready to jump off into their path. They were just yards away from him. There was blind hate in their eyes.

Just as they sprang forward the doors slid shut. The train lurched. Berto pounded on the glass of the doors and shouted something in Spanish, running alongside the train as it gathered speed.

Anson sank onto the turquoise plastic bench next to Julia. He leaned his head against the wall and worked at catching his breath and slowing his racing heart. They still weren't out of the woods. Did she know that? He turned his head to look at her.

She was slumped onto the bench with her head back, framed by a mass of graffiti. Her skin was deathly white and her eyes were dark and frightened. When she shifted to meet his gaze with a sideways glance, there was something else besides fear or relief there—something he just couldn't deal with yet.

"They know which train we're on," he said quietly. "It's an express so they won't have many stops to guess at. There's a chance they could catch up with us again."

"I know," she said. She drew in a deep breath and closed her eyes. "Manhattan suddenly seems very small, doesn't it?"

She shifted Tonio in her arms, and he caught himself admiring her. God, she was tough. He was just beginning to appreciate exactly how tough.

"How about this," he suggested. "We get off at Grand Central, grab the shuttle to Times Square, and get a cab to Port Authority—"

"And get on a bus leaving town," she finished the sentence for him.

He nodded. "I think that would be safer than trying the airports. Who knows whether they have other guys watching."

"I agree," she said. "But you don't think I'm stupid enough to include you in my plans, do you?"

He'd expected it, but still the words hit him like a blow to the midsection. "You think I turned you in."

"Didn't you?" Her voice sounded flat and cold against the clattering train noise.

"No. At least not intentionally. I was . . . looking into your history, asking questions. Someone must have tipped off the Velascos."

"You were investigating me."

"Yes."

"How long had you known who I really was?"

He swallowed hard, but still had to clear his throat before he could speak. "Since the beginning."

"Since the Houston Airport?" Her tone was one of startled revulsion.

He nodded.

"So you were working for them and following me when I left Mexico City?"

"No! No. I was never working for them. I just knew who you were. I just—"

"Never mind," she said, wearily shaking her head. "It doesn't matter."

"It does matter," he insisted helplessly. "You matter. Tonio matters—"

"Save it," she said coldly. "I've got more important things to worry about right now."

"I want to help you." His voice had a strange catch in it, and he couldn't seem to swallow it away. "I wouldn't turn you in."

She shot him a cool, sarcastic look.

"All right, think of it this way," he pleaded. "I know you're going to get on a bus. That's pretty dangerous information if I'm on their side. If you keep me close you can watch me—make certain I don't make any phone calls or anything."

She was silent, measuring him with her eyes.

He held open his coat. "Search me. No radio transmitters, no hidden microphones, no spy stuff. My being with you isn't going to tip them off. And I can help you." He pleaded with his eyes. "Please let me help you."

"Why?" she asked, and the tone of her voice cut into him so deeply that he winced.

"I need to" was all he could say.

She leaned her head back again as though closing the conversation. "I've never been to Port Authority," she said flatly. "I hope you know how to get us there."

He felt as if he'd just been given a temporary reprieve.

"Your arms must be numb. I could hold the baby."

The corners of her mouth turned up slightly, sarcastically, as though she'd just heard a bad joke, but she didn't bother to open her eyes or respond.

God, what a mess he'd made of everything. What a mess.

Julia jerked into wakefulness. Her heart pounded and her breathing was short. She'd been having a nightmare. For a moment she was confused, disoriented, but then the rocking and muffled road noises settled into place in her consciousness and she leaned back and relaxed.

She was on a bus heading toward the bright lights of Atlantic City. Tonio lay stretched out, sleeping on the seat beside her, and in the row in front of her the curls on Anson's head were visible over the top of the seat.

They were safe for the present. All was well. Or at least, almost all was well.

She closed her eyes and tried to fall back to sleep. She didn't want to think. She didn't want to face the dull, continuous pain that threatened to eat her inside.

But sleep would not come to save her from the torment.

He had known all along. He had been pretending all along. Nothing he'd felt had been sincere.

How had she been so stupid? How had she ignored the clues, the danger signs? He had always been too knowledgeable about Mexico and Mexican problems. He had been too vague about what his interest in Mexico was. Small things, but still they should have added up to some warning in her mind.

And he had been too easy—too ready to be satisfied with what little information she furnished about herself. He had accepted her hazy half truths and her unwillingness to talk about her history too quickly. She saw that so clearly now. He should have asked her more questions. He should have been more curious. He hadn't followed the natural pattern of behavior. He had been unnatural from the start.

No wonder he'd maintained contact but had tried to keep his distance. No wonder he hadn't made a pass at her right away. It hadn't been a developing friendship—it had just been a job, an assignment of some kind. He hadn't wanted to mix business with pleasure. The thoughts sent an acid wave of bitterness through her.

A lie. It had all been a lie. Her whole life felt like a lie.

Trying to fit in to foster homes where she wasn't wanted and listening to the empty words of affection that never erased the rejection in their eyes. Trying to be what Paul wanted and needed. Trying to live up to the image of Julia he held in his mind so that he wouldn't withdraw his love and affection. Then, learning that she had failed him—that in spite of how hard she'd tried to be the Julia he wanted, she hadn't quite measured up.

The pain from her past mingled with the pain from the present and built into a dark weight in her chest.

The love she thought she had found, the companion and friend and soul mate she thought she had found, the forever that had begun to form so gently and beautifully in the back of her mind—it had been a lie from the beginning. She hadn't lost all that. She had never had it. She could stop worrying about it or hurting over it or trying to figure out a way to win him back. She could stop thinking about fighting for Anson's love. It didn't exist. It had never existed. It was a lie.

Anson was a lie. And not only to her, but to himself, as well. For didn't his spying and betrayal indicate that he had somehow sold out to the Velascos? That he had compromised his own principles and sense of right and wrong?

Had he done it all for money? Was he being blackmailed? Was he repaying a debt? She leaned her head back and drew in a deep breath through her nose. Did it matter? The fact was that he had been lying and sneaking and spying and pretending.

Visions of their lovemaking filled her mind. Had it all been pretending? Hadn't some of that caring been real?

Why the hell did it matter? she demanded of herself angrily. She hated him. He had used her and betrayed her and manipulated her. He had taken her love and twisted it around until it was just another tool to aid him in his "job."

She hated him.

The anger felt white and hot and cleansing. She held on to it and nursed it, gathering strength from it. And by the time the bus rolled into Atlantic City she felt determined and positive and ready to fight. She would make a good life for her son and herself, and nobody, *nobody*, was going to stop her.

Chapter Ten

"You can't be serious."

Julia stood in the middle of the Resorts International hotel room and looked from the black-lacquered walls and marble-tiled entry to the wide-screen television, to the white couch wrapping around two walls beneath the wide window, with its sweeping Atlantic Ocean view to the etched-mirror wall and the wet bar.

"We certainly should be inconspicuous here, shouldn't we?" she remarked sarcastically. "The perfect hole-in-the-wall hideaway."

"This is Friday evening." Anson's voice had a new edge to it, and his eyes were heavy with fatigue. "We were lucky to find anything at all."

"What did you have? A prearranged agreement with the Velascos' men—if there's an escape just look in all the most beautiful hotel rooms within a hundred and fifty miles of New York and I'll have her in one of them?"

Anson didn't react. He threw the room key down on the marble dining table with a weary sigh and crossed the room to the phone.

"I'm ordering food," he said. "Do you want any?"

"I'll do my own ordering," she snapped and carried the baby through the door into what she presumed was the bedroom.

She stopped and stared around the room in stunned silence. The large sumptuous bed was raised on an angled platform in the center of the room. Beside it was an overstuffed chaise for reclining, and directly opposite it was a deep black marble whirlpool bath that could have held a party of four comfortably.

And everywhere there were heavy, beveled mirrors. They sculpted the ceiling in tiers and framed the head of the bed and formed a gentle curve around the back of the tub.

"Who's paying for all this luxury?" she called over her shoulder to Anson.

"I don't know," he called back. "We both have cash. Why? What does it matter as long as we're safe?"

"Because we have to decide who gets the bedroom," she announced airily.

"You can have the bedroom," he said quietly, and she whirled to see him standing in the doorway behind her.

She expected him to survey the extraordinary room and make some comment, but instead he just looked at her. It was a steady, even gaze that gave away nothing, but it made her intensely uncomfortable.

"Have they brought up the crib yet?" she asked uneasily.

"No. You'd have heard them if they had."

"Did you order anything to eat yet?"

"Yes."

"Well, then, I guess I should order myself something now."

"You can't eat holding the baby," he said. "Can I help you lay him down somewhere?"

"He'll roll off if I put him on the bed or the couch," she said shortly, brushing past Anson to go back into the suite's living room area. She heard Anson rummaging around behind her, opening and closing closets and cabinets. She didn't ask what he was doing.

He walked into the living room with an armful of folded blankets.

"This carpeting is thick and soft," he said, "and we could just use these blankets and make him a bed on the floor until the crib comes."

Julia didn't actively agree, but she didn't protest, either. He seemed to read that as consent, and she watched while he carefully arranged the bedding in a far corner. When he was finished she laid the sleeping child down without comment. She resisted the urge to sigh with relief as her arm muscles rejoiced in the long-needed break. She pointedly avoided his eyes and gave him no thank-you for his efforts.

She picked up the phone, ordered and listened to the puzzled tone of the room service person asking if this was an additional order for the same room or a change of order. She resented having the impracticality of her stubbornness pointed out to her, and it added to her general sense of frustration. She slammed the phone down and stalked toward the bathroom for escape.

Two large rooms and a bath were not enough. She needed to be farther from him. She didn't want to look at him. She didn't want to feel the pain. She didn't want to be reminded of his lies and betrayals.

The bathroom was as spacious and elegant as the rest of the suite. There was more black marble, and her reflection stared back from mirrors on several walls. There was a large, glass-doored shower and a counter with a thoughtful selection of soap and cologne and various useful items. The toilet and bidet were enclosed in their own separate space with a heavy paneled door to shut for privacy.

She rummaged through her purse and selected offerings from the hotel's supplies in an effort to freshen up. Still she felt frazzled and worn and gritty. The enormous marble tub beckoned from the bedroom. But she would eat first. Maybe food would ease the dull ache in the pit of her stomach.

When she stepped back into the living area, the crib had arrived.

"They wanted to take it into the bedroom," Anson explained, "but with you in there in the bathroom..."

She nodded, again consciously refusing to thank him.

"I think I'll just have him sleep out here, anyway," she said. "If he woke up in the bedroom and saw that tub, he'd yell for a bath all night."

Anson nodded, and she took perverse pleasure in the fact that she hadn't bothered to ask him if it was all right to leave the crib in the area he would be sleeping in.

Room service arrived with both orders and she watched in silence as Anson directed the man to the table and dealt with the tip and the thank-yous and ushered the man out and bolted the door.

She sat down at the table and began to eat. The food had no meaning for her. She didn't want to be sitting across from him. She didn't want to be so accessible to his steady gaze. She didn't want to be so near to his strong, expressive hands.

But she refused to be the one to be inconvenienced by moving. She stubbornly refused to be the one to carry her meal to the bar or coffee table. So she focused on the food and ate, with silent mechanical motions, and ignored those blue eyes and the twisting they caused inside her whenever she met them.

The silence hung between them, punctuated by the clink of silver against china and the tinkling of the ice cubes in their glasses. It was strained, but workable at first. Then it changed.

His body language became increasingly more agitated. His breathing changed; she didn't actually hear it but she knew it just the same, she was so attuned to his rhythms across that small table. The very air between them changed. He cleared his throat.

Her heart bounced around crazily in her chest and every muscle in her body tensed as though she might need to spring away like a deer at any moment. She didn't want to hear whatever it was that he was going to say.

The phone rang and they both jumped, their eyes meeting briefly in fear. He stood and crossed to the bar to answer it.

"Hello?"

She could see him relaxing as he listened. She could see the relief in his face, and she released her own fear and let out the breath she'd been holding.

"Yes," he said. "Yes, we got the crib. Everything is fine. The room is wonderful."

She stood quickly and retreated to the bedroom, using the opportunity to escape. She could feel his eyes as she pulled the door shut behind her. She was safe for the moment from whatever he'd been about to say.

Julia piled her hair on top of her head and opened the packet of bubble bath from the hotel's stash. She stripped and climbed into the enormous tub while it was still filling. Leaning her head back, she lost herself in the rushing sound of the water and the liquid warmth seeping steadily up around her. She let the water rise almost to her chin before she lazily reached out to turn the gold handle to off.

She floated there, lost in some hazy world that was devoid of pain and fear. The water cooled and she roused herself to add more from the hot tap. The new current of heat swirled around her and she drifted again.

Curiously she felt at peace. The world might be shattering and closing in around her, but she had not collapsed. She had not fallen into a state of despair or helplessness, or had reverted to hoping for a savior. She had faced the truth—that all she really had to depend on was herself—and she had accepted that and tapped in to her own resources. She was not helpless. She was not inadequate.

No matter what happened, she had herself. She knew that now. And she knew that she would never let anyone take that from her again.

"That's it!"

Her eyes flew open and she sat up with a gasp. Anson loomed over her, his face angry and his body stance hostile and challenging.

"Is Tonio awake?" she asked in an almost reflex reaction.

"No."

"Then what are you doing in here?" she demanded, using her arms to cover herself beneath the fading bubbles.

"You're hiding from me in here," he accused. "You're ignoring me!"

"I'm taking a bath!" she shouted back at him.

"For an hour?"

"I'll take as long a bath as I want," she announced hotly.

He reached down, wetting his shirt sleeve, and pulled the plug.

"Your bath is over," he said. "Now get out or I'll pull you out."

She was nearly speechless with anger. The water level sank around her, exposing the curve of her breasts, and she reached frantically for her towel. He grabbed the towel ahead of her, and held it just out her range.

"Get out and I'll give it to you," he offered.

Clenching her teeth, she stood and stepped out of the tub, quickly reaching out to snatch the towel from him. She wrapped herself sarong-style in the wide, soft rectangle of terry cloth and was instantly grateful for its size.

"Now get out of this room while I dress," she ordered him.

"Oh, no," he said, shaking his head for emphasis. "I'm not walking out of here so you can lock yourself in. I was just lucky that you didn't lock the door the first time. I'm staying right here until you agree to listen to me. I don't give a damn whether you're dressed or not."

She whirled and stalked to the foot of the bed. She wasn't about to drop the towel and dress in front of him. Perching on the edge of the bed, she hugged herself tightly, every muscle in her body clenched. Her huddled reflection taunted her from dozens of surfaces. "All right. Talk!" she ordered him. "But make it fast."

Anson looked at her as she sat on the edge of the wide bed, her bare shoulders glistening with beads of water and her masses of thick dark hair falling haphazardly from a clip on top of her head. Her eyes were as dark as the gray of a stormy sea.

His anger faded as he faced the wall she had built in front of herself. What could he say? He raked his fingers through his hair and swept the room with his eyes. Where to begin? His reflection jumped out at him from the mirrored surfaces and there was no escape.

"I know what you think," he began hesitantly. "I know what it looks like. And I'm not claiming I'm totally free of guilt, but I want you to hear the truth."

He looked into her eyes. They were cold and unforgiving, and he faltered a moment in the face of their hardness. Could she ever forgive him? He drew in a deep breath.

"Almost everything I've told you is true. I've just left out parts. I *was* orphaned and raised by my aunt and uncle. What I didn't say is that their name is Obregon and they live in Mexico City."

There was a tiny flicker of recognition in her eyes as he said the name.

"I was in Mexico City consulting on a legal clinic. It was my cousin's Miguel's brainchild." He paused a moment. "I was there at the ball that night. My uncle had insisted I go with them. They had had plans to attend for months and I didn't want them to cancel and they wouldn't hear of me staying home alone and—" He cut himself off when he realized he was rambling. "Anyway, I was there. I saw you come in with the Velascos and I followed you. I couldn't take my eyes off you."

Shaking his head helplessly, Anson continued, "I know it sounds crazy, but I felt something the moment I saw you, and then I just couldn't help myself. I was curious. I was intrigued. I was fascinated. I even saw you get an envelope from some sleazy character out on the patio," he admitted.

She recoiled, disbelief and revulsion stirring in her expression. "You were spying on me, hiding, watching me like some sort of perverted—"

"It was an accident. I swear, it's not like it sounds. I was outside getting air when you came out and I didn't want to scare you or bother you and I thought you'd go right back in and then instead this guy joins you and I didn't know what to do and—oh, what the hell," he said. "It doesn't matter now, anyway, does it?"

The disgust on her face faded into suspicion and wariness. Tiny questioning lines began around her eyes and he was afraid to even consider what they meant.

He extended his hands in a gesture of resignation and surrender. His words didn't matter to her. He would cut them short and get this over with.

"So I asked around and listened to the stories about you and when I saw you by chance in the airport I knew exactly who you were and I thought I guessed what you were doing." His voice had become a monotone, as though he were reading from a book.

"I couldn't turn you in. The evidence against you wasn't clear enough and the alternatives were muddled. But I couldn't walk away and take the chance that you might somehow hurt the baby with your schemes. So I finally decided to keep tabs on you, to monitor you and make certain things were going well and Tonio remained healthy and happy."

"Keep tabs on me? Is that what was going on between us?" she asked, her tone as deadly as a coiled snake.

"That's the way it started," he admitted. "Then things changed and I realized I cared about you."

"Oh." She laughed hollowly. "Was that before or after you made love to me?"

"Before," he answered quietly, bowed before her righteous anger. Did she have any idea of the power she held over his emotions?

"But your allegiance to the Obregons overcame your silly emotional attachment and you just had to turn me in," she chanted sarcastically. "Or maybe you or your uncle owed the Velasco family some kind of debt or your aunt owed Leticia her life or you just suddenly came to your legal senses or—"

"Stop it!" he ordered her. "I didn't turn you in. Not intentionally, at least. I'm not sure what happened, but I called my cousin Miguel while you were playing mermaid in here in the tub and he's looking into it from that end. I told him the entire story and asked him for help. He has a lot of connections in Mexico City and he has no obligation to the Velascos. All we can figure is that I must have called the wrong person in Mexico and tipped the Velascos off with my investigation. Otherwise I don't see how they suddenly—"

"Your investigation?" She laughed again. "Your spying, you mean. Your sneaky, dirty spying. And don't tell me you weren't going to use whatever filth you dug up. Don't tell me—"

"Yes, I was going to use it!" he shouted.

She cringed slightly and he saw it with something akin to satisfaction. At least he was touching her in some way. "I was trying to help you," he insisted. "Maybe I was spying. Maybe some of the digging I did was just to satisfy my own need to know. But mostly I was looking for something that could help you, something that you could use to fight them with."

"Why?" she demanded. "Why would you suddenly want to help me? Because you felt so guilty about all the lying? Because you felt guilty about using me and seducing me and—"

"Me using you! Me seducing you! That's a laugh! You were the one who did the using, lady, not me." He shook his head in disbelief.

"I know you've had it tough and you had what you thought were good reasons for everything you did, for every person you tricked and every lie you told. But the fact remains that you've walked over a lot of people," Anson pointed out.

"And you've lied to me and used me in every way possible. That's what you intended from the start, isn't it? I made myself available and you took full advantage of that availability. Then, when I had no more use for you, you threw me out on my ear with a speedy goodbye and not a backward look. Ha! Don't talk to me about lying and using people because, baby, you wrote the book!"

"I never should have trusted you," she said in a quavery voice.

"You didn't," he said bitterly. "Maybe if you had things would have been different."

She seemed to crumple before his eyes. Her arms sagged at her sides and her head bowed and he could see the glistening tracks of tears sliding down her cheeks. Her misery reached down inside him and made him instantly sorry. Why did he always want to lash out at her whenever she hurt him?

"Julia..." he cried softly. "Oh, Julia..."

Without thinking, he reached out for her. His fingers touched the soft bare skin of her shoulders and the shock of her physical reality jolted him. But he couldn't make the same mistake twice. He should never have made love to her in the first place. He couldn't let himself want her now. Intimacy without trust was a destructive and terrible act. It could cause them to truly hate each other.

But he needed to hold her, to hug her close to him and find some peace in the sharing of warmth and nearness. Anson gripped her forearms and gently lifted her up from the bed. She rose easily, as though she had no will of her own, but still she did not look up or meet his eyes.

"I never meant to hurt you," he said. "Please believe me."

She tilted her face up and finally he could see her eyes. They were wet from tears and vulnerable and filled with a pain that was both terrible and beautiful at the same time.

"How can I ever believe you?" she asked. "And how can you ever believe me?"

He cupped her face with his hands, holding it up to him, and he leaned over and kissed her softly on the lips.

"Can you believe that?" he whispered. "Can you feel the truth of it?"

"I don't know about believing, Anson, but I—I've learned how to feel. You've taught me that."

Her eyes changed, meeting and discarding a hundred fleeting thoughts that he would never be privy to. How much he would never know about her... how much he would spend his life wondering and regretting. And how many things he wanted to say, but couldn't put into words or pin down into sentences.

She lifted her arms to circle his neck and her towel loosened around her and fell to the floor. A moan escaped his throat as he felt the press of her naked body against him, and he closed his eyes and held on to the fragile magic of the moment.

Julia let her head fall back and gave herself to the fiery trail of his lips as they traced a path down her neck and found the hollows and curves of her shoulders.

"Anson, Anson," she whispered over and over and the longing she felt was part desire and part bittersweet yearning for what could never be.

He lifted her easily, as though she were weightless, and placed her gently across the bed. She lay there, hanging in some plane of existence where love was all that mattered. Where the sight of his body as he undressed and the feel of his warm skin as he lay down beside her and the smell and taste and texture of him was the sum total of reality.

She ran her fingers through the crisp hair on his chest and over the width of his shoulders and the lean muscled strength of his arms. She twined her fingers in his hair and captured him, locking his eyes with her own. Her breath caught at the intensity of emotion she saw smoldering there.

He kissed her lips softly at first, then demanded more and more until she was dizzy and drunk on just the taste of his mouth.

He cupped her breasts in his hands and drew back to look at her. "You're so beautiful," he breathed.

She pulled him down toward her and guided him. He held her so they were almost kissing, lips barely brushing, and their building cries mingled and became one.

Anson held her, listening to the rhythmic rise and fall of her breathing. He was glad she was able to sleep. She would need all the energy she could summon in the coming days. He needed the sleep just as badly, but he was so tired that he was almost beyond sleep.

He wished he could feel as though their brief physical closeness had made a difference, but he was afraid that it hadn't. There was still a huge gulf between them. Too much lying and mistrust had passed between them.

He loved her, he was certain of that. But he couldn't honestly say that he could forget everything and start fresh. In the past he'd been accused of being hardest on the people he loved, and he knew it was true. He expected more from the people he loved. And he took disappointments at their hands harder than he ever would at the hands of others.

He also knew that he had the tendency to attack whenever he was feeling hurt or threatened. That made it difficult to even talk to her without the scene turning into a full-scale battle. Like the one they'd just had.

How much could people hurt each other and still keep the love between them alive? Had they already hurt each other so much that neither of them would ever be able to forget or forgive?

Real love was surprisingly hard. It required so much.

Could he be as flexible and devoted to the preservation of the relationship as love apparently required?

God, there were so many questions! And he had no answers.

He didn't know what was possible or what he was capable of, much less what she might be thinking.

This was one situation where logic had no use, where rational problem-solving methods lost their effectiveness. There were no answers he could think of, no action he could take to set it all straight. All he could do was wait and see what happened.

A lot of it depended on Julia, and how she felt and what she believed was possible.

Gently he pulled away from her and eased himself from the bed. He tiptoed through the darkness into the living room to check on the baby. Tenderly he pulled the covers tighter around the sleeping child. Tonio tossed, flinging his body into a new position and sucking noisily on his fingers. The baby had been so tired that he'd slept through two meals, but Anson was afraid he'd awaken soon and want food immediately.

Food for Tonio gave him something to think about, something concrete to focus his anxieties on. He tiptoed into the bedroom for his clothes and dressed quietly. He stopped on his way out, wondering whether to leave her a note in case she awoke, but quickly decided against it. Flipping on lights and rummaging for pen and paper might wake Tonio prematurely. As silently as possible he pocketed the room key and slipped out into the light of the hall.

He would buy some juice, some crackers and whatever else he could find. And it might be wise to stock up on extra diapers, as well. He went through a mental list as he rode the elevator down from the eighth floor. Then maybe, when he got back, he would be able to fall into the deep sleep he knew he needed.

Julia awoke with a start in the empty bed.

"Anson," she called softly, but there was no answer.

The bathroom door was open and dark. She got out of bed, bending to retrieve the towel on the floor, and wrapped it around her as she went. She opened the door to the living area.

"Anson," she called again, but there was no answer from the dark room.

Tonio thrashed fitfully in his little crib. That was a sign he'd be waking soon. She might as well not go back to bed.

She gathered her clothes and carried them into the bathroom. She was still groggy, and her thoughts felt dull and slow. She stepped into the shower and let the spray play against her skin. Gradually she felt sharper and ready to function.

She dried herself and dressed. Her clothes were rumpled and stale, but she had no other choice. As she brushed her tangled hair, she studied her puffy eyes in the mirror.

Why would he have left the room? Knowing how tired he was, she wondered why would he have been up at all.

Suddenly she stopped and stared at herself in the glass. A horrible suspicion was reflected in her eyes.

He wouldn't have set her up, would he?

She didn't want to even consider it. She didn't want to believe such a thing about him. But how could she ignore the possibility? Trust was a luxury she simply could not afford at this point.

A chill passed through her, and she dropped her hairbrush on the counter. She rushed out the door, stricken with the immediate need to check on her baby.

Chapter Eleven

The arm that shot out to circle her chest knocked the wind from her. By the time she recovered enough to struggle or scream a hand had clamped tightly over her mouth and nose. She clawed at the arms with her fingers but they were thick and immovable. There was no air. She couldn't breathe.

"If I take my hand off your mouth will you be quiet and do what we tell you?"

She went limp and nodded. Stars were exploding in her head from lack of air and the room was beginning to spin.

The hand left her face and Julia hungrily fought to get the air back into her lungs. The overhead light snapped on, blinding her briefly and she was shoved onto the bed.

"Just sit there and shut up," Vinnie said.

She could tell by the bandage on his head and the red gleam in his eye that he was very, very mad at her for the stunt with the pottery jug.

Berto stepped in from the living room. He, too, looked very angry at her.

"All right," he growled in his accented English, "where is the señor attorney?"

Her mind raced. Which would be best, the truth or a story? Which would buy her more time or offer more chances for escape? If they thought he was coming back immediately, would things be better or worse? If they thought he wasn't coming back at all, what would they do? And did she dare hope, that maybe, just maybe, he hadn't arranged all this and he was coming back?

"Tell me!" Berto ordered her, waving his gun around in a carelessly threatening manner.

"I don't know," she admitted hesitantly.

"What do you mean you don't know?" Vinnie shouted.

Berto glared at him and raised his gun sideways as if to bash it into Vinnie's head. "You will wake the town," he said through clenched teeth.

Vinnie cringed and shrugged apologetically.

They both stared at her, and she dropped her head and sobbed. It wasn't hard to do in her terrified state.

"He left me," she told them between sobs. "We had an argument and he got mad and said he was going back to New York and he didn't care what happened to me."

There was a moment of silence while the men considered this new piece of information. They didn't question her at all.

"What now?" Vinnie asked. "Should we just forget 'bout him, then? Huh, Berto?"

She risked a peek up at them. Berto looked undecided.

"Quiet, while I think about this," he ordered Vinnie.

She drew in a deep breath as though to signal recovery from her sobbing. "I should have left him handcuffed there in my apartment," she announced angrily. "I suppose he called you and told you where we were before he left."

"Nah." Vinnie chuckled. "This operation's first class, you know? Phone taps and everything. He called some relative in Mex City and they had an ear on that phone, kinda for insurance, you know? And it paid off like a daily double. They traced that call right here and got the room number and everything for us. Pretty smart operators, huh?"

He sneered evilly at her. "And I guess that makes the two of you pretty dumb."

"If you would keep your mouth closed, your brain would have more of the chances to work," Berto told him in broken English.

"Well, whaddaya think?" Vinnie asked. "Should we cuff her and wait in case he shows up or what?"

"The *niño* goes to the nurse and onto the plane before all else," Berto said, as though talking to himself. "That is the job that is most important. After that is happened, we take care of our extra work."

"So what's that mean, Berto?" Vinnie whined. "Am I s'pposed to cuff her up or what?"

"I am thinking," Berto said. "I do not trust to leave her here with you till I return. You are too stupid to keep her. She could hurt you and run away again, and take the *niño* away from the nurse before the plane goes." Berto frowned and scratched his head. "Yet I cannot stay with her myself and send you to the airport because I do not trust you with the important task of delivering the child."

Berto paced back and forth. "So what job can the American do? I ask myself. How is he to make himself useful and prove to Berto that he deserves to be paid?"

Vinnie tugged nervously at the collar of his shirt.

Suddenly Berto turned and looked from Julia to Vinnie. His lips were shaped into the imitation of a smile. "I have it," he announced proudly. Leveling his gun at Julia, he ordered, "Quickly! Gather the *niño*'s things and prepare him for the cold. We are all going out together to see the beautiful city."

Julia gathered up what little was left of the baby supplies and packed them into the diaper bag. She carefully eased Tonio's limp little body into a warm quilted snowsuit, hoping that he didn't choose now to wake up.

"I will carry the *niño*," Berto announced.

Julia swallowed her protests and lifted Tonio from his crib. She showed Berto how to snuggle the baby against his chest for the best chance of keeping him asleep. Then she tucked all the baby blankets she had around the sleeping child, anchoring them against Berto's body until almost none of Tonio was left to see at all.

"Hold her close," Berto ordered Vinnie. "And keep your gun in her side. With her thick fur coat it will not show at all."

Julia stepped out of the elevator and looked around. There were people here and there, laughing together in pairs or walking across the long, plushly carpeted stretches toward the main casino. She had no idea of the time, but in a casino the hands of a clock lost all meaning for people, anyway. No one would stop to think that it was unusual for a woman and two men and a baby to be going out at whatever hour it was. No one would even notice.

Vinnie gripped her elbow tighter and jammed the gun into her ribs. She drew in a deep breath and began to walk. She looked at Berto, holding the sleeping baby against his chest. Tonio was wrapped in so many blankets that he was barely visible. She hoped he wouldn't awaken when they stepped out into the cold. If he did he was bound to be frightened by Berto's strangeness.

She had stopped wondering where Anson was. That didn't seem to matter anymore. What mattered was that this time she was really going to lose her child. And once he was over the border and back with the Velascos she stood little chance of reclaiming him.

There was only one consolation—she didn't have to worry about his safety. Whoever the nurse was, Julia was certain she'd been hired for her competence. And these two oafs beside her were more than aware of Tonio's value. He was the key to their getting paid.

Nothing would happen to her baby. He just wouldn't be hers anymore. She felt numb and dead inside.

The cold sea air struck her face as they stepped through the front doors onto the windswept boardwalk. January nights were too cold for romantic strolls, and the entire stretch was completely deserted. She looked over at Berto, but the bundle he held didn't stir.

What now? They didn't sound as if they were taking her back to Mexico with them. What were they going to do? Berto had probably thought of some safe place to stash her and Vinnie while he saw the baby off on the plane. Then he would come back and let her go.

They walked in silence. The roaring surf pounded against the beach just yards from where they walked, and the cold air whipped off the water and across the stretch of open sand to blast into them. The sable kept her reasonably warm. She had finally found a situation in which she was grateful for its bulk.

"This is good," Berto announced, stopping suddenly at a building that was built from the boardwalk down to the water, cutting off a section of the beach view.

He leaned toward Vinnie and said something that she couldn't hear.

"Hey!" Vinnie protested. "Not by myself! We're s'pposed to be in this together."

Again Berto leaned close to him and spoke too softly for her to hear.

"Yeah, I know." Vinnie was agitated and nervous. "I know how much more it is. And I know I screwed it up before but how was I—"

Berto grew angry and insistent, but still he kept his words too low for her to overhear.

Julia waited, anxious for them to hurry with whatever it was so that Tonio could be on his way to the nurse. She didn't trust Berto's patience or ability to deal with a hungry, fussy toddler. She knew that the best thing for the baby would be to remain asleep until the nurse took over.

"All right, all right," Vinnie finally agreed. He turned toward her and gave her an unnecessary shove. "Down those steps to the sand. And watch it—I'm right on your tail."

So that was it, she thought, Berto was having them wait together on the beach. It was a fairly smart idea, she supposed. She could never scream louder than the surf and even if she did there was no one to hear her. Vinnie looked awfully cold, though. No wonder he had argued against the idea. She wondered if he'd last.

She took one final look at her bundled child, then started down the stairs. Her heart was a stone in her chest.

"Around there," Vinnie ordered, indicating the building.

He wanted her to walk around the building so they couldn't be seen from the boardwalk. It was a sensible idea, but she was certain they'd be even colder down so close to the water.

The walking was slow in the sand and the force of the wind made it hard to breathe. She walked slowly, unmindful of either the cold or the sand.

"That's good," Vinnie instructed.

They were only feet away from the pounding surf, and she could barely hear his words.

"Take...coat," he said.

"I can't hear you," she shouted.

"Take off your coat," he yelled, holding the gun at attention.

"You're crazy," she protested. "I'll freeze to death!"

"Drop your coat—" he moved the gun very close to her face "—drop it onto the sand."

Her heart was pounding in her throat, and a horrible suspicion was dawning on her.

"New orders," she'd heard them say, and "more money." *My God, was Leticia really willing to carry it this far?*

She let the coat fall and hugged herself in the biting wind.

"Now walk," he ordered. "Straight out into the water."

"This isn't very smart of Berto, is it?" she asked him frantically. "They'll find the body so easily."

"It's smart," Vinnie said with a cruel gleam in his little eyes. "With your baby and your boyfriend gone you just couldn't take nothin' no more so you took a midnight dip. No proof of anything."

The barrel of the gun looked big and black and so close to her face. She turned away from it and gasped at the vast, cold darkness of the water stretching out before her.

Vinnie's beefy hand shot out and shoved her forward. Icy water rushed into her shoes.

"Move it or I'll shoot you," he yelled, without either regret or hesitancy in his voice. "It don't make no difference to me. Somebody decided he wants you gone bad enough to line my pockets with a lotta cash. One way or the other I'm gonna do my job. But if I was you I'd be thinkin' a bullet hurts a lot more than a mouthful of cold water."

Anson had been torn as to what to do.

He'd come from the street, loaded down with filled grocery bags, and rounded a corner just in time to see Julia getting off the elevator with Berto and Vinnie. Her face was pale and set and she kept glancing over at the bundled child in Berto's arms.

He overcame his shock just in time to duck around a large sign and avoid discovery. Then he dropped the sacks into a planter and carefully began following.

How in the hell had these jokers tracked them down so quickly? He couldn't believe it!

He followed them out the doors and onto the dark boardwalk, hanging back to keep from being seen. His mind raced for a plan. What could he do against the two of them? He doubted he could scare up any help in time to do any good, so it was all up to him.

He tried to guess at their intentions, but he had no idea what was going on. Why hadn't they simply left Julia tied or cuffed in the room? Maybe they just wanted to be absolutely certain this time that she didn't interfere with the baby's leaving so they were keeping her close until the last minute.

They'd stopped walking suddenly, and the two men leaned close to talk. The discussion appeared to end and Julia and Vinnie headed down the stairs onto the sand. What the hell was going on?

Berto turned and crossed the walk toward the buildings and the street. He was taking the baby in another direction, and Anson guessed that he was probably heading out to the airport to bundle Tonio onto a plane.

Anson stood a moment weighing his choices. Should he go down after Julia or should he stick with Berto and try to grab the baby? What would Julia want him to do? He knew she would be willing to try anything to keep the baby off that plane.

He started after Berto. The man ducked into a casino, probably to call a cab from a warm spot, Anson realized. He put his hand on the door to follow him in, then stopped.

Something was wrong. He could feel it. He turned and stared down at the spot he'd last seen Julia. Why was Vinnie taking her down by the water?

He started across the walk to the railing. They were nowhere to be seen. But then, he couldn't see the stretch of beach blocked by the building, either. He ran down the steps and across the sand, around to the end of the building.

Stopping at the edge he stood and listened. There was nothing but the sound of the wind and the crashing waves. Slowly he eased himself around the blind corner.

He could see them now. They were dark shapes in the night. Vinnie was standing on the sand holding his gun out. There was something crumpled on the sand next to him.

Anson's heart leaped into his throat and he started forward. But it wasn't Julia on the sand. Julia was waist deep in the water, falling and fighting for her balance, buffeted by the wind and the icy waves breaking against her. She was facing out to sea, totally unaware of his presence.

Quickly Anson crossed the sand. He had the advantage of surprise. Vinnie obviously wasn't expecting any intrusions and the darkness and the sounds of the wind and water completely covered the approach. From the corner of his vision he saw Julia fall again, but he willed himself not to respond.

Hang on, Julia, hang on just a few more minutes, he pleaded silently.

Then he sprang forward, diving toward Vinnie's legs in his best tackling maneuver. The gun flew out of Vinnie's hand and the stout body gave with a crack at the knees. Anson threw his arms around the thick body and hung on for dear life. Over and over they rolled in the sand, locked together and clawing for holds on each other.

Vinnie's big square hands found Anson's throat and began to squeeze. But he'd seen where the gun landed, and it was within reach now. Anson stretched his arm and frantically felt for the weapon in the sand. He couldn't breathe. He wasn't going to make it. He had a vision of Julia fighting against the icy water.

His fingers touched the cold metal. He gripped it solidly and raised it, jamming its barrel into Vinnie's face. The pressure on his neck stopped. Vinnie fell back and he glared.

Anson stood, pointing the gun as he rose. His throat burned and he couldn't seem to get his voice to work. "Get up," he croaked, motioning with the gun.

Vinnie stood, his watchful frightened eyes glued to the gun. "Get her," Anson ordered him, forcing the words from his aching throat.

Julia, unaware of the drama that had been played out behind her, had finally succumbed to the force of the waves. She half-floated in the water, and was unresponsive as Vinnie waded out to her and jerked her to a standing position. Then he threw her over his shoulder in a fireman's carry to bring her out of the water.

The squat man fell to the sand with her at the edge of the water, and Anson rushed forward to bend over them. Vinnie's teeth were chattering. Julia was very still.

"Carry her up farther," Anson ordered.

Vinnie stood and again hefted Julia over his shoulder. Anson followed them up toward the building, then around the corner and on toward the boardwalk. He stooped to scoop up Julia's coat as he went.

"Lay her down on that bench," Anson told him, "and cover her with this coat."

He dropped the coat and kicked it toward the shivering thug. He had seen enough detective movies to be very aware of how easily Vinnie might surprise him and take the gun back. Especially when he was scared to death about Julia and nervous about holding the gun and not completely certain he could make himself pull the trigger.

"Give me your handcuffs," he demanded as soon as Julia was covered. Hopefully the bumbling fool hadn't left them back at Julia's apartment.

She stirred and began to choke and cough. Vinnie tensed and Anson knew if he made one move to help Julia the thug would use the opportunity to jump him.

"The cuffs!" he shouted, waving the gun for emphasis.

Vinnie held them out.

"Put one around your wrist," Anson ordered.

Vinnie's face fell. He'd obviously been counting on Anson's reaching out. Reluctantly he snapped the metal circle around his left wrist.

Anson thought for a second, then instructed Vinnie to throw the keys down. The man did as he was told.

"Now—" Anson motioned with the gun "—move over here and fasten the other side to the railing."

With a look of total defeat Vinnie reached out and locked the other circle to the metal railing.

Relief washed over Anson. They were safe now. He gingerly set the gun down and rushed to Julia's side. Gently he gathered her into his arms. Her skin was deathly cold and she was barely conscious.

He listened to her breathing. It seemed steady enough, and she didn't appear to have taken in much, if any, water. He picked her up, gathering her fur coat tightly around her, and rushed for the nearest casino and warmth.

"Put me down," she said weakly as he pushed through the door into a brightly lighted entryway.

He crossed to a bench and sat her down. She managed to stay upright, so he relaxed a little. Her skin was ghostly and her hair was dripping and her eyes were rimmed in red.

"Will you be all right here a minute?" he asked. "I'm going to call the police."

"No!"

She was beginning to shiver now, and he had to lean close to understand her words.

"No police. They'd just keep us with questions. Hold us up. Waste time. And what could they do?" She paused to let her teeth chatter a minute. "Need to get to the airport," she insisted.

"I'll get you some hot coffee first. And a towel and—"

"No!" She stood, shaking her head. "There's no time. They'll be gone."

He held her arm tightly to keep her from stumbling as they walked through the casino toward the street. Her wet hair attracted curious glances.

"Good night for a swim, huh?" the cabbie remarked drolly as they slid into his back seat.

Anson ignored him.

"The airport, fast," Anson said. "And could you please turn up the heater as high as possible."

Julia had never been so cold in her life. She couldn't control the shivering. It was so violent that she felt as though her body was trying to turn itself inside out. Her own health seemed so trivial at the moment, yet she knew that she would do Tonio no good if she was sick.

"I need to get out of these wet clothes," she told Anson. "Will you help me?"

He nodded, but his brow furrowed in question.

She shrugged out of her coat and pulled it around in front of her. "Just hold it up," she said, "like a tent."

Anson held the coat and she wriggled out of her soggy things. The driver nearly ran off the road trying to keep track of the action in the rearview mirror.

She slipped the coat back on and securely fastened its toggle closings. The lining was damp from contact with the wet clothing, but the improvement was immediate. Now her body warmth felt as if it had at least a fighting chance for recovery.

By the time they reached the airport, her teeth had stopped chattering and the fits of shivering were sporadic and spaced far apart.

But it had all been for nothing. Tonio was gone.

She stared up into the night sky and hoped that the nurse had him warm and safe and contented in the private jet. And she hoped that Christina would be there in Mexico City for him to hold and comfort him. Just when she was certain that she was beyond tears, she felt the wetness streaming down her cheeks.

Pulling her close, Anson said, "Come on. We're going to rent a car. I went to one of those instant money machines while I was out and I robbed my savings account, so we're flush. I think renting a car is our safest bet at this point."

Julia nodded, trying to concentrate on the plan and put aside the helpless sadness she felt.

"At this point I don't think we could get any authority to intervene and risk antagonizing a powerful family across the Mexican border. I mean, no one is going to go down there after anyone, right? So there's no point in trying to call in legal help."

Julia nodded again. She was having trouble following the conversation. She felt dizzy and feverish suddenly.

He stopped and peered down at her.

"We need to get you into a bed," he said. "I'll rent a big car so you can sleep on the way."

"On the way where?" she managed to ask.

"On the way back to New York," he said. "We'll be harder to find and safer there, and we can regroup and plan our next move."

She nodded. It made sense. And, if she wanted to catch a flight to Mexico City, then the New York airports were the places to be.

"Just don't make any more phone calls," she warned Anson. "They had a tap on your cousin's phone. That's how they traced us."

"Miguel wouldn't—" he began.

She held up her hand and shook her head wearily.

"I don't think he knew. I don't think it was his fault."

"And how did you find out?" Anson asked.

"Vinnie likes to talk. I just asked him if you called them and gave them directions and he was eager to brag about what a high-class operation this was, with phone taps and the works."

"And did you think I called them and turned you in?" Anson asked her carefully.

"Yes," she answered sadly. "I didn't want to believe it, but I couldn't help but think..."

He nodded and bowed his head a moment.

"I guess you were right," he said hollowly. "I guess we never will be able to trust each other. The history's just not right, is it?"

She didn't respond. What could she say? She'd told him the truth, that she had doubted him. She hadn't wanted to, but she had nonetheless. She couldn't make that truth change or go away just because it was such a critical wound for them both.

"We need a safe place to get some rest," she said finally. "We won't do Tonio any good if we collapse from exhaustion."

He didn't say anything. She looked sideways at him and saw the lines of fatigue and defeat etched into his face.

"How long since you've slept?" she asked gently.

He shrugged and changed the subject. He talked about minor things. Things that didn't matter to her in the least—like how dummies the level of Berto and Vinnie could pick the lock on a hotel door, and how expensive it must be to tap everyone's phones.

Then he switched to how lucky it was that he'd gone back to the ocean to check out what was happening with her and Vinnie instead of following Berto, and how badly he wanted the Velascos to pay for all this.

"So where did you go when you left?" She couldn't help wanting to know.

He looked at her a moment.

"I was afraid the baby would wake up and be hungry. I couldn't force myself to go to sleep, so I decided to go out shopping. Someone in that hotel has found two grocery bags full of snacks and juice and disposable diapers by now."

"I'm sorry," she told him. "I just couldn't help but think—"

"You don't have to apologize."

"What you said... about us not having a history of trust," she began hesitantly. "That's the problem, isn't it? We can't ignore all the history."

"Do you think Tonio is scared?" he asked her finally, and his own fear for the baby wrenched her heart.

"He's fine," she assured him. "Whoever the nurse is, you can bet she knows exactly what to do to keep the baby happy and occupied. That's what she was hired for."

Julia smiled at him in reassurance.

"The airport people said it was a private jet that took off," she reminded him. "Tonio is probably wallowing in the lap of luxury this very moment without a care in the world."

"I hope so," Anson said softly. "I hope so."

"And he'll be well cared for at the Velascos, too," she admitted. "It's not a very loving atmosphere, but Leticia is strict about hiring good nurses."

"I can't imagine them doing all this." Anson shook his head. "How you must hate them."

"It's not them," Julia said. "It's not the whole family. It's all Leticia. She's like a madwoman."

"And no one ever tries to stop her?"

"Not so far."

"It's all so insane, all this bloodline business."

"To Leticia, I guess the question of blood is everything."

When they finally had the full-sized sedan rented and ready to pull onto the road, he insisted that he was all right to drive. She didn't argue. She was too feverish and faint to care. She waited until he was certain of his directions and needed no help reading road signs. As soon as he was headed north on the open highway she crawled over into the back seat and didn't stir again until the New York skyline was in full view.

Chapter Twelve

"Rise and shine!"

"Where am I?" Julia asked groggily.

"The Big Apple," Anson said. "Now come on, we've got a little walking to do."

Julia climbed out of the car and looked around groggily. "Are we at an airport?"

"La Guardia," he answered. "I thought we'd leave the car in long-term parking in case they've traced it. We'll walk up to the departing area in the terminal and take a cab to a hotel."

"You're really getting tricky," she said with admiration.

"Comes from watching *Three Days of the Condor*," he said.

"What?"

He looked at her and grinned. "Come on, woman. If you're gonna be my sidekick on this caper, you're gonna have to move faster!"

"I can't believe you're not dead," she told him as they climbed into a cab.

"I am," he said. "What you're seeing is a zombie."

As soon as they were checked into the airport hotel, Julia insisted that he take a shower and go straight to bed. She puttered around the room while he was in the shower and then, after he was tucked in, she climbed into a hot tub.

She still felt awful, but it was less awful. She no longer felt as if she was a candidate for pneumonia; she just had a lingering sick feeling that was as much like a bad hangover as anything.

She scrubbed herself till she was pink and washed and dried her hair. Anson was sleeping soundly.

Julia pulled on her coat and slipped out of the room. If she was on her way into battle, then she at least needed some clean clothes. She didn't intend to launch an attack on Mexico City wearing nothing but a grim look and a sable coat. She had promised Anson she wouldn't make a move while he was asleep, but certainly that couldn't extend to shopping, could it?

It was funny how life went on. She might be worried sick about her son and recovering from an attempt on her life and planning an insane attack on the Velascos, but she still couldn't stop thinking about how desperately she wanted a toothbrush.

Hailing a taxi, she had him head for the nearest shopping area. She took her time, confident that Anson would sleep for ages. She bought a sackful of supplies from a big drugstore, then went from aisle to aisle in a discount department store buying an assortment of underwear and shirts and jeans. Anson's sizes were all a guess, but she didn't worry about it.

Doing something productive made her feel good. Action made her feel good. She was not helpless. She was not defeated. Tonio was her child, her son, and she was more than ready to fight to claim him.

She called another taxi to take her back to the hotel. She knew what she had to do, but she didn't know if she could do it alone. Not that she would blame Anson at all if he wanted out at this point. In fact, getting out was probably the smartest move he could make...and above all else, Anson was a very smart man.

Anson turned over and sat up, fighting his way out of a bad dream. Julia was being hurt. The baby was crying. Vinnie's face leered at him. And he couldn't do anything to stop any of it. The worst part of the dream was the helplessness.

He looked around the semidark room. Julia wasn't there. He padded to the bathroom and looked inside. It was empty. He realized that her coat was gone.

A terrible rush of fear hit him. Had she gone alone? Had she gone down to face them by herself? She had promised she wouldn't do anything while he slept—but then, why should he trust any of her promises?

He pulled back the drapes and looked out the window. The scene below told him nothing. He fumbled for the phone and called the airline. A pleasant voice informed him that there was a flight in four hours. There had been no connections in the past several hours that someone could have taken to Mexico City. He booked a reservation and hung up the phone.

Julia couldn't have gotten anywhere if she had run off without him. She was going to be stuck with that same flight schedule he'd just heard. The flight in four hours was the only choice for the day.

He propped the pillows up behind him on the bed and leaned back to think. He had to find her. He would never forgive himself if something happened to her. Just because he knew that the relationship between them couldn't work didn't mean he could just stop caring about her or about Tonio.

He squeezed his eyes shut and tortured himself with thoughts about how much Tonio must be missing his mother.

"Oh, you're awake!"

Julia was surprised to see him sitting up in the bed when she stepped into the room.

"I thought you'd sleep forever."

Anson's laugh was tinged with relief as she dumped her sacks on the bed.

"Is that where you were?" he asked incredulously. "Shopping?"

She threw him a new toothbrush and a pair of socks. "Just tell me you aren't glad to have those," she challenged him playfully.

"I guess we both have a compulsion to shop when we can't sleep," he said with gentle sarcasm.

"And," she mentioned carefully, "maybe we both have a compulsion to believe the worst when we don't know something." She could tell by his behavior that he'd thought she'd run off without him.

He looked at her silently without bothering to deny what she was hinting at.

"Well," she said with a lightness she didn't feel, "not trusting each other will probably help to keep us on our toes, right?"

He neither agreed nor disagreed. Suddenly he was enormously interested in her treasures and began claiming things for himself.

"Hey, you got my sizes right!"

She wiggled her eyebrows. "You forget," she teased, "I know that body of yours pretty well by now."

It was the wrong thing to say, and she knew it even before she'd finished the sentence.

There was a yawning silence they couldn't fill.

Quickly she moved to the phone and picked up the receiver. "I'd better check on connections to Mexico City," she announced to justify herself.

"There's only one choice," he said flatly. "I've already booked it for one, so just change the reservation to two. It shouldn't be any problem."

She stared at him a moment, grasping the meaning of his having made the reservation. Understanding what he had thought and what he'd been planning.

She finished with the phone and dressed in her new clothes. The jeans were a good fit, but she had to roll up the arms of the shirt. The cotton felt good against her skin.

"All right, sit down over here," he ordered her, perching on one side of the small table in front of the window.

He had a pen in his hand and he smoothed out a sheet of hotel paper on the table in front of him.

She took the seat opposite him and searched his face. He looked better now that he had rested. But he still had faint circles beneath his eyes and a shadowed look to his expression. Somehow it only added to the wonderful depth of his face.

She had to remind herself not to reach out and touch him. She had to remind herself of his inaccessibility. They had come together in those passionate moments in Atlantic City, but that joining had not been a new beginning. It had been an ending, a letting go—a bittersweet, final journey into a world they could never have together.

She had to remember that and not let herself get tangled in his eyes or lost in the need for his warmth. She had to remember that and respect and honor the temporary bridge of truce that had been so fragilely spun between them.

"Julia reporting for duty," she announced, tossing off a military salute. "Have the fortress-scaling instructions arrived?"

"The courier has just left them," Anson said, joining in the false levity. "Now if we could just read Japanese..."

Anson's throat was very tight, and he was having a hard time avoiding her eyes. She looked so beautiful with her hair falling softly about her face and her dark gray eyes shining with purpose and determination.

He had to remind himself that love was real and significant and one of the greatest joys in life—but love wasn't all there was to a relationship. Love did not make everything else all right.

They hadn't stood a chance. He could see that now. Their karma had been wrong or their horoscopes off or their cosmic timing out of whack. What the hell... What did it matter now, anyway? The fact was that it hadn't worked—in spite of all the good parts, it just hadn't worked.

He had to forget all that now and concentrate on the business at hand. The important thing now was rescuing an innocent baby from the clutches of some apparently unscrupulous and evil people.

"Let's go over what we know," he said, his tone all business now. "It's obvious we can't go at this in a perfectly legal and sane way—that would get us nowhere."

She nodded agreement.

"Somehow or another I need to get in there and steal him back," Julia said. "That's the only way I can see. And I have to do it fast, before they expect anything or have a chance to develop some elaborate protection measures."

"If there was only someone we could ask for help," Anson said. "Someone in Mexico City."

"Christina would help us. I'm certain of it."

Anson's eyebrows raised in question. "Isn't that the one who's married to Arista?"

"Yes, but she's married in name only. She would never support him in this."

"I don't know. She could give us away and—"

"No. If Christina agrees to help us, I'd bet my life on that. And if she doesn't agree, I'm certain she wouldn't report our asking, either."

"You know," Anson pointed out hesitantly, "getting the baby back and away isn't all there is. This fight could go on indefinitely. There has to be a way to put an end to it and get them off your back once and for all. You can't hide the rest of you life."

"I know." She sighed deeply. "But what can I do? What can I fight them with?"

"Facts," Anson announced firmly. "There's one thing I'm certain of after all my digging—something doesn't smell quite right in that barrel of fish. It just doesn't add up right. And I think the key to it is Arista."

Julia shook her head in disagreement.

"Juan is too stupid to be behind much," she said. "Leticia is the brains in the family."

"It doesn't necessarily take brains to be rotten," Anson said. "Or even to be scheming and rotten. Some people do it just by instinct."

"So what do we do?" Julia asked. "We have three and a half hours till plane time, but what can we possibly do?"

Anson sat back and gnawed on his lower lip a moment. He had lost all his notes along the way, but that didn't matter. He was fairly certain he had everything committed to memory.

The only thing he didn't have was the report on Arista that he'd been expecting. His state department connection had promised him a detailed report on the man. Arista was not that important to them yet, but his name had come up in several other ongoing investigations, and he had been flagged as a troublemaker in training.

The connection had been hesitant to offer anything over the phone but had promised to messenger a full report to Anson at his office the next day.

That would have been Friday.

And of course he'd spent Friday running through subways and then romping around Atlantic City. Today was Sunday already. How time flew. And that report was no doubt sitting on his desk waiting.

But he had no doubt in the world that his office was being watched. So how was he going to get it?

Julia waited. She understood Anson's reasoning and she knew she should be more concerned with the future but right now all she could seem to focus on was getting Tonio back.

Anson suddenly looked up and smiled.

"How are you at scrubbing floors?" he asked her.

She stared at him in total bewilderment.

"There's a report in my office," he explained. "Something that came Friday. It's about Juan Arista, and my hunch is that it could be very important to us."

She nodded but still didn't completely follow his train of thought.

"They could be watching my office, but they wouldn't be looking for the cleaning lady, would they?"

She smiled and jumped from her chair.

"I don't do windows, though," she insisted as they headed out the door.

Julia watched the passing city sights and wondered why she wasn't scared. These men had orders to do away with her if they caught her. What if someone was watching the office and saw through her cleaning woman ruse?

But she simply wasn't frightened anymore. She had gone beyond all that. If anything, what she was feeling now was eagerness.

They had rented another car and had swung by a junk shop on their way to the office. Now she was armed with a bucket and mop and she had on an old tattered cloth coat, and had her hair tied up in a scarf.

Anson pulled up several blocks from the office.

"You mean I have to walk?" she teased, knowing full well he couldn't pull up in front and let her out.

"Let me look at you," Anson ordered. She posed for him with wide eyes.

"Here," he said, slipping his reading glasses on her. He studied the effect a moment, and she saw a sudden shadow of fear cross his face. "Maybe this isn't such a—" he started to say but she was already out of the car and on her way.

As she walked she reached out and let her hand trail along a grimy city wall until it was black. She reached up and smudged the grime on her cheeks and forehead for good measure.

She was feeling pretty confident when she inserted the key into his outside door and let herself into the building. The halls were echoing and quiet. Her heart stepped up a beat.

She took the elevator up and fumbled through his keys for the door to his office suite. Suddenly the wooden door opened in her face.

"What do we have here?" a big burly black man said with a grin.

Her heart stopped completely, then skidded into something close to the speed of light.

She squinted up at the man and screwed her mouth up.

"Just cleanin'," she said curtly. "Outta my way."

The man made a face as though to say he thought she was a pain in the neck, but he stepped aside and let her enter.

"That ain't one of our friends is it?" a voice called from the back.

"Nah, Vinnie," the black man replied. "It's just some cleanin' woman."

Julia's knees felt like jelly. Vinnie was there.

"Well, get on with it," the black man ordered her.

The floor she was standing on was carpeted, so it was obvious she couldn't start there. She headed toward Anson's office just as if she belonged there.

Vinnie was watching the television in the break room. She had to pass right by him. She ducked her head and prayed as she crossed the hall.

Nothing. No reaction. He hadn't seen her.

The black man appeared in the doorway and eyed her suspiciously, so she attacked Anson's tiled floor with a vengeance. It would probably be the cleanest floor in New York when she finished. The man finally tired of watching her and walked away.

Quickly she grabbed the manila envelope from Anson's desk. It was right on top as they'd hoped it would be. She tucked it into her waistband at the back of her jeans and pulled the old coat back on over it.

She picked up her bucket and headed back out toward the front.

"You ain't finished, are you?" the black man asked.

She started to mutter something about clean water, but then she heard the footsteps coming from the back. Vinnie rounded the corner and she dropped the bucket and ran just as he met her eyes.

She could hear them slamming out of the office after her. The elevator was there. She rushed into it and pressed the first floor button. Nothing happened. She pressed the close button. She jumped up and down to trick it into thinking it had a load. Finally the doors began to slide shut. She caught a glimpse of Vinnie's beet-red face as they slammed.

As soon as the doors opened on the first floor, she bolted. She had no idea how close they might be behind her. She raced down the half-empty sidewalks and around corners until she reached the car.

She jerked open the door and threw herself in. "Go!"

Then she began to laugh. And she laughed all the way to the airport as she recounted every scary detail. And she laughed boarding the plane. Beating Vinnie had made her feel powerful and almost immortal.

* * *

Anson watched her sleeping, her seat tilted back and her head resting against the window. He couldn't believe her story about the office. He couldn't believe how much courage she had.

He opened the envelope and pulled out the contents again. The reports on Arista were comprehensive and filled pages. Juan had been a playmate of some very bad boys in the States. There was a wealth of information on his activities in both countries and even within the Velasco business concerns.

There was enough information to hang the man with.

They had already agreed on their strategy. They would call Christina on her private line as soon as they arrived in Mexico City and find out exactly where Tonio was and what was happening. Then, if Christina agreed to help them, they would formulate a plan with her for getting the baby. If she didn't agree... they would formulate a plan, anyway.

And once they had Tonio they would go to the Obregons' house for safety. He was certain if he told his uncle the whole story they would receive protection and help from that quarter.

Then, once the child was safely out of the Velascos' hands, they could proceed with their attack strategy. They could have it out with the conniving bunch once and for all and put an end to the harassment and the threats against Julia.

He settled back into his seat with a feeling of contentment. These charges against Arista were exactly what they'd needed to tip the balance of power in their direction.

Everything was going to be fine, just fine.

Chapter Thirteen

"Christina?"

"*Sí?*"

"Oh, God, I'm so glad you finally answered. This is Julia. I'm in Mexico City." She paused to catch her breath. "Have they got Tonio there?"

"He is here, but I do not understand. I was told you sent him here. I was told—"

"Forget what they told you. They tracked me down." A sob escaped her in spite of her feeling of control. It was so comforting to hear Christina's voice. "They tracked me down and they took him from me by force. They even tried to kill me."

Christina gasped and Julia could imagine her gripping the phone, her dark eyes filled with horror and worry.

"I've come to get my baby back," Julia said. "Do you think it's possible for me to sneak into the house?"

"Oh, Julia! They fill the grounds with many men to watch. It is too dangerous for you! You must not try. You must—"

"I have to. Please. Time is short. Will you tell me about the guards?" Julia paused and took a deep breath. "I'll understand if you don't feel you can help me in any way. Believe me, I'll understand."

There was a moment's silence.

"You will not do it without me," Christina said in an even, determined voice. "Let me think a moment."

Julia looked over at Anson, waiting anxiously for the outcome of the call. She nodded at him and he broke into a smile.

"The men..." Christina began hesitantly, "are all on the outside. So the bigger problem is the getting into the house for you. I am so afraid for you, Julia."

"I'm not alone," Julia told her and looked up at Anson as she spoke. "There is a man with me. A man you will like very much. He is Ignacio Obregon's nephew and he lives in New York."

"That is good. That is much better. Two can possibly do this thing."

"Do you have an idea, then?"

"Yes. We continue to get our deliveries just like it is any other day. So you must find a small truck—how you say?—a van. And you must find some clothes to wear that are suitable. And you must make yourself look like a man. Can you do all this?"

"We'll do it," Julia assured her. "At this point the assignment sounds simple."

"What?"

"Nothing. I've just been through so much that nothing seems impossible anymore."

"Good. Then I will go down and say that I am expecting a delivery for Juan. He is at the office all day, so you do not need to fear him."

"All right. And when we come to the gate Anson can talk to them and announce a delivery for Arista. His Spanish is perfect."

"Yes," Christina agreed. "And say it is something valuable that needs to be signed for."

"We'll see you soon," Julia promised. "And thank you."

Christina didn't say goodbye, she just hung up.

Money was no object at that point, and in Mexico City the free use of money can make anything easy. They had rounded up a small panel van and two sets of dark coveralls and some empty boxes, which they stuffed with rags and taped shut.

Julia pinned up her hair and secured it under a cap. Again she rubbed dirt on her face and donned Anson's reading glasses. She looked at herself critically in the van's large side mirror. It was not great, but it would have to do.

They rolled up to the delivery gate at the back of the Velasco estate in less than two hours after the phone call.

"Delivery for Señor Arista," Anson announced in Spanish as he fished in his pocket for a phony delivery form they'd conjured up.

The guard looked them over and waved them through.

The grounds were swarming with armed men. Julia's heart sank at the sheer overwhelming numbers they would be up against in their escape.

"Delivery for Señor Arista," Anson said again, climbing out of the truck and handing the form to a guard at the door to the house.

"I will take it," the guard barked.

"Oh, no. This is very valuable. My boss would be angry if anything happened. I must have Señor Arista's signature... or possibly that of his wife."

The guard looked irritated. He stared down at the form and then up at Anson.

"Go ask for the attention of Señora Arista," he finally ordered one of his men.

Julia breathed a sigh of relief and slumped down farther in the van seat.

Christina appeared in minutes and gave a superb performance signing the paper for Anson.

"My husband has been quite anxious about this delivery," she said in Spanish. "It is fragile and irreplaceable. I think the delivery service should be responsible for carrying it to his room and if something should happen they will find it is on their shoulders."

The guard nodded a hasty agreement.

"Very well, then," she addressed Anson. "Please have your man help you and bring it into the house."

Julia scrambled from the van and ran around the back to meet Anson. Together they lifted the box carefully out as though it were heavy.

Christina's eyes were frantic when they met Julia's, but her voice was calm.

"My husband will be furious if anything should be damaged," she said. "Now carefully follow me inside and up the stairs, please."

Julia kept her head down and turned away from the open kitchen door as they passed by it. The lively conversation among the group of servants gathered around the table neither slowed nor changed tone as they passed by the door. Their entrance into the house had completely escaped notice.

Her knees felt suddenly weak, and she stumbled on the stairs under the slight weight of the phony box. She was so close to Tonio now... so close.

Silently they followed Christina into the Arista suite and dropped the boxes on the floor. Christina turned toward her, eyes filled with tears, and shook her head.

"Oh, Julia," she said, and the words wrenched her chest.

She stood there swallowing against her own tears, and studied her sister-in-law's face. The woman had aged since last Julia had seen her. Her jet hair was streaked with gray, and her forehead and mouth were traced with the lines of despair.

"I'm so sorry for everything!" Julia cried and threw her arms around Christina's neck.

Christina stood stiffly a moment, then hesitantly raised her arms. Slowly, tentatively, she lifted them, circling Julia's back lightly.

"I missed you," Julia said simply.

Christina sobbed out loud and tightened her arms, holding on to Julia and returning the hug with a flood of feeling. It was the first time Julia had ever really embraced Christina, or any of her in-laws, for that matter. That small reminder of the Velasco family's coldness revived her and filled her with renewed strength. The Velascos would not raise her son. The señora would not destroy Tonio as she had Paul.

"The baby?" Julia asked, pulling away and searching Christina's face.

Christina swallowed and wiped away her tears with a lace-edged handkerchief. She straightened her shoulders, gathering her dignity, and cleared her throat.

"In the nursery," she said. "Come—the way seems clear. The security men are all on the outside."

"How is he?" Julia asked.

"I do not know," Christina answered sadly. "Mother has kept him secluded in the nursery and not allowed me to visit yet. She said she did not want him overly excited after his journey."

Julia exchanged a look with Anson. She knew him so well now. One glance and she could convey her pent-up anger at the señora to him, and in his brief return glance she saw understanding and a reminder to stay calm.

Christina checked the hallway and motioned for them to follow. Quickly they covered the distance to the nursery door, their footfalls muffled by the thick carpet. Christina put one hand on the knob and held the other up with the index finger to her lips signaling for quiet.

"I saw the nurse in the kitchen," she whispered, "but just in case..."

She cracked the door open and peeked inside, then hurriedly stepped into the room, motioning silently for them to follow.

The draperies were closed and the room was in semi-darkness. It was very, very quiet, so quiet that it sent a shiver up Julia's spine. Her eyes adjusted and she could see the crib and the mound of blankets and the outline of Tonio's sleeping body.

A tender swelling of emotion rushed through her, and she started for the crib.

"Wait," Christina whispered, grabbing her arm. "How will you get him away?"

"We'll have to sneak back down through the house with him," Anson explained softly. "Then..."

Julia looked at him. As far as she knew there was no answer to that part yet—not after seeing the watchful horde of security men ringing the grounds.

"Then I'll create some kind of diversion to distract the guards and make them all run around to the front so Julia can get the baby into the van. Once she's driven off the grounds through the back I'll follow her on foot."

Julia stared at him. "You'll never get out."

"I will create the disturbance in the front," Christina announced firmly, "so you can leave together in the van."

"The señora will never forgive you," Julia said.

A dark determination settled over Christina's features.

"No matter," she said tonelessly. "How much worse could she make my life than it already is?"

Suddenly the door flew open and the overhead light snapped on. Julia raced over to the crib and threw back the blankets to grab her child. But it wasn't Tonio—it was a large plastic doll. She dropped the blankets and turned back toward the door in shock.

Leticia stood there, looming in the doorway with the smug expression of a cat studying cornered mice.

"He's not here." She paused and smiled coldly at Julia. "I had hidden cameras installed in this room. They connect to a monitor right beside my bed."

Leticia turned slightly to pull the door shut behind her. "But I decided to keep him somewhere else, anyway. Just in case."

The woman smiled again and then fixed Christina with an icy stare. "So. My own daughter betrays me."

"No, Mother," Christina said in a surprisingly level voice. "I'm not betraying you. I'm simply standing up to you for once. I can't let you do something this wrong."

"Wrong!" Leticia's eyes blazed. "You call it wrong to rescue my grandson from this—" she pinned Julia with her wrath-filled stare "—this immoral, ill-bred slut! This scheming, evil witch?"

"You are wrong, Mother!" Christina cried. "All of you were wrong. Julia never—"

"Shut up!" Leticia ordered. "You've failed as a woman. You've failed the Velasco family and you've failed me. I won't listen to your pitiful lies."

"Then listen to *me*," Anson said in a voice as hard as steel. "Or can you face the truth?"

Leticia swung her eyes toward Anson, as though recognizing his presence for the first time. "And who are you?" she demanded hotly. "Some hired criminal?"

"I'm an attorney," Anson replied coolly, "and the nephew of Ignacio Obregon."

Leticia's eyes widened briefly in surprise, then narrowed again. "So? What could you possibly know of all this?"

"I've been investigating this whole situation, and I've turned up some rather interesting facts. Starting with Arista, your esteemed son-in-law. Juan's been a bad boy. Such a bad boy that my government has noticed him. Of course you couldn't know this, but Juan was caught pilfering earthquake relief funds a few years ago. He knew better than to ask Señor Velasco for help. He knew what the señor would do if he found out Juan was bringing dishonor to the family in such a way. But he was desperate for a quick cover-up, so he embezzled funds from the family's business to buy a fix."

Anson smiled grimly, as though he thought Juan's stupidity amusing. "It was such an easy way to raise capital that he kept it up, dipping in here and there in the family resources to finance his bungled schemes and then juggling facts and figures so no one would notice. When the señor announced suddenly that he was promoting

Juan in the business and relieving him of responsibility for the records and accounts, Juan panicked. He needed a lot of cash to feed back into the accounts and set things straight before someone else took them over and discovered the shortages."

"What bearing does this have on the matter at hand?" Leticia demanded. "Why should I listen to any more of it?"

"Mother!" Christina exclaimed incredulously. "You are hearing that Juan is a criminal and has been stealing from the family and you disregard it!"

"Juan will be dealt with!" Leticia snapped. "But his activities have nothing to do with this moment."

"But wait," Anson said. "There's more. Are you afraid to hear the rest?"

Leticia glared at Anson but she kept her mouth shut in a thin, hard line.

"Again, señora, I'm sure all this is new to you. I'm sure you would never condone criminal activities like these, and that you are as shocked as I was when I learned of them," Anson commented with raised eyebrows.

"Juan went to organized crime in the States for a quick loan to protect himself. The men he contacted play very rough, and they have some lucrative interests in Mexico. A connection with the Velasco name was valuable to protect and cover up those interests."

"Juan would never compromise the family name!" Leticia insisted hotly. "Never!"

"But he did," Anson said. "And do you know how he convinced those men that he was a good investment? That he could deliver the family name and the family influence to them? You have to remember, this was before Mariano left and before the señor had even considered retirement. At that time, Juan's future in the family didn't look particularly glowing."

"Enough! Enough!" Leticia took a step forward as though she might strike Anson. "I will listen to no more. I will not allow Juan's name to be defamed any further."

"Why are you defending him, Mother?" Christina cried.

Leticia whirled to face Christina. "Because Juan alone has supported me and stood by me in this family. Because Juan, like me, had had to earn a place as a Velasco, and understands the sacred duty we have to protect the name and the family from the onslaught of unworthy interlopers that threaten us."

Leticia's eyes were burning and her righteousness made her look as formidable as some medieval monarch whose throne had been challenged. "And because Juan saw the danger and warned me. He brought me the truths about my—" she paused, raking Julia with a scathing glance, "—about this woman before anyone else suspected. Because of his dedication and vigilance I knew what she was almost from the start. And because of his tireless efforts my grandson will be saved from her. I only wish..." Leticia's grand presence deflated somewhat into an air of sadness. "I only wish I could have known everything in time to save my Paul from her influence. I know now that she stole my son from me and made his life a hell."

She turned back toward Anson, drawing herself up regally again. "You have no truths for me, señor attorney. I know all I need to know. And I am thankful to Juan because with his help I am saving my grandson and thus preventing this evil woman from destroying yet another Velasco with her poisons. And maybe if your helpless male body was not so filled with lust for this creature your mind might not be so blinded to the true facts."

Anson had a look of amazed disbelief on his face. "You really believe all that, don't you?" he asked. "Well, you're right about one thing—you are threatened. The Velasco name is threatened. But it's not by Julia. Do you know how Juan convinced the mob?"

Leticia took a half step backward, as though she were physically afraid of the answer.

"Juan guaranteed them that he could get full custody of the Velasco grandson—that's how. He told them he could get complete control over the heir to the entire Velasco empire and so would end up with all the cards in the game. Tonio was Juan's ticket into the big leagues.

"All he had to do was discredit Julia with the family so that she'd be paid off and thrown out. He thought it would be easy. After all, she was nothing but a naive little widow in a foreign country—and an orphan at that. He never dreamed she'd put up a fight and he never imagined that she wouldn't be willing to put a price on her baby's head.

"Everything went wrong. But Juan didn't give up. He couldn't afford to. Those men in the States play too rough for him to fail. So he arranged a kidnapping. And when it looked to him like Julia and I were becoming too threatening, he ordered our deaths."

"Madre de Dios," Christina breathed.

"That's not true!" Leticia cried. "Juan wanted the child to make Christina happy—because she couldn't have one of her own."

Julia could no longer control the rage building inside her. She almost felt as though she could attack this vicious, destructive woman with her bare hands.

"You're sick! You're actually pointing a finger at your own daughter now! Well, I've had enough of your twisted visions, and your accusations and your blame. I have some truths for you now, Señora Velasco, and they're truths you've never had to face, because everyone is too cowed and frightened of you to stand up and shout them.

"Just look at the wreckage you've made of this family! You've punished your daughters cruelly for not giving you grandsons. Teresa's guilt over having daughters instead of sons has made her into a miserable, unpleasant woman, and I see now that she and her husband have finally deserted you. They've finally realized exactly who the source of their misery is."

"They'll be back," Leticia declared, knowing sarcasm in her voice.

"Will they? Now that Teresa can't have any more children? Now that they haven't a prayer of making you happy? I don't think so. The Diaz family may not be as successful as the Velascos, but at least they know how to love their grandchildren, regardless of sex. I don't think Teresa and Mariano will ever live under your roof again. And look at Christina," Julia said in a strong voice.

Leticia's eyes swung to her daughter, and even in the midst of an angry confrontation there was a dismissal there. Christina was not important in her eyes.

"You've never appreciated Christina," Julia accused. "She's the only one of your children who's ever loved you and defended you through everything, and you've never once thrown her one crumb of approval. You saw her as a failure for not attracting proposals, so you pushed her into an unhappy marriage of your choosing. Then when she couldn't have children, you simply dismissed her as having no worth at all.

"Why she's still here with you is a mystery to me. But now that she's seeing you more clearly—now that she understands how wrong you are in your treatment of me and Tonio, don't count on her staying much longer," Julia ended triumphantly.

"Stop it!" Leticia screamed. Her eyes and the veins on her forehead were bulging. "My daughters are none of your business!"

"Oh. Well, how about the effect you had on my husband's life then?" Julia drew in a ragged breath, trying to control the unreasoning fury she felt. She wanted to keep her thinking clear and she wanted to make her words count.

"You're right, you know. Paul should never have married me. That knowledge is still painful for me, but I can face it now. Now that I know you as I do, now that I see just what you're capable of, I can look back and understand.

"Paul married me for the wrong reasons. He married me because I was young and idolized him. He needed that hero worship. He needed to replace you with a woman who looked at him with eyes full of love instead of judgment. He needed to replace you with someone who made no demands and loved him for what he wanted to be rather than what his family thought he should be.

"And the mistake he made with me was that he was behaving like you. He found me at a youthful, vulnerable stage and decided that was all he ever wanted me to be. That was the Julia he wanted, and when he couldn't keep me like that he wasn't happy with me anymore." Julia swallowed hard. "He didn't love me anymore. Just like you've done with all your children.

"You've had set ideas about what you wanted each child's life to be, and when they didn't live according to your plan you withdrew your love. Paul hated you. He never talked about it. He didn't have to. But everything is so clear to me now.

"I know now that the other reason he married me, and maybe the biggest reason, was because I was the exact opposite of what you wanted for him in a wife. And I understand now that the reason he didn't want children all those years is that he didn't want to give you the grandson he knew you wanted.

"His entire life was designed to spite you. His choice of schools, his choice of friends, his choice of careers—it was all to spite you. And the clinic, and the dedication to the poor... that was the icing on the cake. The problems came because in living his life solely as a statement against you, he forgot to live life for himself."

"You are demented!" Leticia raged. "My son did not hate me! Paul was confused and misguided. He was confused about the great responsibility he had as the only surviving Velasco male. The responsibility to carry on the family's proud traditions, and the responsibility to preserve and protect the bloodlines and name of one of the oldest lines in Mexico. The weight of that responsibility bore down on him after his brother's death, and his youth and inexperience caused him to feel inadequate.

"Paul did not hate me! He simply saw me as the symbol of his obligations and duties. He chafed against me as a schoolboy rebels against a beloved taskmaster."

"Chafed against you?" Julia laughed hollowly. "He didn't speak to you for fifteen years! He left home and refused to acknowledge your existence. He denied his place in the family. He renounced you as a mother. You call that chafing?

"He didn't speak to you until he knew he was dying. And even that was something to use against you. He actually took pleasure in telling you—he enjoyed being able to devastate your plans in such a horrible way. He—"

The door burst open and a panting Juan Arista flung himself inside. His silk shirt was soaked with perspiration from his flabby body. Beads of sweat ran down his face from his hairline and gathered on his upper lip. He was waving a very shiny, very large, gun.

"Ha, ha! I heard they were coming. I raced from the office as soon as I knew." He chuckled and wiped his forehead with his shirt sleeve. "We've caught them, Leticia. I told you. I told you!"

Julia held her breath. Anson's face was frozen. Leticia was as still as stone, and Christina wavered between a look of horror and one of disgust.

"How did you hear they were coming?" Christina asked her husband in a voice that was too calm.

"On your phone, my dear wife." Juan pronounced each word separately, with cruel delight. "My sweet, timid little model wife."

"You listen on my private phone?" Christina's voice was filled with revulsion.

Juan waved the gun between Anson and Julia.

"We've got them now, Leticia. We can put them away forever with the charges the señor can bring against them."

"You wouldn't—" Christina began.

"Shut up!" Juan shouted at her. "You've betrayed your mother and your husband. You've disgraced your family. Only your being a Velasco saves you from the same punishment. When this is over..."

Juan's eyes narrowed and gleamed as he threatened his wife. He moved toward her a step and shifted the gun, ever so slightly, away from Anson and Julia.

Suddenly Anson lunged. Juan spun to meet him, but a fraction too late. The men's bodies collided. The gun clattered across the floor. Julia's eyes followed it, but then snapped back to the men. Juan had knocked Anson off balance in the collision and was using his weight advantage to pin Anson to the floor. His fat, sweaty hands were around Anson's neck, squeezing.

In a split second Julia made her decision. She leaped onto Juan's back, pummeling his head with her hands and scratching his face. She couldn't let him hurt Anson. Juan turned and broke his grip to lash out at her. The opening was all Anson needed to take the advantage. In moments Juan sat dazed on the floor, one hand holding his bleeding mouth.

"Stand up, Juan." The order rang out in the confusion.

The words were hard and cold and they startled Julia with their intensity. She turned to see Christina holding the gun with both hands. Her grip was steady and the weapon was leveled at her husband's chest. Her eyes blazed with a deadly light.

Juan struggled clumsily to his feet and stood cowering before this new Christina.

"So you listened on my phone. And you encouraged my mother in her madness. And you sent men to take the baby in New York. And you ordered them to harm Julia. What other crimes are you guilty of?" Christina asked him, as though she was ready to believe anything.

"I could shoot you now, you know," she told him coolly. "I could kill you and I would still be protected. The Velasco lawyers would protect me with some story or another. And I could be rid of you. I could be a respected widow."

"I did it for you, Christina," Juan whined. "I knew how much you wanted a baby. How terrible it was for you because you were nothing without a child to raise. And yet that woman was going to have a Velasco to raise! It wasn't right. It wasn't fair!"

"Enough lies! You never cared for my feelings. The only reason you were ever concerned about my barrenness was because a child would have ensured your own place in the family."

Juan's eyes traveled frantically around the group of faces. "She made me do it!" he screamed suddenly, pointing at Leticia. "She made me do everything. It wasn't my fault." He was babbling like a child now. "I didn't want to make up those stories about Julia. I didn't want—"

"Stop it, Juan!" Leticia ordered fiercely. "You are despicable. I gave you a chance at a position in this family and look what you have done with it. And now, how do you repay me? With lies and accusations.

"Julia was not my choice but I was determined to accept her and tolerate her as the mother of my grandson until you began planting the hints and bringing me the awful stories. I see now how you used me, and it sickens me. When I think of what you were doing... what I allowed you to do, it fills me with shame and disgust.

"You did want custody of Antonio for your own gain! And you spread your slime over the entire family to achieve your end. You are not worth spitting on. I gave you a start—raised you up from that weak, unimportant family of yours and gave you—"

An evil grin spread across Juan's twisted face. "Weak unimportant family of *ours*, cousin. Or did you forget that we share relatives? That you were cut from the same cloth?" he sneered.

"Enough! I wash my hands of you."

"Oh, no." Juan shook his head and his eyes took on a maniacal gleam. "Queen of the Velascos. If I am finished, so are you."

His eyes narrowed briefly. "I studied Paul and Julia so that my evidence would contain enough grains of truth to be believable. I looked into their lives and learned much about them." He grinned maliciously.

"I talked to many people. I talked to a woman who lives on her own farm and has an income for life. A woman who used to be a maid in this household. A woman who is loyal to you yet with the secret she holds."

Leticia's face went completely white, and she swayed slightly, reaching out to grip the back of a chair for support.

"Yes, I tricked her into telling me. And I know the biggest reason Paul hated you. The reasons he would never speak aloud to a living soul and kept buried down inside to torture himself. I know the truth that he and the maid shared with you."

"No!" Leticia's cry was strangled.

"The maid remembered the note word for word," Juan continued. "The note she found that day next to your eldest son. The note she gave to Paul when she called him up to his brother's room in panic.

"And she remembers how Paul wept and called you, and how you came into the room and saw not the death of a beloved son, but the failure and shame of it instead. She tells the story so sadly. She sees you as a saint protecting the family's honor when you changed the room and the body to make things seem different. When you swore your young son Paul to secrecy and destroyed the note." Juan's eyes were bulging and his face was flaming. "The suicide note your older son wrote and dropped beside his bed that day."

"I had to destroy it," Leticia sobbed. "I couldn't let the shame touch the family. I had to protect..." Her sobbing dissolved into moans and she sank into a chair.

A silence fell over the room, punctuated only by Leticia's pitiful weeping. Juan appeared to suddenly deflate. He leaned back against the wall, and his entire body sagged.

"Anson, if you would take the gun and watch him, I will go to call my father and the police." Christina's voice held a newfound strength.

"Not the police," Juan pleaded. "If you do not care about me, Christina, consider the family. What harm you will do the name of Velasco by airing all these family difficulties."

"Difficulties? Is that what you see here, Juan Arista?" Christina asked him. "I do not see difficulties. I do not see shame being brought to a name. I see a villain. I see an unprincipled criminal who should be brought to justice and punished."

Anson moved into position and accepted the weapon from Christina. "I ought to feed you to your pals Vinnie and Berto," Anson told the cringing Juan.

Christina bent over her mother and took hold of her shoulders. She shook the older woman gently but firmly, as if commanding the attention of an hysterical child. "Mother. Mother! Where is Tonio?"

"My room." The voice was thin and pathetic, and Leticia looked incredibly old and beaten. "I was keeping my grandson safe in my room. He needs to be safe so he can grow up and take the place of his father."

Christina crossed the room and placed her hand on Julia's arm. "Go to him now. Go to your son. There is no more trouble that cannot be handled. You are free from all of us now. You can teach your son a better way."

Chapter Fourteen

Julia finished the last of her packing and straightened with a sigh. There hadn't been much to do. She had come with little more than the clothes on her back. The French wool traveling suit she had on now was Christina's. Her sister-in-law had insisted she take it.

"Where are you guys?" she called as she carried her things down the stairs.

It was amazing how the house had changed in character once Leticia had gone. The servants hummed and laughed. There was music. Even the very light seemed brighter and cheerier.

"We're in the dining room," Christina's voice called back to her.

Julia opened the French doors to the formal dining room and laughed at the sight of Tonio crawling rapidly underneath the huge table and his aunt dodging here and there, trying breathlessly to catch him.

"What game is this?" Julia asked.

"You mean you do not know?" Christina asked in mock wonder.

"It should be clear to all that Tonio is a rabbit and I am a fox who likes to bite the stomach of rabbits."

"Oh, of course, how foolish of me not to recognize both of you."

Christina straightened and eyed her carefully a moment. "There is hot tea in the kitchen, Julia. The kind you like. Would you have a cup with me?"

"What about Mister Rabbit down there?"

Julia smiled and peeked under the table. Mister Rabbit peeked back at her and dissolved into a fit of giggles.

"We will close the French doors so he cannot run away in that direction and we will leave open the door to the kitchen. Mister Rabbit will grow tired of hiding and soon he will be in the kitchen with us, no?"

"Yes," Julia agreed, but wished she had an excuse not to sit down with Christina.

She could see the concern in her sister-in-law's eyes and she simply didn't want to discuss her problems. She didn't want a good listener. What she needed was a good hypnotist! Someone who could wipe her mind clean of all the pain.

She followed Christina into the immense kitchen. It was a sunny room with waxed, clay-tile floors and long stretches of counters and chopping blocks. A stainless steel commercial refrigerator from the States hummed in one corner and the indoor charcoaler was from the States, as well. The room looked even bigger now that it was empty of servants.

Julia took a seat at the scarred wooden servants' table.

"I don't think I've ever been in here when there weren't servants working," she remarked. "It feels strange, doesn't it?"

"Yes, you have," Christina laughed. "I will never forget it! That first week you came to live here and Mother caught you in the night down here..."

"Oh, yes, I remember. I had an unbearable craving for a banana-and-honey sandwich, and I was trying to find a banana in this maze..."

"And mother with her, how you say..." Christina indicated her head.

"ESP, or maybe mind reading," Julia filled in for her.

"Yes." Christina smiled. "She came down in the night to catch you at the act and only your bigness with the baby saved you."

Julia shook her head.

"All that was so hard to get used to—all your mother's absolute rules. I never could bring myself to wake a servant to fix me a midnight snack."

Julia shrugged.

"It did break me of the snacking habit, though," she admitted ruefully.

"When you were caught making a banana sandwich in the night—that is when I knew I was to like you," Christina said shyly.

Julia watched silently as Christina finished placing the tea things on the table. She knew better than to offer help. Christina was enjoying the opportunity to play hostess.

"Where is everyone?" Julia asked.

"I sent them away for the afternoon. The house is good empty, no?"

Julia nodded. "It's so peaceful and calm. This house was always filled with such tension."

"Yes."

Julia sipped her tea. The cup was English bone china, and the handle felt so fragile in her fingers.

"I told the driver to come back in time to take you for your plane," Christina said.

"Thank you."

"I am very much excited about coming to visit you and Tonio in New York. As soon as all is put into order here, I am coming on the trip."

"I know. And we'll be waiting."

Christina cleared her throat and nervously turned her cup around and around in its saucer.

"Mother was not always like that," she said quietly. "I am sad for so much of what she did to you...but so many of the thoughts were Juan's, not her own. And of course she knew nothing of Juan's orders at violence."

Christina drew in a long breath.

"It is strange. She was from a rich family that was never 'accepted.' They were newly rich and uneducated and they made their money in the wrong ways. She was always ashamed of them.

"My father was never the one for the bloodlines. He was too much preoccupied with other things...in his own world, as you say. The name was not of heavy importance to him, but as soon as he gave my mother the Velasco name as her own, that name became her religion. And the importance of it grew and grew for her with the passage of time and the disappointments in other parts of her life."

"Those disappointments were of her own making," Julia reminded her. "Her children weren't failures and disappointments. Remember that. Her unreasonable expectations were the problem."

"Yes. I know that is true, but still..."

"I know. She is your mother. And it hurts to have her see you as a failure. It hurt all of you. It drove Paul away and it alienated Teresa. And it killed your older brother. Don't let it destroy you."

"No. There is no danger now. Seeing Juan beaten at his evil games has given me great strength. It has made me see that good can win."

Julia smiled. She knew exactly what Christina meant. But did she herself believe that good could win? Sometimes. Not always.

Tonio came rushing through the door from the dining room and stopped, delighted to find them. He chuckled and quickly headed back out through the door as though he expected pursuit.

"He never grows tired," Christina remarked in amazement, and Julia had to laugh at the understatement. "There must never be calm with him in your small apartment, no?"

"Only at nap time," Julia said.

They sipped at their tea in silence a moment.

"And will you call him?" Christina asked meaningfully.

There was no use pretending she didn't understand. It would be a waste of time.

"It wouldn't make a difference."

"One never knows."

"I know. Too much happened. There were too many disappointments... too many lies."

"But there is still love. I see it in your eyes."

"Love isn't enough sometimes."

"Love is what there is that is... solid. It is what holds people together stronger than blood or false vows. It is the reason I will try to make a new start with my mother and help her to see things and begin again."

"That's different," Julia insisted. "She's your mother. Nothing can ever change that blood bond between you."

Christina shook her head emphatically.

"Have you not seen through all this that the blood ties do not offer any guarantees? It is love that binds. It is love that makes us tolerant and flexible. It is love that allows us to forgive."

Julia carried her cup to the sink and turned to watch Tonio sneak up on Christina. His aunt pretended not to see him. He grabbed her leg and she jumped as though frightened. The child shrieked with delight and then scrambled underneath her chair.

Christina stood and carried her own cup to the sink. Then she turned and moved the chair to expose Tonio. He looked surprised and made a move to scamper away.

"Come, nephew," she said, capturing him and scooping him up into her arms. "Your Aunt Christina has a surprise for you and we will leave your mama alone to think a while."

"And so you will be leaving us again soon," Ignacio said, pulling a chair beside Anson in the library.

Anson nodded and smiled.

"I am sorry we did not have the opportunity to become better acquainted with Julia. She sounds like an extraordinary woman."

"Yes," Anson agreed. "That she is."

"There has been much learned from these lessons, Anson. Your aunt and I are ashamed at our blindness and unquestioning allegiances. We are thoroughly chastised."

Anson studied his uncle carefully. Words of this sort were rare from Ignacio.

"Julia Velasco might be an extraordinary woman, my son, but she is also a very lucky one. She is lucky to have found such a brilliant and courageous young attorney to help her set things right."

Anson swallowed hard against the sudden lump in his throat and blinked against the burning in his eyes.

Ignacio stood and Anson stood beside him.

"Your Aunt Helen and I are very proud of you, Anson Wolfe. Very proud indeed."

Ignacio gathered him roughly into a bear hug, and Anson hugged him back as hard as he could. He had waited twenty years to hear those words.

His uncle left with mutterings about going to the office, and Anson settled again into the wing chair. How much longer should he stay? How much more rest and recuperation could he stand?

Work sounded like the best medicine now. Work sounded like the best way to forget.

How rigid and inflexible his whole life suddenly appeared. How could he ever hope to relate to people or learn tolerance or forgiveness if he clung to his old black-and-white notions.

But then he really didn't have those notions anymore, did he? Somehow they had softened and melted during all this insanity. Knowing Julia had taught him so clearly that there are many shades of gray to right and wrong.

He should have taken her lying for what it was—a survival measure—and not projected that into something sinister and dark. Just because she was willing to lie and pretend to protect herself and her child didn't mean that she was an untrustworthy, insubstantial person. What a fool he'd been to think that way.

And how much his accusations and lack of understanding must have hurt her. It was good that she was through with him. It was a healthy sign. How could she possibly love a person who had judged her so unfairly.

Anson heard the distant ringing of the phone. It was nothing unusual. The Obregon phone rang frequently. He heard a housekeeper answer it and then heard the soft Spanish voice telling the caller "One moment, please. I will go for him."

He waited to hear his uncle's name called out but instead he heard, "Señor Anson. *Teléfono*."

The words startled him from his window gazing. He stared at the extension on a side table near him. His pulse picked up a bit and his palms felt suddenly damp. Hesitantly he picked up the receiver and lifted it to his ear.

"Hello," he said in Spanish. "This is Anson Wolfe."

"Hi," a voice replied in English. "It's Julia."

Her voice was light, and she rushed right on as though the call was nothing more than an ordinary, everyday chat.

"I'm leaving this afternoon for New York, so I thought I'd just give you a call and let you know how everything is before—"

"Where are you?" he cut in. His voice echoed back at him in the still room and he knew he'd spoken too forcefully.

"I'm at the Velasco house. Christina convinced me to stay here with her. I mean... we're the only two left, so it's not uncomfortable or—"

"What happened with Leticia?" He knew he sounded too ponderously professional, but he couldn't help it. He couldn't do the light banter with her. Not with all the emotions he was trying to keep bottled inside.

"Well, after you and your uncle left... and the police carted Juan off, it got pretty quiet around here. I was afraid that the señor might suffer some kind of collapse—you know his health isn't that good—but instead the whole thing seemed to give him this new power. I've never seen him so authoritative. He had a long conference with Leticia and Christina in the library, and he insisted that they tell him everything."

"He didn't know what was going on?"

"Not a thing. It was all Leticia and Juan."

"So then what happened?"

"He made this eloquent speech of apology to me and said he would understand if I wished to sever all connections with the family. He said he was arranging psychiatric treatment for Leticia at the ranch and in no time he had her loaded onto a helicopter and they were gone."

"And will you sever connections?"

"No. It might take me a while to trust them...but, I'd like to give it a try. I want Tonio to have relatives...to have family. And you know, it's a very funny thing... At one point I thought revenge against Leticia would be so wonderful, but it's not.

"I don't hate her anymore. I just feel sorry for her. She blew everything, but some of her motives were actually very reasonable in a nineteenth-century sort of way. I really can forgive her."

"And what will Christina do now?"

"That's the best part," Julia told him excitedly. "Christina wants to run the medical clinic! She's going to be terrific at it too and I—"

"Yes," he said shortly.

"What?"

"Yes, that's very nice. Everything has worked out well for everyone."

He had to get off the phone. He had to get away from her voice.

"Except us," she said sadly.

The words stopped him, caught him short of breath a moment. What did she mean by that?

"Now what do you mean?" He kept his tone professional, chiding her as he might a childish client.

Impersonal. That was the key. He had to keep it impersonal. He had to cover up. He would not break down. He would not beg or plead or argue. He loved her too much to put her through anything else.

"Things have certainly worked out well for you and for Tonio," he pointed out. "And as to myself, I've managed to reach a new understanding with my uncle and aunt through all this. So you see—we've all profited in ways."

"Yes," she agreed dully. "I guess everything has turned out for the best."

"Absolutely," he insisted firmly. "If everyone is happy, then of course it's for the best."

"*Is* everyone happy?" she asked timidly.

What was all this about? What was she thinking?

"It would appear so," he said carefully.

"Do you ever wish that you could just go back and start something over?" she said sadly. It was more a statement than a question.

"Sometimes," he said. "But that's usually an impossibility, isn't it?"

"Yes," she said. "I imagine you're right."

He listened to her talk about packing and being glad to get back to New York and he hung up the phone and stared unseeingly at it. The craziest ideas were jumping around in his mind.

Julia sat down in the plastic Houston airport chair and let Tonio crawl off her lap into the empty seat next to her. She ached. Every cell in her body ached.

Could she live in New York knowing he was in the same city? It was a huge place, but still, wouldn't it be continual torture? How long before she didn't have the urge to pick up the phone and dial his number? How long before she didn't want to walk past his office just to catch a glimpse of him?

She had hoped for so much when she'd called him at the Obregons' that morning. Christina's talk about love had made her start hoping.

She'd hoped they could put together some fragile, tentative start at a new beginning. But he hadn't given an inch. His distance had been like a wall between them. And she felt as though she didn't have the right to try any harder to break through it. If that was the way he wanted it to stay, she would respect his wishes.

But it was going to be so hard.

Just to know that she could walk into his office and look into those blue, blue eyes and watch the quizzical expression on his sharply intelligent features and see him reach up to run his fingers through all that wonderful curly hair in that boyishly unconscious way of his...

She felt as if something was chipping away inside her, and soon there would be only tiny pieces and eventually nothing but dust.

How was she going to keep herself from inventing reasons to see him or talk to him? How could she force herself to respect his wishes?

She bent over to fish in her purse for a toy. Something, anything, to keep Tonio occupied. She was afraid he might discover the ashtrays soon or climb down from the chair and toddle off like a streak.

She felt around the bottom of the bag. Diapers, cheese snacks, tissues, a little comb, a scratch-and-sniff book. The beat-up rubber squeak chicken he still loved. Where was that talking mouse Christina had given him as a going-away surprise?

A vision of Christina holding Tonio and surprising him with the silly stuffed mouse made her feel briefly warm inside. Christina had promised to come visit them in New York soon. Very soon, she hoped.

Her fingers connected with the mouse's furry body. She pulled it out of the bag. As she did, she heard Tonio laugh in delight.

"You like your mouse, don't you?" she was saying as she straightened in her chair. But Tonio wasn't paying the least bit of attention to her or to her presentation of the talking toy. He was leaning over the back of the row of chairs toward someone sitting directly behind her, and he was stretching his arm, reaching his hand out.

She whirled around.

There sat the most beautiful man, with slightly curly, ash-brown hair laced with the most striking silver gray. He turned and looked at her with the bluest eyes she'd ever seen, and he reached up unconsciously to rake the hair back off his forehead with a strong, expressive hand.

"He's got a good grip," the man said.

Julia nodded. She was afraid to speak, afraid to break the spell of this magic.

"I think he likes me," the man offered and he reached out to take the mouse from Julia.

"What's this, huh, big boy?" he asked Tonio as he held up the toy and pulled the string that doubled as the mouse's tail.

Tonio's eyes widened and he stared at the toy, ready for what he knew was coming.

"What's your name?" the squeaky little mechanical voice said, and Tonio laughed in delight.

Anson handed the toy to Tonio, and turned slowly back toward Julia. He was so close. She could hear him breathing. She could reach out and touch his cheek or brush his lips with the barest of movement. His expression was intense and filled with so much hope, so much longing, that she could barely speak.

"I could use a friend in New York," she said. "I hope that's where you're going."

"That's where I'm going," he answered. "But I want more than a friend. I want someone I can trust and love... someone I can believe in."

"Oh, so do I," she cried, and she reached out to him and pulled him close, wetting both their faces with her tears. "I'm ready to believe."

Take 4 Silhouette Intimate Moments novels FREE

Then preview 4 brand new Silhouette Intimate Moments® novels —delivered to your door every month—for 15 days as soon as they are published. When you decide to keep them, you pay just $2.25 each ($2.50 each, in Canada), *with no shipping, handling, or other charges of any kind!*

Silhouette Intimate Moments novels are not for everyone. They were created to give you a more detailed, more exciting reading experience, filled with romantic fantasy, intense sensuality, and stirring passion.

The first 4 Silhouette Intimate Moments novels are absolutely FREE and without obligation, yours to keep. You can cancel at any time.

You'll also receive a FREE subscription to the Silhouette Books Newsletter as long as you remain a member. Each issue is filled with news on upcoming titles, interviews with your favorite authors, even their favorite recipes.

To get your 4 FREE books, fill out and mail the coupon today!

Silhouette Intimate Moments®

Silhouette Books, 120 Brighton Rd., P.O. Box 5084, Clifton, NJ 07015-5084

Clip and mail to: Silhouette Books,
120 Brighton Road, P.O. Box 5084, Clifton, NJ 07015-5084*

YES. Please send me 4 FREE Silhouette Intimate Moments novels. Unless you hear from me after I receive them, send me 4 brand new Silhouette Intimate Moments novels to preview each month. I understand you will bill me just $2.25 each, a total of $9.00 (in Canada, $2.50 each, a total of $10.00)—with no shipping, handling, or other charges of any kind. There is no minimum number of books that I must buy, and I can cancel at any time. The first 4 books are mine to keep. *Silhouette Intimate Moments available in Canada through subscription only.*

BIMS87

Name _____ (please print)

Address _____ Apt. #

City _____ State/Prov. _____ Zip/Postal Code

* In Canada, mail to: Silhouette Canadian Book Club,
320 Steelcase Rd., E., Markham, Ontario, L3R 2M1, Canada
Terms and prices subject to change.

IM-SUB-1B

SILHOUETTE INTIMATE MOMENTS is a service mark and registered trademark.

Silhouette Special Edition

COMING NEXT MONTH

#385 FORBIDDEN FRUIT—Brooke Hastings
Noble Lady Georgina felt obliged to marry her social equal. But when her grandmother hired macho, working-class Mike Napoli to chaperone Georgina, attraction soon outranked obligation!

#386 MANDREGO—Tracy Sinclair
Elissa had vowed to avenge her father's ruin. Her plot led her to an island paradise—and into the arms of her enemy's bodyguard, dangerously attractive Troy Benedict. Could revenge possibly be so sweet?

#387 THE MIDNIGHT HOUR—Jude O'Neill
Sassy Cleo and wise-cracking Gus were once partners in mystery writing and marriage, but their famed collaboration had led to calamity. If they reunited, would they be crafty enough to write themselves a happy ending?

#388 THE BABY TRAP—Carole Halston
Ginny Sutherland wanted a baby—without the complication of remarrying. Still, she'd need a male temporarily, and virile Ed Granger might just be the man for the job....

#389 THE SUN ALWAYS RISES—Judith Daniels
Restaurateur Catherine Harrington didn't want to love and lose again, but wandering, "no-commitments" Nick O'Donovan was convincing her to take the risk....

#390 THE FAIRY TALE GIRL—Ann Major
When her fairy tale marriage failed, Amber Johnson left the Bahamas with her illusions destroyed. So how could she believe rancher Jake Kassidy's promise that with him she'd live happily ever after?

AVAILABLE THIS MONTH:

#379 VOYAGE OF THE NIGHTINGALE
Billie Green

#380 SHADOW OF DOUBT
Caitlin Cross

#381 THE STAR SEEKER
Maggi Charles

#382 IN THE NAME OF LOVE
Paula Hamilton

#383 COME PRIDE, COME PASSION
Jennifer West

#384 A TIME TO KEEP
Curtiss Ann Matlock

ATTRACTIVE, SPACE SAVING BOOK RACK

Display your most prized novels on this handsome and sturdy book rack. The hand-rubbed walnut finish will blend into your library decor with quiet elegance, providing a practical organizer for your favorite hard- or soft-covered books.

Only $9.95

Approximately 16" x 8" when assembled

Assembles in seconds!

To order, rush your name, address and zip code, along with a check or money order for $10.70* ($9.95 plus 75¢ postage and handling) payable to *Silhouette Books*.

Silhouette Books
Book Rack Offer
901 Fuhrmann Blvd.
P.O. Box 1325
Buffalo, NY 14269-1325

Offer not available in Canada.

*New York residents add appropriate sales tax.

Silhouette Desire

Available May 1987

Still Waters
by
Leslie Davis Guccione

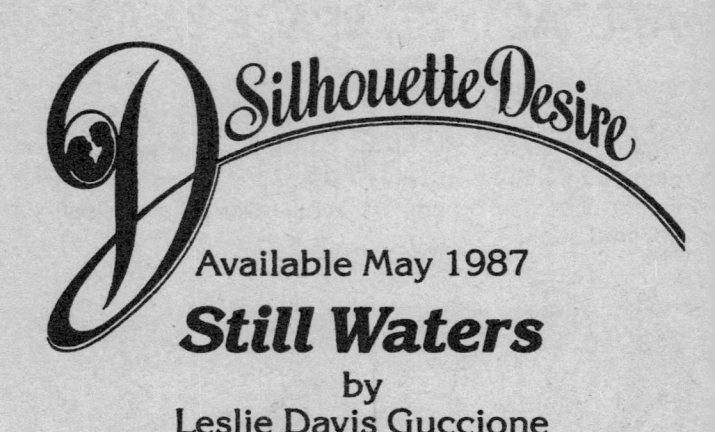

If Drew Branigan's six feet of Irish charm won you over in *Bittersweet Harvest*, Silhouette Desire #311, there's more where he came from—meet his hoodlum-turned-cop younger brother, Ryan.

In *Still Waters*, Ryan Branigan gets a second chance to win his childhood sweetheart, Sky, and this time it's for keeps.

Then look for *Something in Common*, coming in September, 1987, and watch the oldest Branigan find the lady of his dreams.

After raising his five younger brothers, confirmed bachelor Kevin Branigan had finally found some peace. He certainly didn't expect vibrant Erin O'Connor to turn his world upside down!

D353-1